Best Wishes!
Amber Penn

TAKE *my* HAND

AMBER RENEE

TAKE *my* HAND

TATE PUBLISHING
AND ENTERPRISES, LLC

Published by Tate Publishing & Enterprises, LLC
127 E. Trade Center Terrace | Mustang, Oklahoma 73064 USA
1.888.361.9473 | www.tatepublishing.com

Tate Publishing is committed to excellence in the publishing industry. The company reflects the philosophy established by the founders, based on Psalm 68:11,
"The Lord gave the word and great was the company of those who published it."

Book design copyright © 2013 by Tate Publishing, LLC. All rights reserved.
Cover design by Ronnel Luspoc
Interior design by Caypeeline Casas

Published in the United States of America

ISBN: 978-1-62510-793-0
1. Fiction / General
2. Fiction / Action & Adventure
13.04.08

For Mrs. Winton. Thanks for the push.

CHAPTER

1

Jonathan Watkins rushed to Labor and Delivery at the local hospital in Austin, Texas; the double doors banged into the wall as he hurried through. He had been in the middle of a city council meeting when his mother-in-law had paged him. His wife was in labor with their first child. Jonathan couldn't believe it. He couldn't believe he was going to be a father.

"Beth…Watkins…please," Jonathan gasped to the nurse at the front desk.

There were a few clicks on the keyboard, Jonathan tapping his finger impatiently, as the nurse looked up the information.

"Room 1231," the nurse smiled. "Down the hall and then to the right."

Jonathan was nodding and moving away before she was done speaking. He moved down the hall, turned left and noticed the numbers on the rooms. He grunted in frustration, turned around, and moved in the other direction. Finally coming to the room marked LD 1231, Jonathan stopped for a moment. Slowly, he pushed the door open and walked in. As quietly as possible, Jonathan moved the privacy curtain out of the way. His wife looked up at him, her face shining with sweat, and smiled.

"I'm so glad you made it," Beth said, her voice full of emotion, blonde hair falling from the braid meant to hold it.

"I wouldn't miss it," Jonathan assured, moving to the bedside and kissing his wife's damp forehead. "It caught me off guard, the page. You were fine this morning, and you still have five weeks to go."

"Well," breathed Beth, "the doctor did say expect anything with our first child." She moaned as another contraction overtook her body.

Beth's mother smiled at her daughter and then moved to leave, whispering to Jonathan that she would let him take over now. She walked out of the room just as the nurse was coming in. Jonathan watched as the nurse looked at the monitors, checked vital signs on Beth, and looked over the IV fluids. Jonathan glanced back at Beth as she moaned from another contraction.

"Oops," she suddenly said. "I think my water just broke."

The nurse smiled at her, pulled the sheet back, and then her smile slipped some.

"What's wrong?" Jonathan asked.

"Well, it looks like the fluid has quite a bit of meconium in it," the nurse replied. "That means the baby has had her first bowel movement." She quickly helped Beth get cleaned up, placing dry absorbent pads under her. The nurse then moved to leave the room.

"I will be right back. I have to go let the doctor know."

Jonathan watched as she walked out. He moved to Beth's side and took her hand again as another contraction came. He coached her as best as he could, holding her hand, putting cool cloths on her forehead, and wiping her tears when her emotions became too much.

Suddenly, an alarm sounded on one of the monitors in the middle of Beth's contraction. Jonathan glanced over at it and then back to his wife. The concern in her eyes was apparent, and mirrored his. Jonathan was sure that alarms going off while having a baby couldn't be a good thing.

Just then two nurses came in, one of them the one from before. Jonathan stepped out of the way as they set to work. The extra nurse changed Beth's position, let her IV fluid free-flow, and paged the doctor overhead to their room. The nurse from before checked to see if Beth was dilated further and gasped.

"Call OR stat," she demanded of the other nurse. "I have a prolapsed cord."

Jonathan watched in horror as the other nursed rushed from the room. The first one left her hand where it had been while checking Beth and instructed her to put the head of her bed all the way down and then had Jonathan stuff pillows under Beth's rear end.

"What is going on?" Jonathan demanded, watching as the number indicating his daughter's heart rate continued to drop.

"The umbilical cord has come out before the baby," the nurse said, stuffing another pillow under Beth. "We have to get her out now before the pressure cuts off the blood supply entirely."

"What?" Beth screamed.

Just then the doctor came in, full OR garb on. "Let's go, now!"

Another nurse ran into the room just then and worked with the other two as they prepped Beth for surgery, the first still holding the baby's head up to try and keep off the pressure. Jonathan didn't know what to do. Beth was looking at him with such fear and worry that he wanted to weep for her.

A few more cords unplugged, Beth was being wheeled out of the room, tears flowing continuously. She glanced back at Jonathan, fear etched in every line of her face.

"I love you, Beth," Jonathan called. The door swung shut behind them.

Jonathan moved to the counter by the sink on shaking legs. He leaned on it with most of his weight, fear and worry nearly causing his legs to buckle. Would Beth be okay? Would their daughter be okay?

"God, please," Jonathan prayed, "be with my wife and child. I only ask you to spare their lives. Please, bring them both back to me."

●

Five doors down, Paige Monroe sat in her bed holding her one-hour-old son, Lucas, his dark hair standing up at odd angles. Her husband, Owen, was working on calling every person in their address book. It was a rather large address book. Owen and Paige both came from Georgia originally. They had known each other in high school. When Owen went off to the Army and Paige to the Navy, they lost touch. However, fate brought them together again in Austin, Texas. Paige had been discharged from the Navy and had become a nurse, working in Austin. Owen came to Austin after his discharge for a meeting at the local branch of the FBI. He had just recently been hired and was looking to settle. After meeting up with Paige and having dinner, Owen put in for an immediate transfer. That had been eleven years earlier.

For five long years, Owen and Paige had struggled with conception difficulties and two miscarriages. Finally, thanks to modern technology, they were able to conceive. It was rough from the start. Nausea and preterm labor plagued Paige the entire length of the pregnancy. In her sixth month, she was admitted to the hospital dehydrated and exhausted. Her doctor advised bed rest. To make matters worse, Paige had gone nearly two weeks overdue.

That morning when her water had broken, Paige expected to have a long and drawn-out miserable labor, just like the pregnancy had been. However, to her and Owen's surprise, she had been nearly ready to push upon admission to the labor and delivery unit. They had barely had the chance to start her IV, and she was pushing. Ten minutes later, Lucas had been born. He had come out screaming his head off, all nine pounds, eleven ounces of him. The nurses had been shocked at his size; amazed, Paige had been able to push him out so easily. Paige was just thankful that he was so healthy since she herself had been so sick.

Paige looked up at Owen, now pacing the room, talking on his Bluetooth and gesturing with his hands. She smiled when he caught her eye and then looked back down at Lucas. His little mouth was smacking like a fish, so Paige lifted him up closer to her so that he could nurse. Silent tears started to fall from her eyes. She assumed that Lucas would be their only child due to the difficulties that they had faced. That didn't matter to Paige, however. She felt blessed by God to have just the one healthy child that she now had. Paige felt certain that between his father raising him to be strong and military-ready and herself teaching him to be a true southern gentleman, Lucas would grow into a fine man. Not to mention, hopefully, intelligent, as both she and Owen both were.

●

Beth looked up at Jonathan and then back down at their daughter, Sarah. Her tiny little body lay in the warming bed, surrounded by tubes and monitors. The sounds of the Neonatal Intensive Care Unit assaulted Beth's ears. Leaning a little farther forward in the wheelchair, Beth reached out to gently touch Sarah's hand. She was so tiny.

Sarah had been born at four pounds, four ounces. Her heart rate hadn't initially recovered once she was born by emergency C-section. The doctors had to resuscitate her, helping her breathe, and even doing chest compressions at one time. Beth had tried to get them to tell her what was going on, but they had hurried off with Sarah and hadn't been able to tell Beth much of anything.

Now Beth knew. She knew that her daughter was sick. Not only had her umbilical cord come out too soon and been wrapped around her body twice, thus causing the problems with her heart rate, but she had also aspirated a large amount of the amniotic fluid. The doctors had explained to Beth and Jonathan that the meconium in the fluid was now in her lungs and was what had made her unable to breathe on her own.

Sarah now laid in the warming bed, a breathing tube down her throat and lines running into her umbilical cord for fluids and medicine. Her little body twitched like she was in pain and she frequently grimaced like she was trying to cry, but couldn't because of the tube in her throat. The doctors were cautiously optimistic about Sarah prognosis. They weren't sure when she would be able to breathe on her own. They weren't sure when she would get better. They did, however, continually tell them that she was in good hands and they were doing everything they could.

Beth slumped back into her wheelchair. It had only been about eight hours since Sarah was born, and Beth was starting to feel pretty sore. She gripped Jonathan's hand. He looked down at her and nodded. He gently touched Sarah's hand once more and moved to start wheeling Beth back to her room.

While Jonathan pushed her, Beth couldn't help but think back on her pregnancy. She and Jonathan had gotten pregnant nearly right away. They had waited some time to start their family because of Jonathan's desire to advance his political career. Once they decided to have a baby, it was only two months later when Beth found out that she was pregnant. Things had gone on without a hitch after that. Up until going into preterm labor, Beth didn't have one thing wrong with her pregnancy, not even morning sickness. It had been a dream. But that dream was over now. Now Beth couldn't even be sure whether her precious daughter would survive.

●

Paige sat waiting for Owen to bring the car around. Lucas was two days old, and they were on their way home. He was currently tucked into his car seat, asleep at the moment. Paige couldn't believe how wonderful it was to have her son, safe and sound in her arms. Paige had been so worried during the pregnancy that something would go wrong, and she wouldn't get this joy of bringing her son home. He was such a beautiful child.

Just then Owen arrived with their vehicle. He quickly jumped out, lifted Lucas's car seat into the car and then helped Paige in the back next to Lucas. He pulled out of the parking lot of the hospital and continued to drive five miles under the speed limit the entire way home. It made Paige smile. About halfway there, Lucas woke up but did not cry. He simply blinked a few times, like he was still bewildered to be out in the world, and then looked around.

They arrived home to the welcome of their families. Paige smiled at everyone, overjoyed to introduce them to Lucas. They talked, laughed, ate and oohed and aahed over the new baby. Paige walked over to Owen at one time while her sister was holding Lucas and took his hand. He looked down at her, happiness and pride practically seeping from his very soul. Paige could relate. She couldn't imagine life getting any sweeter. She had her son; she had her healthy, perfect baby boy.

●

Beth stood with Jonathan beside the incubator in the NICU that was holding Sarah. She no longer had a breathing tube, a welcome change that morning for her four-week birthday, but the doctors had brought them even more distressing news.

"She seems to be doing all right breathing on her own, finally," he had said. "Now we have to get her strong enough to eat on her own. She is tolerating the feeding tube with the pumped breast milk. We just have to get her to take a nipple. Our only concern now is her eyesight. We did a preliminary study, and it appears that she may be developing what we call ROP. It stands for retinopathy of prematurity. What this means is that the retina of the eye starts to detach. We won't know the full extent for some time."

"What will that mean for her eyesight in the future?" Jonathan asked.

The doctor looked grave. "We have caught it fairly early and can monitor and try and treat it, but sometimes there is just nothing we can do. It could lead to blindness, should it detach entirely."

Beth gasped. Tears spilled over down her cheeks. Was it too much to ask that her daughter grow into a normal child? Was it too much for her to live as well as grow healthy? Sarah twitched in her bed just then. She grimaced like she was in pain and then squeaked out the tiniest of cries. Jonathan and Beth looked at one another, tears in their eyes. It was the first time they had heard Sarah cry.

Suddenly, Beth didn't care what the future held, as long as her daughter survived. As long as God saw fit for Sarah to live, Beth would take whatever else came their way. She knew that God would provide for them. Beth unlatched the little opening to fit her hand through to touch Sarah. Her little hand came down on Beth's finger and grasped it softly. All Beth could do was cry.

CHAPTER

2

Six-year-old Lucas Monroe smiled at his parents and then at his birthday cake and presents. Paige could not believe that her son was six already. He was enjoying second grade, already the brightest in his class. Lucas had shown great potential intellectually. Paige and Owen had actually started him in kindergarten when he was three (turning four midyear in February). His teachers were amazed at how bright he was. They were all nervous for him at first, but he soon proved himself smarter than most of the children two years older than him. Paige knew that if he kept it up, Lucas would graduate high school at sixteen. That made her nervous, but she knew that with proper guidance, Lucas would do well.

Paige was also proud of how well Lucas behaved. She had been raising Lucas to say please and thank-you, sir and ma'am, and how to treat loved ones and friends. He behaved perfectly in public and was very thoughtful and helpful. Paige was always washed with compliments for her young son, convincing her that he was going to be the perfect gentleman one day.

Owen, on the other hand, was bursting his buttons over the fact that his son was the perfect military trainee. He was slowly teaching Lucas martial arts, self-defense, and how to defend others. Owen also hoped that as Lucas grew, he could be taught search and rescue and military tactics. The idea was to prepare Lucas for the Army to follow in Owen's footsteps, but only time would tell. He knew that between his training and what Paige was teaching the boy, Lucas would grow up to be a great man. Owen now found himself with his fortieth birthday around the corner and a family he would die for. The guests cheered as Lucas blew out his candles. The Monroe household was a happy one.

●

Beth Watkins watched as her daughter stubbornly tried to buckle her own shoe; Sarah's sightless eyes stared off into space, her face twisted with concentration. Beth sighed. She could still remember the day that the doctor had told her and Jonathan that Sarah's eyesight was gone forever. After the initial test on Sarah's eyes, they had tried to do what they could to preserve Sarah's sight. A follow-up test once she was older showed at that time that the retinas in Sarah's eyes had detached entirely. The doctors had told them that it was the combination of being premature and having to be on oxygen for so long that had damaged Sarah's eyes. Beth had been devastated at the loss of her daughter's sight, but grateful that she had survived.

Beth and Jonathan had gotten over the shock of having a blind child. They had agreed to help her enough to teach her and keep her safe, but no more than that. Sarah had quickly grown to want to do things all on her own anyway. The biggest problem they had faced in the past was change, new obstacles. They had moved twice in the six years since Sarah had been born. Beth had tried to help her daughter adjust and learn the new house, but Sarah still had problems. Walking had been difficult for Sarah to learn; toilet training had been even harder. The biggest problems they faced were small tasks like buttons, ties, buckles, etc.

Now that she had turned six, Sarah was going to be starting her kindergarten lessons with a tutor for the blind in the fall. She was progressing well and even showed promise as a pianist. Beth herself had been playing for years and it only took Sarah hearing her play Beethoven's Moonlight Sonata once before she was begging to learn how. It seemed to help Sarah a little, actually having something she could do that seeing people also did. It really seemed to help boost her confidence. Each year that passed seemed to make new things, and old, easier for Sarah, but Beth still worried. She worried about Sarah's future, about love and marriage. Would there be someone there to help Sarah after she and Jonathan were gone? Would the world be too much for her? Jonathan was campaigning for governor of the state of Texas. Beth worried whether or not a public life would affect Sarah. How would they help her through the publicity? How would they keep people from taking advantage of her? How would they keep her safe?

●

Lucas looked at himself in the mirror. He had just returned from his junior karate class. The instructor had discussed with Lucas's father about moving him into the intermediate class. The instructor had said that he never had a student move up after only five classes, and certainly never a ten-year-old. Lucas hoped to go into the Army like his father one day. He had seen his father's medals. Lucas longed to serve even at his young age . However, little did Lucas know something else was stirring in him as well. He had a deep longing to protect, even now before he fully understood.

●

Sarah winced as she gingerly let her fingers slide over the fresh scrape on her knee. She had, once again, tripped over the unfamiliarity of her new home. She and her parents had moved; it was the third time in ten years. She was proud of her father, now the governor of Texas, but Sarah longed for a friend. Moving because of her father's career aspirations had proven friend making a difficult task. Not to mention she was hardly ever around kids her own age. Sarah worried that it would be even harder now that her father was the governor and she would have an "assistant" as her parents put it. Sarah knew that it was actually someone to keep an eye on her. Her father was the governor, and even he didn't have an "assistant." Sarah sighed. She hoped that they would stay in this place long enough for her to make at least one friend. Maybe she could even go to school.

As Beth bandaged Sarah's knee, she looked up into her sightless eyes. Beth hated that every time they moved, Sarah had to relearn the house. She always tried to set up the furniture the same but never quite succeeded. Beth hoped that this would be their last move for a long time. Sarah spoke of nothing but making friends and having sleepovers. Beth knew that she was concerned about the effects of her father being governor and her "assistant" would have on her chance of friendship.

Beth was proud of Sarah for supporting her father even though each move was difficult. The campaign had been long and difficult for all of them. Jonathan's competition tried to bring Sarah into the debates, making it sound like Jonathan would not be able to do his job properly with a blind child to care for. However, Jonathan had still won by a landslide. Now his next goal was to work toward a second term, and then, though he rarely mentioned it, Beth knew that his long-term goal was to be president.

CHAPTER

3

Sarah took a deep breath as she prepared to enter her new school. She let her cane help guide her as she followed her mother to the office. They had arrived a little early for the first day of school so Sarah and her mother could meet with the principal to talk about Sarah and her needs. As Sarah followed her mother, her ears were immediately assaulted by the new sounds once she entered the door. She could hear laughter; she could hear adults talking. Then piano music caught her ear. She had heard it before, of course. Her mother had been teaching her to play. It thrilled Sarah to think that she might be able to take formal lessons. It was one thing that Sarah did well and it didn't matter that she was blind.

Sarah heard another door open. Her cane bumped either side of the door jam, telling her which way to go. Sarah stepped forward and soon was knocking her cane into a chair. Moving around to the front of it, she sat down. She heard her mother sit next to her. Sarah tried to sit still, to be a good girl, but she was so excited to finally be in a real school.

"I see you are adept at using your cane," the principal was saying. "My name is Mrs. Jenkins. I am the principal of the school. Tell me, what is it that you hope to gain from your schooling?"

Sarah bounced a little in her seat and then righted herself. She had to sit still, be a lady. Sarah turned her attention in the direction of Mrs. Jenkins voice to reply.

"I really love music," she started. "I would love to take formal lessons on the piano. I would love to learn other languages. I really like animals and flowers. Besides that, I would like to be with other kids. I would love to have friends."

"We've had Sarah with a tutor since she was old enough for lessons," Beth explained. "Now that she is older and has expressed so much interest in making friends, we decided to allow her to try a regular school."

"What about Sarah's security? I don't expect any problems from any students or anything, but I wasn't sure about your plans due to her being the governor's daughter."

"Well, we are in the process of getting her an assistant, but the finalizations have been delayed. Sarah didn't want to get a late start on the school year. She wanted to be able to start with all of the other kids. I would really appreciate her being kept a close eye on for this first week. We should have someone by the beginning of next week."

Mrs. Jenkins had some reply, but Sarah didn't notice. She was suddenly very aware of all of the new young voices she was hearing. The other students were starting to arrive for the first day. Sarah started to feel bouncy once more. Her mother and Mrs. Jenkins were discussing a few more things, but Sarah's attention was only captured when Mrs. Jenkins asked her if she was ready to see the rest of the school.

"Oh, yes please," Sarah replied, jumping to her feet.

Mrs. Jenkins and her mother laughed. They, too, climbed to their feet and followed Sarah out the door and back into the hall. Mrs. Jenkins led them through the halls, informing Sarah of her classmates, her surroundings, and her daily schedule and learning curriculum for the year. Sarah didn't know what to expect other than it sounded a lot like her tutoring but with other children.

Her mother had wanted to keep her with a tutor due to the politics and public life, but Sarah had begged. Jonathan had finally agreed to let Sarah attend the school for the blind for her fourth-grade year to see how it went.

They got to the final room, and Mrs. Jenkins knocked on the door. The teacher came out, but she wasn't alone. Sarah could hear another person breathing. Mrs. Jenkins put a hand on Sarah's shoulder and then reached down to take her hand. She lifted it up and placed Sarah's hand into the hand of someone else.

"Sarah, this is Mona. She is going to be in your class and will help you get adjusted to the school."

"Hi," Mona said, shaking Sarah's hand.

Sarah smiled, even though she knew that Mona couldn't see it. It could be heard in her voice, though. "Happy to meet you, Mona. I am Sarah."

Sarah said good-bye to her mother and entered her classroom. Most of her first day was spent getting to know the school and her classmates. Mona helped Sarah around the campus and even helped her at lunch. They began to talk, and Sarah prayed silently that this would be the friend she was looking for. Mona told Sarah how she became blind due to a head injury, and it was her second year at the school. The doctors had said it was temporary but did not know when her sight would return. The final bell rang at the end of the day and out filed the children. Sarah followed Mona out the door and stood with her at the parent pickup spot.

"This is where you should wait every day," Mona explained. "Not only is it easier for your parents to find you but this way the bullies from the private school four blocks away can't get you. They come in all ages. The private school is a very big campus, with three separate buildings for elementary, middle, and high school. They think blind kids are fun to pick on. Their school gets out thirty minutes before ours and most of the time just as we get out here, they are walking by. If you stand here inside the gates, they leave you alone. Although, you do have to get used to some teasing."

"I'm glad you told me," Sarah acknowledged. "I ran into a bully once. I don't ever want to again. I'll be okay once I have my 'assistant.'" Sarah let her sarcasm hang in the air.

"Won't that make you feel weird?" Mona asked. "I don't think I would want someone around me all the time, especially an adult."

"I don't really *want* it," Sarah confessed. "My daddy says I have to. He doesn't want anyone to bother me because of who I am or if they get mad at him."

"Tell him not to make anyone mad," Mona suggested.

"That's what I said." Sarah laughed. "He said that he can't always control that, though. Besides, they are a little overprotective with the whole public life thing and me being blind. I understand why they are doing it. I just think it will be weird."

Mona sighed. "Well, as long as the person lets us stay friends"— Sarah's heart jumped—"I won't care that they're around. It's too bad that they can't disguise themselves as a kid. Or too bad they can't have a kid be with you."

Sarah smiled at this thought. She would much rather have someone her own age watching after her. She felt she stood out enough as it was. But she knew that it was silly. No one her age would be able to help her. Sarah knew that her parents were mostly worried about her after school and things like that. If it was just a matter of waiting with her until her mother arrived, then Mona would suffice, Sarah knew. However, her father had said, in so many words, that he was worried about her safety. No kid would be able to beat up an adult.

The rest of the week passed quickly for Sarah. She and Mona were soon spending all their spare moments together. Sarah was delighted to find out that she and Mona had quite a bit in common. They both loved music, ice cream, and animals. Before their first week together was over, they had become close friends. Some of the kids acted funny when they found out Sarah was the governor's daughter, but it didn't bother her. Sarah was used to being asked about her father. Everyone had always known he planned to run for governor; he had always been involved with city politics. His views on some things had, at times, caused problems for the family, but nothing serious.

Friday afternoon, Sarah went with Mona to the pickup spot. They talked as they waited like normal. Soon, Mona's mother arrived.

"Do you want a ride?" Mona asked. "Your mother is usually the first one here."

"I know. I don't know why she's late. She might have gotten tied up in a meeting or something. She sometimes goes with my dad to luncheons and stuff. I should be here when she arrives." Sarah hugged Mona and stood alone as her friend left.

Sarah wasn't sure where her mother could be. She *had* been the first to arrive all week. Sarah started to grow nervous as the time passed. What if something happened to her parents? What if something was wrong? Just then, someone was coming up behind Sarah and a hand was suddenly on Sarah's shoulder.

"Time to lock up," the person spoke. Sarah didn't recognize the voice. She could hear music blaring, but second hand. It was like the person talking to her was wearing headphones or something.

"But, wait, I can't...my mom isn't here yet," Sarah tried to say.

The person pushing her out the gate either couldn't hear her or wasn't paying attention. Sarah was ushered out of the gates and told to wait on the sidewalk. Sarah was scared. All around her she could hear cars, buses, and other kids. She had no idea how long she would have to wait or what surrounded her. Sarah stood where she had been put, afraid to move, her back against the fence. Her backpack was hanging over her left shoulder, her cane in her right hand. Sarah kept her left hand lashed to the links of the fence. She knew that she couldn't move.

Suddenly, someone was laughing. It was a boy. He was fairly close, off to her right. Sarah felt her heart rate pick up in fear.

She didn't like his laugh. It was mean sounding. Sarah tipped her head in the direction that she was hearing him and then heard what seemed to be two more walk up.

"Did you get locked out?" the first boy asked, chuckling. "Where's your mommy?"

"Leave me alone," Sarah responded, her voice sounding braver than she felt. "My mother will be here shortly."

"Well, she's not here now," the boy taunted. "Let's have some fun while we wait."

Sarah gasped as the boy grabbed her arm. She yanked it away, only to be shoved from the other side by another boy.

"Knock it off," Sarah demanded. "I'll tell my father. He's the governor."

"Oh, so you're Sarah Watkins," the other boy stated from her left. "I heard that you were blind, but I didn't know you went to school here. If you *are* Sarah Watkins, where are your bodyguards?"

"I don't have any," Sarah replied.

"How old are you?" a third voice asked from in front of her. Sarah hadn't even known he was there.

"Ten." She suddenly felt a hand on her arm. Flinching away, Sarah stumbled back into the fence. The boys laughed.

"We just want to play," the first boy informed. He stepped even closer, too close. Sarah could feel the heat from his body on her right arm.

Sarah stepped to her left but sensed the other boy there. She tried to shy away from him as well but had nowhere else to go.

"Stay away," Sarah demanded. Her voice shook in fear, sort of diminishing the effectiveness of her words. "I'll tell my father."

The first boy laughed. "Sure, go ahead. Your daddy ain't here right now, and you don't know what we look like."

They began to push her from all sides; she slapped a hand away as it tried to lift her skirt. Fear seized Sarah. Grasping her cane, she swung with all her might. She felt three separate thuds and heard one boy fall. Turning, Sarah started to run as fast as she could, her backpack falling to the ground. She knew that the sidewalk went on for thirty paces before there was a turn. Her left hand was her guide along the fence surrounding the school; she held her cane out in front of her with her right. Sarah followed the fence; it turned and then came to an end.

Panic rose up as Sarah heard the boys advance toward her, seemingly from every side. They were laughing and taunting her, calling her names. Sarah tried to swing at them with her cane again, but it was pulled out of her hands. She suddenly felt their hands pushing her from every side. One shove landed her on the ground; Sarah quickly covered her head anticipating more.

"Hey!"

The others stopped.

"You leave her alone," a fourth boy demanded. His voice was unique; his accent seemed to almost twang.

"What are you going to do about it?" the third boy hissed. "This ain't none of your concern."

"Yeah it is," the fourth boy informed. "You leave her alone. She's blind, she's not dumb. She feels just like we do. Now get lost before I get mad."

"You're Lucas Monroe, aren't you?" the first boy asked.

"Yeah, so?"

Sarah heard the first boy move away from her; the other two followed. The three of them were chuckling evilly as they moved closer to the fourth boy. Sarah was worried now for the other boy. She hated for him to get hurt because he was trying to help her.

The first boy cracked his knuckles. At least Sarah thought it was him. The sound was far away from her, in the area the first boy seemed to have stopped. She recognized his chuckle.

The boy laughed. "Rumor has it that you are convinced that you are a black belt in karate. Well, now we can tell everyone that you defend delinquents, after we kick your butt, that is. This is gonna be good."

Sarah wanted to yell at him run, but she was too afraid. She couldn't help but be thankful that their attention was turned from her, for the time being. Sarah knew that there was no way the other boy would stand a chance against three others. She knew that when they were done with him, they would come back to her. Sarah wanted to run, but following the fence would take her passed the fighting boys. And she didn't want to go anywhere near what she was hearing.

The first boy told the others to attack, and they listened. There was skin-to-skin noise and one of the boys cried out in pain. Another grunted as if hit with something rather hard. There were two more fist-to-face-type noises (Sarah recognized the sound from TV), and two bodies fell to the ground. Sarah heard the first boy cuss and run forward, and in no time he was on the ground with the others.

"Let's go," the first boy hissed, sounding like he had had the wind knocked out of him. "You're going to regret messing with my space, Monroe!" he yelled as they ran off.

Sarah relaxed slightly as she heard them leave. A presence arose beside her. She flinched.

"It's okay," the fourth boy cooed. "I won't hurt you. Take my hand."

Sarah turned her face toward the sound of the boy's voice. She couldn't believe he hadn't been beaten to a pulp. Reaching out, she felt his hand grasp firmly around hers. He helped her to her feet and then Sarah heard him step back, as if to further show that he wasn't hostile.

"My name is Lucas Monroe. What's your name?"

"Sarah, Sarah Watkins."

Sarah head the boy's breath catch. "As in, the governor's daughter?"

Sarah nodded. The boy was silent for a moment. Sarah heard him swallow; he took a few heavy breaths. She had the faintest notion that he was collecting himself. Shocked over who she was? Or was he angry over how those other boys had been treating her? Sarah couldn't be sure.

"Are you okay?" Lucas asked. Sarah could almost feel his eyes check her over for injury.

"I'm okay," Sarah responded. "I fall all the time."

"They didn't hurt you, did they?" The seriousness in Lucas's voice made Sarah realize he meant more than just shoving.

"No," she responded quickly, shuddering at the thought. "I don't know what they would have done if you hadn't come along, though. Are you a professional? Or in high school?"

Lucas laughed. His laugh made Sarah smile. "I'm only ten," Lucas informed her. "But I have had training from my father."

"How did you get those boys to go away?"

"I fought them off using defensive techniques along with martial arts," Lucas informed, sounding a little smug. "I don't let anyone threaten a girl in front of me."

Sarah felt herself blush. "Well, thank you." Sarah heard Lucas kick his toe in the dirt. He cleared his throat.

"I can escort you back to the school, if you don't mind. I can make sure you get back there safely."

Sarah smiled, her cheeks feeling even warmer. She had never had someone be so nice to her, especially not a boy. Sarah wasn't sure what to do.

"I would like that. Thank you, Lucas."

Sarah heard Lucas come slowly toward her, handing her back her cane. He hesitated and then gently took her arm, and they walked back to the front of the school. Sarah wasn't sure how to act with Lucas holding her arm the way he was. She had never been in a situation like this before. However, new as it was, Sarah was surprised to find she was not at all uncomfortable.

"Your daddy's here," Lucas whispered as they rounded the corner. "He's got the cops with him. Your mom's crying. Call to her."

"Momma!" Sarah called. She heard her mother gasp, heard her running, and then felt her warm embrace.

"What happened? Where have you been? Why were you not in the gate? I am so sorry," Beth gasped. Sarah could tell her mother was hysterical. Her father hugged them both. Sarah could hear the multitude of other people who were there, the entire police force, no doubt. Her parents had a habit of overreacting.

"I was told to wait outside the gates because they had to be locked. Everyone left me. Some bullies chased me around the fence, and I got stuck at the end because I couldn't tell what came after the fence ended. They called me names and pushed me down. Luckily, Lucas showed up. He beat them up, made them go away, and then helped me get back here." Sarah turned to where she knew Lucas had been last.

Beth and Jonathan both turned around, expecting to find an adult or at the very least a high school student. However, they were shocked to find their daughter's savior was a ten-year-old boy.

"Is that true, son?" Jonathan asked.

"Yes, sir," Lucas replied, his voice taking on a respectful tone. He stood at attention as his father had shown him, hands clasped behind his back, in respect to authority.

"Well, we are grateful to you, Lucas," Jonathan said. He smiled as the boy brought his hands around front of him, clasping them like a soldier told to stand at ease.

"You fought the three of them off on your own?" Jonathan asked, making reference to Lucas's slightly swollen knuckles on his right hand.

Lucas glanced down at them and hurried to pull his arms behind him again, determined to not show any weakness or injury.

"Yes, sir," he replied again. "I can give you the names of the three boys that chased her if you'd like."

"That will be fine," Jonathan assured him. "We can take you home and get the names then. I would like to speak to your father if possible."

"Yes, sir. My father and mother should both be home. My mother is a nurse and my father is with the FBI. He had the day off today."

Lucas turned, jogged over to pick up Sarah's backpack that she had dropped, and then moved to where Sarah was, and gently took her hand again. She tipped her face in his direction and smiled slightly. Lucas felt a twinge in his heart; she *was* kind of cute. Lucas led Sarah over to the car where her mother was holding the door open. He then went around to the other side in the backseat and climbed in next to her. Sarah's head was tipped to the side as if she was listening to something outside of the car. Lucas would have bet she could hear her father yelling at the school staff even though the door was shut.

Once they were all in the car, Lucas told them again what had happened and the names, grades, and addresses of the boys who had chased Sarah. When Jonathan questioned him on how he knew so much, Lucas simply replied that his father taught him.

"My father has been teaching me how to protect people since I can remember. I have been taking karate and defensive classes since I could walk."

"Why is that?" Jonathan asked.

"My father trained with the Army Rangers," Lucas continued. "After he was discharged, he entered the FBI. He moved up very quickly and is now a chief detective. That is what I plan to do, sort of. I plan to go into the Army and then the FBI or some other law-enforcement area."

Jonathan was impressed. "How well can you defend yourself? How well do you think you will you defend others?"

Lucas shrugged. "I have been studying martial arts for five years, and my father has been slowly teaching me for as long as I can remember. I know how to defend myself and others either heavily or with little force against foes my size and slightly larger. I can also shoot a gun accurately up to one hundred yards."

Jonathan laughed. "You are quite the child. How did you get those other boys to leave?" Lucas told him, and afterward, Jonathan was even more impressed. He also told them that although he was only ten, he had just started sixth grade.

"You must be a bright child," Beth complimented.

"Thank you, ma'am," Lucas responded, sounding slightly embarrassed.

When they arrived at the Monroe household, Lucas climbed out of the car, jogged around to the other side, and helped Sarah out. He held her arm until they were up on the front porch. He even told her when to step; she had left her cane in the car. Sarah heard the door open, and Lucas guided her in.

"Mom? Dad? I'm home," Lucas called.

Sarah heard heavy footsteps coming downstairs to her right and deeper into the house more. Closer were the hurried footsteps that were lighter, softer. Sarah assumed it was Lucas's mother who was coming up on her left.

"Where were you?" she asked. "I was so worried. Oh, my, Mr. Governor…"

Mr. Monroe came into the foyer just then. He cleared his throat as he seemed to collect himself. "Mr. Governor," he said.

Sarah heard him shake her father's hand. She still had a hard time with people treating her father with such respect and reverence. He was just Dad to her.

"To what do we owe this pleasure?" Mrs. Monroe asked. Sarah heard her move over to Lucas's side.

"Well," Jonathan started, "your son was of some assistance this afternoon to my daughter, Sarah. I took it upon myself to see him home and was wondering if we might speak."

"Of course," Mr. Monroe responded. "Please, right this way, Mr. Governor. Mrs. Watkins."

Sarah turned to where Lucas had been last and smiled when she felt him take her hand. It caused a warm feeling to blossom in her chest. Was this what it was like to have friends?

As they all sat in the den, Jonathan reported to Mr. and Mrs. Monroe (Paige and Owen as they had introduced themselves) of their son's heroics. At the end of the story, Sarah could hear Paige hug and kiss her son. She assumed that Lucas was glad at that moment that she could not see.

"I'm glad Lucas could be of service to your daughter, Governor Watkins. He is quite the boy. I hope that you have gotten Sarah's situation figured out," Owen inquired. "I would hate for a repeat of what happened today."

"Well," Jonathan started, "we have it covered now, but I'm thinking of a different approach. Sarah has expressed many times that she doesn't want an adult around her all the time, so I was thinking about not having one."

Sarah turned toward her father, hope rising in her chest. What was he talking about? She would love to not have an adult around her all the time, but what had changed his mind?

"Isn't that unsafe, sir? What if she needed help? Would someone be able to get to her in time?" Owen sounded concerned.

"Well, the time that Lucas gets out of school puts him walking past Sarah's school just as she is released. I was wondering if you and your wife and, of course, Lucas, would agree to have him wait with Sarah. That way it is less likely to draw attention. I had a watch made for her that has a button linked to the police and fire stations in the area. Sort of a safety net for her if we aren't around. It has a GPS signal in it so that help can come to her. I was thinking that if Lucas were to wait with her, he would be able to provide a moderate defense for her and at the very least provide distraction enough for Sarah to press her emergency button."

Sarah nearly squealed. She could not see, but she knew enough about the voices of people that she could tell Lucas was nice looking; well, he had a cute voice, anyhow. Besides, he treated Sarah nicely, and that was more than she could say for some people. The thought of him waiting with her every day was almost too much to bear. She now had the possibility of having two friends. Plus, now she didn't have to have an old person with her all the time.

Owen sighed. "Well, that's fine with us if it is okay with Lucas."

Lucas looked at them all and then moved beside Sarah. She turned her face toward where she felt him standing

"Would that be all right with you?" he asked. "I wouldn't want you to be uncomfortable with my presence."

Sarah smiled. "I wouldn't mind at all. It would actually be more comfortable than having an old person, I mean, adult beside me at all times."

Lucas chuckled. "Okay," he agreed, "I'll do it." Sarah could hear the smile in his voice.

The adults talked for a little bit after that. Jonathan asked Owen about his time in the Army and asked Paige about her time in the Navy. Sarah knew that her father had a deep respect for those in the Armed Forces. She tried to sit still, but Sarah always bored quickly when her parents talked.

"Would you like to go for a walk?" Lucas asked suddenly. He had been sitting so quietly that Sarah hadn't been certain that he was still next to her.

Sarah nodded and smiled as she felt Lucas take her hand again. He helped her to her feet and then led her out of the room. Sarah thought she heard the adults chuckle quietly, but she tried to ignore it and the blush that crept up her neck.

Lucas led her through the house and out a back door. Sarah heard it slide in its tracks as Lucas pulled it open and then closed it behind them. He helped her down the steps of the back porch and into the yard. Sarah was suddenly assaulted with the intense floral scents of the backyard.

"Your mother has quite the flower garden back here, doesn't she?"

Lucas chuckled. "Yeah, she does. It is her pride and joy, next to me. Well, that is what she always says, anyway." Lucas sounded embarrassed again.

"I love flowers," Sarah told him. "Could you take me closer?"

"Sure." Lucas took Sarah's hand once more. He guided her to the garden and through the gate of the picket fence surrounding the flowers. He stopped her just inside, not sure if she wanted to walk among them or not. Sarah closed her eyes in apparent pleasure. Her head tipped back slightly as she sniffed the air.

"I smell roses, tulips, honeysuckle, and jasmine. Is that freesia too? Wow. What a garden."

Lucas laughed. "I will have to take your word for it. The only thing that I know for certain is the roses."

Sarah giggled. "You must be pretty smart, though, to be ten and in the sixth grade already."

Lucas scuffed his toe in the dirt. "Well, I do my best," he replied a little embarrassed.

"I was glad that my parents finally let me go to school this year. I was getting tired of being with the tutor. Not that she wasn't nice, but still."

Lucas nodded, and then remembered that Sarah couldn't see. "I can see where that would get old," he replied.

"So what else do you like, Lucas?" Sarah asked. "Aside from martial arts and running around helping people like Hercules."

Lucas laughed softly, sounding slightly embarrassed. He took Sarah's arm again as they walked for a while around the garden and then around the yard. Lucas told Sarah about his love of martial arts, how he loved to shoot guns with his dad at the shooting range, and how he was even learning archery. He also loved movies and music. Lucas told Sarah that he loved sports and hoped to play on the football and basketball teams for his school when he got older.

Sarah in turn told him about her likes: flowers, music, playing piano, animals. She also told him about how she had been born too early and had been sick. She told him that was how she had lost her eyesight. Lucas hadn't asked, but Sarah knew that he had been wondering. Everyone always did.

It seemed like a short time later that Sarah's parents were call-ing her name. Lucas took her hand and led her to the car. He helped her in as her mother held the door.

"I'll see you on Monday," Lucas promised. All Sarah could do was smile.

When Monday came, Beth informed the school of what had been decided and that Lucas would be there from now on. She informed the school that Lucas was to be allowed inside the gate and was to wait with Sarah until someone came to pick her up. She then told Sarah that Lucas would meet her at the front door every day unless he or she was informed otherwise. Sarah hoped that Lucas would want them to be friends as much as she did.

Monday afternoon Sarah walked out the front doors of her school. Her pace was more hurried than usual, her excitement over being near Lucas again spilling over to her feet. She stood on the step and waited.

"Take my hand," the familiar voice drawled beside her.

Sarah couldn't help but smile as she took Lucas's hand and allowed him to lead her down the steps, Mona giggling beside them.

CHAPTER

4

A giggle escaped Sarah's lips as she hurried as fast as she could down the stairs toward the Christmas tree. She had always loved Christmas. The smells, the tastes, the presents; it all added up to happy memories. This year, however, she was even happier. Not only did she have a good friend, Mona, but she also had Lucas. He had waited with her every day but one since the agreement. The day he missed, he had been ill. Sarah's mother teased that she had a crush, but Sarah assured her they were just good friends. The thing that Sarah liked best was that they shared interests and even birthdays. Sarah found it interesting that they were almost the exact same age; Lucas was one hour older. She found herself wanting to know more about Lucas, even more than she already knew. Sarah wanted to spend more time with him, talk with him, laugh with him. They didn't get much time alone with Mona always around.

Waiting anxiously for that afternoon when Lucas was to come over, Sarah hoped that he would like the gift she was going to give him. Luckily for Sarah, her and Lucas's parents had become good friends. Over the past few months their parents had entertained each other and had even gone on outings together. As much as she hated to admit it, Sarah felt that she did have a crush. She knew that she was starting to like Lucas, but never having liked a boy, Sarah was nervous about what to do. She was also nervous about whether or not he liked her. She knew they were friends, but the more Sarah thought about it, the more unsure she was of whether or not a boy could like her as more than a friend, being blind and all.

Right on time at four o'clock, Owen, Paige, and Lucas arrived for cocktails before dinner. Lucas walked in, politely greeted his hosts, and then excused himself to find Sarah.

Beth laughed as he walked off. "They are so cute together."

Walking down the hall, Lucas turned into the den and found Sarah listening to Christmas music. She turned toward the sound of his feet, a small smile on her face. It never ceased to amaze him how advanced her other four senses were. Half the time she could hear or smell him coming before he even got near her.

"Lucas?"

Lucas smiled even though she could not see his face. As much as he hated to admit it, he was really starting to like Sarah, though he could not figure out if it was friendship or something more. He did, however, know that she looked very pretty in her crimson Christmas dress. It complemented her honey-colored hair nicely.

"You look really nice," he complimented shyly.

Sarah smiled. "Thank you. I was wondering when you would find me. I have been waiting. Did you bring my present?"

"What makes you think I bought you one?"

"You better have, Hercules, because I bought you one."

Lucas laughed. She had been calling him that since teasing him about running around saving people. "Of course I bought you a gift. We can open them at the same time."

Sarah smiled and held out the brightly wrapped box she had been holding. Lucas moved into the den, stepping up next to the couch Sarah was sitting on. He took the box from her and in turn placed a small box in her hand, sitting beside her on the couch. They were both silent as the wrapping paper was removed. Sarah heard Lucas gasp when his box was opened. He said nothing, but she knew that he was more than happy with the videos she had given him—*Martial Arts: The Complete Story; The United States and Her Defenses; Then and Now: Combat Styles and Tactics; The History of Combat Weapons.*

"Where did you find these?" he asked. "I have never seen anything like it."

"My father is the governor, remember? He made a few calls, found what I wanted, and had it sent to us." Sarah smiled in Lucas's direction and knew that he was smiling too. Gently lifting the lid of her box, Sarah reached inside and felt around. Pulling out the gift, she inspected it with her delicate touch. It was a bracelet, a charm bracelet. Feeling the trinket, Sarah tried to figure out what the charms were but could not. The look on her face must have registered her frustration. Lucas reached over and took her hand. Guiding her fingers along, he introduced her to each of the decorations.

"This one is a music note, because I know how much you love music. This one is a rose because you love the way they smell. This one is a candy cane because you love the way they taste. This one is a kitten because you love the way they feel. And this one..." Lucas paused, clearing his throat a little, "this one is a heart to let you know that I will always be around when you need me."

Sarah almost cried. She never knew that having a friend could be this nice. For the first time in her life, the world was not scary. She felt safe with Lucas around even if he was only ten. Gently, Lucas took Sarah's hand in his and hooked the bracelet around her wrist. Sarah rotated her wrist back and forth, loving the way how it felt. Hugging her friend, Sarah knew that she would always be watched over as long as Lucas was in her life.

"I can tell your parents were from the South," Sarah said, pulling away.

"What do you mean?" Lucas asked.

"I don't mean it as a bad thing," Sarah apologized. "I know that people from the South are usually raised to be respectful, to be loyal and strong. I just mean that you make me feel safe. You are polite and courteous. You remind me of a young man from the Old South, like you see in the movies. I like you that way. My mom says that not many boys are like that now."

Lucas shrugged, blushing a little and glad Sarah couldn't see it. "I guess I learned from my dad and mom. As long as I can remember, my dad has taught me two things, how to protect and how to love. He has been teaching me what he knows since I was five. I've always been interested in what he does, and since I love and respect him so much, I have taken it very seriously, as with his advice on how to treat people, especially girls. He always told me to love them like it was your last day and cherish them like it was their last. He always treats my mom like that, so I guess I adapted it. My mom always says that I am mature for my age. She has always told me to be polite and courteous, yes sir, yes ma'am, that sort of thing."

Sarah laughed. "My mom says that about me too. I'm glad your dad taught you what he did or else we may not have become friends."

Six weeks after Christmas, February 7, was Sarah and Lucas's eleventh birthdays. When each was asked what they wanted to do, they replied the same. They wanted to spend the day together. An agreement was made for the two families to go out for pizza and then ice skating at the sports complex.

Once at the pizza place, Lucas led Sarah to the private room for dinner. Pulling her chair out, he made sure Sarah was situated before sitting across from her. He failed to see the amused looks on their parents' faces.

Lucas looked at Sarah. He had grown quite fond of her cute face and soft, golden hair. He had long since gotten used to the sightless stare of her blank, yet pretty, green eyes. She was currently tipping her head this way and that as she listened to everything around them.

Sarah turned in his direction, her smile faltering some. "Are you still here, Lucas?"

Lucas smiled. "Of course. You know I wouldn't leave without telling you." Sarah's smile came back full force, making Lucas smile as well.

"Can I ask you something?" Lucas whispered.

"Sure," Sarah replied, leaning in to whisper as well.

"I haven't ever made you uncomfortable, have I?"

Sarah leaned back, a surprised look on her face. "What do you mean? What could you have possibly done to make me uncomfortable?"

"I don't know," Lucas responded. "I don't mean uncomfortable in a…well, bad sort of way. I just don't ever want to do anything to hurt your feelings, like a comment or helping you when I shouldn't. I don't want to be rude, but even though I like being with you and being your friend, I don't have any other blind friends, so I am not sure what the correct protocol is."

Sarah laughed. "You have never stepped on my toes before, Lucas. I will let you know if you do. Usually you seem to know when I need help, and when I don't, even before I do. But, you know what I've realized?"

Lucas grinned. Knowing Sarah, her revelations could be anything. "What?"

"I don't know what you look like," Sarah whispered.

Lucas couldn't tell if she was joking or not. "Well…I know. That's because, um, you're blind."

Sarah burst into fits of giggles.

"Well, you are," Lucas retorted, amusement in his voice.

"I know that, silly," Sarah laughed. "I mean I have never seen what you look like in the way that I see. Would you mind?"

Lucas was taken aback. He knew that blind people used their hands as sight, reading braille and such. But he had never had his looks felt before. However, he knew that it would make Sarah more comfortable. Anything for Sarah. Lucas leaned forward across the table.

"Go ahead. My eyes are blue and my hair is light brown, not that you know what colors look like." Lucas rolled his eyes at his ridiculous color comment.

Sarah smiled, not seeming to mind, and reached out her hands so her delicate fingers could form a picture of Lucas. Her touch began at his forehead, moving to his eyes. Long lashes tickled Sarah's fingertips. High cheekbones met at the base of a distinct nose. A strong jawline and defiant chin underlined soft lips. Sarah reached to his ears; not too big. Soft hair gently laying at the beginning of a strong neck, leading to broad shoulders.

Sarah grinned. Now she *knew* that if she could see, she would find Lucas attractive.

Paige had noticed her son lean forward and for a moment feared he was going to kiss Sarah. But he stopped; Sarah reached for his face.

"What is she doing?" Paige asked Beth

Beth glanced at her daughter. "She's seeing what he looks like." Beth laughed. "She must have decided it was time to find out."

Jonathan and Owen joined their wives in watching Sarah "look" at Lucas. They laughed when Sarah leaned back and smiled.

"She must be pleased with what she sees," Beth whispered coyly.

"Well, he does take after his father," Owen teased.

Later that evening, Sarah sat on a bench with her ice skates on, not knowing if she was capable of skating. She could hear the parents talking off to her left; other kids could be heard all around. Sarah could smell the ice, could hear the grate of blades against it. Someone walked passed her just then, laughing loudly. It made Sarah jump.

Suddenly, Sarah was afraid. She had no idea who else was there. She knew that her dad could have rented the entire rink for the night, but Sarah hadn't really wanted him to do that. Sarah knew that they stood out enough as it was. Most everyone in

Texas knew what her father looked like. They hadn't had problems in public before, so why should tonight be any different. Sarah felt bad renting the place for the whole night when it was just a few of them. She hadn't wanted others to not be able to skate this night. However, she was beginning to doubt her insistence on not renting it out. Sarah hated to think she was going to make a fool of herself in front of others. She couldn't be sure of who would be watching her. She also did not know where Lucas was, except for the fact that he was on the ice already.

Standing slowly, Sarah gathered her balance and wobbled straight ahead; she could smell the ice even more. Her fingers touched the wall bordering the ice rink. Inching along the side, Sarah found an opening and stood with her hand extended. She waited.

Beth saw her daughter find her way to the entrance of the ice. She fought the instinct to go and help her. She almost gave in as she watched Sarah stand with her hand extended, waiting for help.

"She's not waiting for help," Jonathan assured his wife. "She's waiting for Lucas." He smiled and pointed to the boy heading for their daughter.

The sound came of blade against ice as someone slide to a halt in front of Sarah; she held her breath.

"Take my hand," Lucas instructed.

Sarah smiled at the sound of his voice, took his hand and allowed him to lead her onto the ice. She had not skated since she was six. She had a small fear of doing so because of the fact that the last time she had gone skating, her mother had been leading her and had let go of her hand. Sarah had coasted for a while, calling to her mother. Beth had tried to get Sarah to listen to her voice and skate alone, but Sarah had panicked and had fallen. Sarah was afraid to skate alone now. Lucas knew of her fear and had promised to never let go.

Slowly, Sarah relaxed as Lucas skated backwards, leading her around the rink. Each time around he went slightly faster until they were going at an overly moderate speed. Sarah laughed, happy that she had let Lucas talk her into trying ice skating one more time. Her happiness was interrupted, however, when she felt Lucas slow down.

"Carl is here," he informed her. "He has Trevor and Jack with him."

Sarah felt her body go cold, and it had nothing to do with the ice. The three boys that Lucas spoke of were the three that had chased her the day she and Lucas had met. They had not stopped teasing Lucas about her, and they had even tried to get to her again. They had tried to wait for her after school a few more times, but Lucas had always been there, standing between Sarah and those who threatened her. Sarah could not figure out why they hated her so much. She guessed it was a combination of being blind and being the governor's daughter. She was always glad that Lucas was around when they showed up. Sarah heard them skate onto the ice and laugh as they went by.

"Let's go sit down," Sarah suggested, her voice quivering slightly.

Lucas agreed, so they started back around the rink to get to the gate. Out of nowhere Sarah heard skates come up behind them. Laughing, the three boys rushed passed and pulled Lucas with them, his hand tearing out of hers, the force of the tug nearly causing her to fall.

"No, let him go! Lucas!" Sarah managed to stop herself and froze.

Without Lucas guiding her, she had no idea where to go. She didn't even know where she was on the rink. If she moved she risked hitting the wall or another skater. Sarah could hear the other skaters on the ice. She could hear Lucas yelling and the sound of a struggle. Suddenly, a hand grabbed hers, but it was not Lucas's. Sarah tried to pull away but couldn't. The boy laughed

as he pulled her for a bit. Sarah screamed as he let go. Trying to
stop, Sarah stumbled and fell. Sliding across the ice she started to
brace herself to hit the wall.

Lucas nearly fell trying to get away from Trevor and Jack. He
had to get back to Sarah.

"Let me go, " he demanded, slamming his elbow into Jack's
stomach and his fist into Trevor's.

Spinning around, Lucas saw Carl pulling Sarah across the ice.
His blood ran cold as Carl let go. Springing forward, Lucas skated
as fast as he could toward Sarah. He saw her try to stop, falling
onto the ice. She was only a few feet from the wall. Closing the
gap, Lucas slid down onto the ice, grabbed Sarah, and spun all in
one smooth motion, putting himself between her and the wall.

Sarah didn't realize what had happened until they slammed
into the wall. She could feel a hand in hers.

"Lucas?"

Lucas groaned in pain trying to catch his breath. "It's okay…
Sarah…I'm here. I'm sorry I let go."

A sob burst from Sarah's lips as she wrapped her arms around
Lucas's neck. As he hugged her back, Sarah could hear her
mother and Paige calling their names and trying to get across
the ice. She could also hear her father and Owen telling Carl,
Trevor, and Jack that if they did not leave her and Lucas alone,
there would be charges filed and penalties enforced. Sarah could
hear who must have been the boys' parents apologizing less than
convincingly, and then starting to shout back. Soon, the staff of
the skating rink was involved.

"I want to go home," Sarah whispered to Lucas. "Please, I
want to go home."

Lucas nodded and helped Sarah to her feet. Sarah knew that
her mother was on her right side; she could feel her mother's
hand on her elbow. Sarah wasn't letting go of Lucas, though. He
had his right arm around her, his left hand holding hers. Guiding

her back across the ice, Lucas did not let go of Sarah's hand until she was safe in the car; her mother climbed in beside her.

"I'll see you tomorrow," Lucas promised. "I'll be there."

CHAPTER

5

FIVE YEARS LATER

Sarah sat in her room, eyebrows scrunched in concentration, as she worked at French-braiding her hair. She had to stop and start again twice before she felt it was good enough. As it was, she would have Mona confirm it when she got there. Mona's sight had returned two years after Sarah had met her; she now attended school with Lucas. Mona had confessed to Sarah that she liked the blind school better and that Lucas seemed to be the only one in the private school that was not stuck up.

However, due to the fact that Mona's father was a high-priced business attorney, she really had no say in the matter of her schooling. She and Sarah were still good friends, spending at least three afternoons a week together. Mona had made sure to confirm Sarah's suspicions of Lucas's good looks as soon as her sight had returned. She had gone on about it for at least an hour, describing his every little feature in detail, even down to the little dimple that appeared when he smiled.

Sarah could not believe that she and Lucas had been friends for over five years already. She was in her sophomore year of school, and Lucas was a senior. Sarah kept trying to imagine what it would be like to be even more than friends with Lucas. He was the only boy that had ever treated her normal, except for the blind boys. Sarah had only ever wanted to be with Lucas and knew that she always would. She guessed Lucas felt somewhat the same, but she couldn't be sure.

He still took her hand and still looked after her. He had graduated to walking her home on some days; other days, like when he had sports or something, he would still wait with her outside of the school until a car came for her. He simply told his coaches that her safety was more important to him than any game in the world, and if they wanted him to play badly enough, they would let him arrive late. They always did. Lucas was not only smart but an incredible athlete, already receiving college offers. His coaches practically worshiped him. Soon he would just be able to drive her himself. Lucas had told her that the biggest downfall to being advanced in school was being younger than all his classmates and being the last one eligible to get his license.

Sarah couldn't decide if she considered Lucas her boyfriend or not. He kissed her cheek on occasion and was always the perfect gentleman. However, he had never expressed any deeper feelings other than friendship and had never kissed her on the lips. Sarah was confused; her mother told her it would work out in its own time. All Sarah knew was that she never wanted to be without Lucas. He had been somewhat of a guardian for her without her having to have adults around all the time. The extra help was always there but mostly out of sight; in five years they hadn't once been needed. Sarah's father was assured that Lucas was probably better anyway, more so now that he was older. Jonathan was almost as proud as Owen of how Lucas was turning out. The families were still close, and Sarah wondered if she and Lucas *could* ever be anything more than friends.

Just then Sarah heard the doorbell peal. Her mother's shoes clicked across the hardwood floors of the great room as she moved to answer it. Moments later, the door was opened and

Sarah heard Mona greeting her mother. The two talked a bit while Mona moved into the house and then Sarah could hear footsteps on the stairs.

"Hey, girl," Mona greeted, coming into Sarah's room. "Your hair looks nice. You're getting better at it."

Sarah smiled. "I was going to ask you how it looked. The last football game was so windy. I wanted to make sure my hair was contained tonight."

"I thought you were going to cut it?"

Sarah shrugged. "I decided that I wasn't going to. I didn't really want to."

Mona chuckled. "Or Lucas didn't want you to."

Sarah stayed quiet. She could feel a slight blush creeping up her neck, but she ignored it. Getting to her feet, Sarah moved across her room to get into her closet and find clothes for that night. She was a little nervous. Lucas had a football game, and it was the one to determine which team went on to the state championship. Sarah knew that Lucas wasn't very optimistic about their chances of winning. The team they were playing had already beaten them once. However, Lucas's team had beaten them as well, so it was pretty evenly matched.

Sarah had been to every game that she could go to. Lucas had been playing since he had started junior high and this was his second year as quarterback and captain for the varsity team. It unnerved Sarah to the point of nausea to listen to the games and not be able to see. She always made sure that someone was with her so that if Lucas took a hit, she would know right away if he got up or not. If he went down, Sarah would hold out her hand or grab someone else's arm and wait for the pat on her hand that meant Lucas was up and okay.

Sarah knew that what she felt for Lucas went beyond friendship. She could feel it to her core, in her heart. Never having been in love before, Sarah wasn't sure if she could call it that. However, even if she did call it love, it seemed so much more than that. It was like a physical need, like air or something. That was what Sarah felt; she felt like she couldn't breathe when Lucas wasn't at her side.

"What's the matter?" Mona asked.

Sarah sighed. She wasn't ready to confess to anyone what she was feeling. "I'm just nervous about tonight. I always worry that Lucas is going to get hurt."

Mona stood up off the bed, moved across the room to stand behind Sarah, and placed her hand on Sarah's shoulder.

"He'll be okay, Sarah," Mona assured. "He's a tough cookie. No worries."

Sarah sighed again, turning to walk out of her closet. She then pulled her shoes on and followed Mona out the door. After a quick good-bye to her parents, Sarah left the house with Mona and climbed into the passenger's seat of Mona's new car.

"Daddy got it for me when I passed my test," Mona told Sarah. "It has the 'new-car smell' and everything."

Sarah laughed but didn't say anything. She knew that a first car was something that she would never have any experience with. Things that she was going to miss out on were always things that Sarah tried not to dwell on.

While they drove, Sarah listened in amusement as Mona went on and on about Josh, the boy she had been dating for the last few months. He was in Lucas's class, so he was older than Mona and Sarah. Mona loved that about him, primarily because her parents hated it.

Once to the school, Sarah followed Mona through the gates, letting her cane guide her. A few people said hi to her, but she knew that most of them just stared. She could always tell the amount of people that stared based on the scuffs and snorts that Mona made.

"As if they have never seen a blind person before…" she would usually mutter.

There seemed to be an unusual amount of people staring tonight. Sarah smiled as she heard Mona snort for about the twentieth time. She slowed her pace so that she fell back in step with Sarah.

"Ya know, one would think that they had never seen you here before," Mona stated in a mock whisper.

Sarah laughed. They were getting closer to the bleachers. Sarah could hear the hollow metallic banging as people moved up and down. Sarah could smell the grass, could smell the warm autumn air. The day was overcast; Sarah couldn't feel direct sunlight on her shoulders anyway. Lucas had always told her that it was better that way, easier to see the ball.

"Here we are," Mona said, just as Sarah's cane bumped the bottom step of the bleachers.

Sarah reached her hand out, grasped the cool railing to the steps, and started up, aware that Mona was behind her. Sarah made her way up the stairs and then down to the second set of steps upward. She knew the distance by heart. Seven steps up and Sarah took her seat to her left. It was the same place she always sat; it was always reserved for her.

"Hello, Mr. and Mrs. Monroe," Sarah greeted.

Owen huffed in mock irritation and then laughed. "How did you know we were already here? Smell us or hear us breathing?"

Sarah giggled. "I actually heard you whisper to Mrs. Monroe to be quiet to confuse me while I was coming up the steps."

Owen laughed again. Sarah situated herself next to Paige; Mona on her other side.

"Was Lucas nervous about tonight?" Sarah asked Paige.

Sarah heard Paige chuckle softly. "He says that he isn't, but he is. He spent most of the afternoon in his room listening to his music very loudly."

Sarah smiled. Lucas did like to listen to his music quite loudly, much too loudly for Sarah's sensitive ears. As if on cue to the music conversation, Sarah could hear the band getting their instruments around. She prepared herself and only flinched a little as they started to play.

The crowd erupted in cheers as the players started to run out onto the field. Sarah heard the tearing of the paper as the players smashed through the covered hoop the cheerleaders always decorated for each game. Sarah immediately felt better just knowing that Lucas was closer. She listened as the two teams warmed up, running and pumping one another up.

Finally, the referee called for the captains. Sarah knew that Lucas would be going out to the center of the field. She tilted her head a little, leaning as if to get even closer to Lucas, and heard Mona stifle a giggle. Sarah didn't care. She felt whole with Lucas around.

The visiting team won the coin toss and kicked off. Sarah sat on the edge of her seat while the game began. It was intense, to say the least. Sarah was even aware of Paige and Mona flinching at her side. Every time the announcer would yell "And the QB takes a hit!" Sarah would grab their arms until one of them would pat her hand, reassuring her that Lucas was okay.

By the time the final quarter started, Sarah was a nervous wreck. The opposing team seemed to have it out for Lucas. It seemed every time he threw the ball into play, he got tackled to the ground. More than once he was slow to get up. Twice it was an entire ten seconds before Paige touched Sarah's hand.

In the final minutes of the game, Lucas's team had the ball and the score was tied. The crowd was going insane; Paige, Owen, and Mona were on their feet. Sarah stayed seated, all of a sudden very scared for Lucas. The other team had been so hard on him. It made Sarah very nervous about how desperate they would get.

There was so much noise. Sarah couldn't differentiate between anything that she was hearing. The announcer was about to lose his mind. Sarah tried to listen to him so at least she would know what was going on.

"There's the hike...Monroe is looking for an opening...he runs...Turner is open...Monroe throws...Turner is in the end zone—ooh, Monroe is hit—it's good! Touchdown!"

The audience erupted just then, driving Sarah's ears nearly to their breaking point; she had to stuff her fingers in them momentarily. She couldn't be excited about the win, though. She had heard the announcer say that Lucas was hit. Sarah held out her hand and waited. And waited. And waited. Sarah got to her feet. She turned slightly toward Paige.

"Paige? What is going on? What is it?" Sarah's heart was pounding. The audience was starting to fall silent.

"What is it?" Sarah demanded.

"He's...he's not getting up," Paige chocked.

"Dear Lord, no," Sarah breathed. She fell back into her seat. Mona sat beside her with an arm around her shoulder. Sarah could feel her body shaking in fear.

"Trainer!" She heard a referee call.

Sarah could hear the hurried footsteps of the team's medic running out to the field, along with another person, probably the coach. The seconds ticked by like hours for Sarah. Tears started to run down her face. Paige reached down and took her hand, but there was too much tension in her grasp to reassure. Sarah heard more people running out.

"EMS is going out there," Mona whispered.

A small sob of fear escaped Sarah's lips. What would she do without Lucas? What if he was paralyzed? What if he was in a coma? What if he got amnesia and never again remembered who she was? Sarah couldn't breathe.

"Lucas, don't leave me," Sarah whispered so quiet she knew that she was the only one to hear. Sarah closed her eyes and prayed, and prayed.

Finally, Paige gasped. Sarah's eyes popped open, though she knew it wasn't going to change anything. She waited. And then Paige sighed in relief.

"He's moving," she said. "His legs are moving. They're getting him ready to roll onto the stretcher."

Just then, Lucas screamed in pain. Sarah felt as though she had been electrocuted. Her hand flew to her heart, tears streaming down her face.

"What? What is it? What is wrong with him?" Sarah jumped to her feet.

"It's okay, Sarah," Mona soothed. "He's okay. They are messing with his left arm. Probably a dislocated shoulder or something. Okay, he is on the stretcher. Oh, there it is, he has his fist in the air. He's letting you know he's okay."

Sarah gasped in relief as the crowd cheered in support. Lucas had established a long time ago that he would let Sarah know, through other people of course, that he was okay, heard her or anything else that he had to let her know by putting his right fist in the air. Well, that was something. He was okay enough to remember to let her know.

Mona helped Sarah down off the bleachers. Paige and Owen were right behind them. Sarah held Mona's arm, not really paying attention to where they were going. She was focused on what else she heard. She could hear the EMS speaking. Then she heard it; she heard Lucas's voice.

"No, it's my entire arm," Lucas was saying. "The entire thing is on fire."

Sarah winced at the pain she could hear in his voice. She unconsciously started to drift in the direction that she was hearing Lucas, her arm pulling tight on Mona's. They were closer. Sarah stopped, practically sensing the fence in front of her. Two steps forward, and she was touching it.

"Sarah, what are you doing?" Mona asked.

"Are you okay, Hercules?" Sarah called. She teased him with his nickname, mostly to hide her own fear.

"Sarah!" he hollered back. "Yeah, I'm fine. I think my arm is busted. Meet us at Regional. That is where they are taking me."

"I'll be there," Sarah promised. She turned on her heels, took Mona's arm again, and practically led her to the car.

As it turned out, Lucas was right. His left arm was broken just below the elbow. He had to have surgery to set the bones correctly. He also had a concussion. He spent the rest of the night and part of the next day in the hospital with Sarah at his side every chance she got. When he was finally able to come home, he was out of school for a few more days. Every afternoon Sarah made her driver take her to Lucas's house so that she could check on him. Once he was able to come back to school, Lucas continued to take her home. Sarah tried to tell him he didn't have to, that he could go straight home to rest. Lucas wouldn't listen. He insisted on sticking the course and making sure Sarah got home safely.

Three weeks later (following the football team's loss in the state championship), Lucas and Sarah were out for ice cream one evening. Sarah was having a difficult time with what she was feeling. She knew that she was falling for Lucas; she knew it with all that she was. However, what did he feel for her? Was his behavior strictly due to what he thought were his duties to keep her safe? Or was he starting to have feelings for her as well? Sarah couldn't be sure, and not knowing was driving her insane.

She could currently hear Lucas laughing with someone as he ordered their ice cream. The voice was vaguely familiar to Sarah, like the other person might have been on the football team or something. Sarah was sitting at one of the picnic tables waiting for Lucas to come sit with her. He always made sure she was seated and then went up to order. He never wanted her to stand in line for fear that she might get bumped or something. Sarah smiled grimly to herself. Mona always told her that Lucas did what he did out of love for her. Sarah just couldn't be sure. She wanted to believe it, she really did. But Sarah couldn't make herself believe that he felt the same as she did just because he didn't want her to stand in line. Everyone did that for her, even strangers.

Sarah tilted her head. She could hear Lucas starting to move toward her. She could tell it was him by the way he walked. He had a specific gait pattern that Sarah had come to recognize. He walked with a confidence that not many people held, but yet he dragged his left heel just slightly. Not to mention she could hear his cast scraping against his jeans. He must have the ice cream on a tray, carrying it one-handed.

Sarah turned her face toward where she was hearing Lucas coming from. "Did you remember to get me extra cherries?" she asked.

Lucas chuckled. "How did you know it was me coming?"

"I told you, I recognize you walk. Besides, I can smell your cologne, like always."

Lucas laughed again. "Are my applications still too heavy for you?"

Sarah giggled as well. "No, it is just the right amount, actually. I think I am just more sensitive to it. Besides, I was downwind. I can smell the hot fudge on your ice cream. Double, as usual?"

Lucas laughed and Sarah heard him set her caramel sundae in front of her.

"Twelve o'clock," Lucas said, "spoon is at three."

Sarah smiled. She had long since outgrown the need for people to tell her where her food and silverware were in relation to her position, but Lucas still did it out of habit. Sarah let him. She thought it was cute.

They didn't say anything for a few minutes as they dug into their treats. Sarah was happy to find five cherries on her sundae, just as she liked. She could usually beg Lucas for his as well. Sarah felt her head tip as she listened to Lucas sitting across from her. She could hear the tap of the index finger of his left hand as it thrummed against the table. He did it all the time. She knew that his spoon would be in his right hand. She could tell that he was bouncing his right foot as well, the gravel scuffing as the toe of his shoe moved. He did this when he was nervous or anxious about something. He always seemed to be nervous or anxious when they were in public together.

"What's wrong?" Sarah finally asked as she put her spoon in her empty dish.

"Nothing, really," Lucas replied. Sarah knew that this was his knee-jerk response when there was something wrong and he didn't want to say it.

"Are you sure?" she asked. "You seem awfully uptight. Your leg hasn't stopped bouncing since we got here."

Sarah heard Lucas's leg stop. He laughed.

"I'm sorry," he replied. "There are just more people here than usual, and you know how I get in crowds."

Sarah did know how he got in crowds. He was always more nervous about her safety when there were a lot of people around. He told her that it was because he couldn't watch everyone at once, that he never knew who was around. It always made Sarah extra nervous as well.

"Well, I'm done, so we can go if you want," Sarah suggested.

Lucas sighed. "Yeah, we probably should. It's getting pretty busy, and I don't want you here when the 'night crowd' rolls in."

Sarah heard Lucas stand, pick their dishes up and walk over to the trash. She knew that this specific ice cream place not only had the best around, but was also a popular hangout for teens after the sun went down. There had been more than one instance of fighting reported to police. Sarah had also heard about things happening to girls and various other rumors about things that couples did behind the building. It made Sarah shudder. She was suddenly extra-aware of the sun going down. Lucas was right. It was time to go.

"Well, well, well," a voice suddenly hissed in her ear.

Sarah gasped, flinching away from the speaker. It was Carl, one of the original boys that had given her so many troubles when she was younger. Sarah hated him, even if he had indirectly led to her meeting Lucas. Carl had been a problem ever since that first fateful confrontation outside of the blind school. He hadn't given up his pursuit of making Sarah's life miserable. He never missed an opportunity to harass Sarah, or Lucas for that matter. He was always coming near Sarah, saying obscene things and trying to touch her.

Sarah scooted away from Carl as quickly as she could, sliding right off the bench of the picnic table; her cane clattered to the ground. She stumbled a little in her haste, spinning so that Carl wasn't behind her anymore.

"Get lost, Carl," Sarah spat, sounding braver than she felt. In truth, she was terrified. She wasn't sure where Lucas had gone. Not to mention, Carl was the one person Sarah feared above all others.

"Wanna get lost with me?" Carl asked. He reached out, grabbed Sarah's arm and pulled her toward him. Sarah was just about to scream when—

"Hey!" Lucas yelled. Sarah heard him run toward them. Lucas's strong hands were suddenly gripping Sarah's arms and pulling her away from Carl. It sounded like Carl was pushed away. She was then aware of Lucas stepping in front of her, between her and Carl.

"Don't think for one second that just because my arm is in a cast that I won't be able to defend her," Lucas snarled, his voice low, like Sarah knew it always was when he was angry.

Lucas stared Carl down, feeling the hatred for him seep into his very soul. He couldn't let him near Sarah. The possible consequences were far too painful to imagine. Carl twitched to his right (Lucas's left) as if to try and get passed Lucas on his weaker side. Lucas took his left hand and gently pushed Sarah away to the right. She was so used to his reactions that she didn't even stumble. She could hear Carl's movements nearly as well as Lucas could see them after all.

Carl tried to reach around Lucas to grab Sarah again. Lucas lashed out with his left hand, cracking his cast against Carl's temple. He bit back a groan as his broken arm jarred inside the plaster. Carl stumbled back, righted himself, and acted as though he was going to come back at them. Lucas cocked his right arm, getting ready to hit Carl again if he came any closer. Carl paused, thought about it, and then started to back away.

"Just you wait," he sneered, turning to leave.

Lucas lowered his arm, clenching his teeth against the throbbing of his broken bone. He made sure Carl kept going and then turned to Sarah. She was white as a ghost, both arms extended his way. Lucas's heart clenched. He hated when she was afraid like that. He wished he could make it all go away. He wished that he could make it so that she was never afraid again. Most of all, he wished he knew what wishing all of that meant in regards to what he was feeling for Sarah.

"Are you okay?" he asked.

Sarah nodded, relief washing over her face. She knew that if Lucas was talking to her and asking her if she was okay, then the threat was gone.

"I want to go home," she stated.

Lucas reached out, took her hand and started to lead her home.

After his arm had healed, Lucas decided that it was time to teach Sarah some defensive skills, especially since Carl was so bent on making her life difficult. He wasn't sure how it would work, but he wanted to try. It pained him to think that he may not be around when she needed help. He wanted to feel somewhat reassured that she could at least mildly defend herself. If all else failed Lucas figure that it might take an attacker by surprise to have a blind girl fight back.

So the Saturday after his cast came off, Lucas went over to Sarah's house. He greeted Governor and Mrs. Watkins and then moved to the backyard where Sarah was waiting for him; Lucas had called ahead. He walked up behind where she was sitting in a chair; she turned slightly as she heard him approach. Lucas saw her smile. He could feel the breeze coming from behind him and knew that Sarah could smell him.

"You're late, Hercules," she scolded, though her smile grew larger.

"I'm sorry," Lucas laughed. " Zeus made me finish my chores before I was allowed out to play."

Sarah laughed and got to her feet, reaching for his hand like she always did. Lucas took it, warmth spreading through his entire body like always. He tried to ignore it, as usual. He didn't want to look into it too much. He couldn't get that involved.

"What are we going to be doing?" Sarah asked as Lucas led her out into the yard more. He didn't want to destroy Mrs. Watkins's flower beds.

"I am going to teach you how to defend yourself," Lucas said, pulling Sarah to a stop.

She looked at him incredulously. "How? You do remember that I can't see, right?"

Lucas snorted. "Of course. However, part of my training has been using my skills without being able to see. You have to learn to use your other senses acutely when subject to sensory deprivation."

"Okay," Sarah replied, skeptical. She wasn't sure how this was going to work, but she trusted Lucas. If he thought it would work, thought it best, she would do it. So Sarah stood where Lucas put her and listened as he instructed her.

"So, Sarah, the first thing that you are instructed in self-defense is to anticipate the attack. Since you know nothing other than being blind, this will not be hard for you. You should be able to tell where I am coming from before I am even close enough to grab you."

Sarah's heart kicked up a notch as Lucas circled her, looking at her from every angle as he judged her center of balance and strength. He then taught her how to stand so that she was balanced as much as possible when attacked. He showed her how to lash out with her hand and catch a captor in the nose or throat. He taught her how to punch and kick. He even taught her how to throw someone over her back. Sarah thought that she would pass out when he came up behind her and wrapped his arms around her body. As it was, they had to stop and start three times before Sarah could concentrate enough to get the hang of it. Lucas thought that she was having a hard time seeing him as an enemy; that she didn't want to hurt him. However, Sarah knew that it was not it at all.

"One thing that I want you to remember, though," Lucas was saying toward the end of their lesson, "is to never engage an attacker unless you think that you stand a decent chance. If there is more than one person coming after you, don't fight. Be submissive. If the person is quite a lot larger than you, try something that will take them down for a while. A knee to the groin usually works on men."

Sarah giggled. Lucas cleared his throat and Sarah knew that he was probably blushing a little, or grimacing.

"Do you have any questions?" Lucas asked.

"Can we have lunch now?" Sarah asked.

Lucas just laughed.

CHAPTER

6

Sarah sat in her homeroom, fidgeting. She was supposed to be studying for her English test, but the braille text sat open in front of her, ignored. She was anxious beyond all belief. Today was Friday and the day of the big basketball game. Lucas was captain of the varsity team. He was just as much of a star on the basketball court as he was the football field. After the game was his school's yearly Valentine's Day sweetheart dance. Not only was Sarah nervous about the dance (never having really been to one before), but she was also nervous about the fact that Lucas had asked her to go with him. When his school had had dances in the past, Lucas had always stayed home; well, he had come over to Sarah's. Sarah was both nervous and excited about what it could mean for him to ask her to the dance.

Finally, the bell rang, signaling the end of the day. Sarah jumped to her feet, hurrying as fast as she could out of the classroom and to her locker. She grabbed the books she would need for the weekend to keep up with her homework (since she hadn't gotten any studying done) and hurried out of the school. Once through the doors, Sarah stepped to the side to avoid blocking the exit, held out her hand and waited. She heard a low chuckle that sent a tingle of joy down her spine and felt Lucas's strong hand take hers.

"Did you have a good day?" he asked as he led her down the stairs.

"I did until just recently," Sarah replied a little more urgently than she meant to.

"What happened?" Lucas asked, his voice taking on the tenor it always did when he thought she was in trouble.

Sarah laughed. "Nothing happened. I am just nervous about tonight. I've never been to a school dance before, remember?"

Lucas pulled his hand out of hers and put his arm around her shoulders. That thrilled Sarah. He didn't usually do things like that.

"I'll be there, don't forget. I won't let anything happen to you."

They stopped just then, Lucas sidestepping slightly so that he was in front of Sarah, or so she thought. Sarah's heart was pounding. She wasn't sure what he was doing. Just then she heard a car door open. Then it made sense.

"You passed your test?" Sarah squealed.

"Yup," Lucas responded. "Today was my first day out. Would you care for a *ride* home?"

"Why thank you," Sarah said, allowing Lucas to take her hand again and help her into his new truck. She smiled as she heard Lucas shut the door, knowing that he would go around to his side. She was happy for him that he finally had his driver's license. However, a small part of her wished that when he had stopped in front of her like that, it had been for another reason other than showing off his car.

That night, Mona came over for dinner and to help Sarah get ready. She helped Sarah do her hair and makeup. They had agreed to go to the game fully prepared all but the dress, deciding to put them on afterwards in the bathroom so they didn't get dirty. After they were finished with preparations, Mona drove them to the school.

Once there, Sarah started to get really nervous. She knew that there was going to be a lot of other students around, all of them from the private school. Sarah took a deep breath as she climbed out of the car and followed Mona into the school. She would just have to focus on the fact that Lucas would be there. Sarah could survive anything as long as she had Lucas.

Following Mona into the gymnasium, Sarah could hear the already hefty crowd gathering. Supposedly it was the first chance in fifteen years the school had at beating their archrival. Sarah was proud of Lucas. He was a star athlete, an excellent student, and still had time to help her get home safely. Lucas had managed to not only be the youngest student in his class but he was also graduating valedictorian, as of right now anyway. He planned to attend the local military prep school to start training and continuing his education for two years before joining the forces at the age of eighteen. Sarah hated to think about him leaving the city, let alone the state or country. Finding their seats, she waited with Mona for the game to begin.

Trying to concentrate on Mona while she talked, Sarah couldn't help but hear everyone around her talking as well. Two old ladies behind her were talking about their grandsons, numbers 12 and 16. Two men to the back and left of her were heatedly discussing the win possibility. Suddenly, Sarah heard Lucas's name mentioned. She focused her hearing to the front and right of her.

"I can't wait to watch Lucas sweat tonight," one girl cooed. She had an unpleasant, whiny voice. "He is so fine."

"I know," her friend responded. "It's too bad all of his attention is focused on the delinquent."

They both laughed.

"I guess he's bringing her to the dance," a third girl informed. "I wonder if she can even dance, not being able to see and all."

"Well," the second girl started, "I have never seen her, but apparently she is not that bad looking. Carl said he'd love to take her home."

"He'd take anything home that had a pulse," the first girl laughed. "All I know is that if the blind chick leaves Lucas's side for even a moment, I am taking her place. I am tired of waiting to have him. I don't care if she is the governor's daughter."

Sarah leaned over to Mona. "The three girls to the front and right of me are talking about Lucas. Who are they? What do they look like?"

Mona paused, looking for the culprits. "Oh, them," she groaned. "Those three are in Lucas's class. They think they own every guy in school. All three of them are blonde with *full* figures, if you know what I mean."

"One of them said she wants Lucas. Who is she? Is she prettier than me?"

Mona laughed. "That's Tanya. She hates that Lucas likes you and not her. She's not used to a guy not wanting her. Besides, Lucas is a prize in this school. Smart, athletic, hot, ya know, he's awesome. You're a lucky girl."

Sarah sighed. "We're just friends, I guess. I sometimes think I'm still his job."

Mona scoffed. "I disagree. I have seen the way he looks at you. If it isn't a look of nothing but love, I don't know what is."

Sarah started to respond, but just then the introduction music started playing. The crowd went crazy as the team ran out onto the court. Sarah could hear the squeak of the shoes and could smell the sweat, could feel the excitement and tension pulse through the air.

Mona leaned over. "Lucas is looking for you. Wave your hand." Sarah waved her hand in the air hoping he would see that she was there.

"His fist is in the air," Mona told her. Then, she gasped. "He just blew you a kiss! Holy crap!"

Sarah felt a blush of elation creep up her neck. She could hear the girls from earlier scoffing and muttering in mutiny. Feeling bold, Sarah got to her feet. Smiling in smug satisfaction, Sarah blew a kiss back to Lucas with as much enthusiasm as she could. A nervous giggle escaped her lips as she settled back. She could feel Mona staring at her.

"Where did all that come from?" she asked. "I don't think I have ever seen Lucas smile that big."

Sarah shrugged, trying to be nonchalant. She wasn't sure what to say. She hadn't ever told anyone, not even Mona or her mother, what she was beginning to feel for Lucas. She knew that they both suspected, but Sarah kept it to herself. She needed to be able to sort out her own feelings before she spoke them out loud.

"I haven't figured that out yet," Sarah replied quietly. She heard Mona stifle a giggle, but Sarah was saved by the blow of the whistle to start the game.

The first half of the game went smoothly. Both teams played well, keeping the points difference within five. By halftime, the home team was up by three. Mona led Sarah out into the hall and to the bathroom. Sarah felt her way around until she was finished with what she came to do. Opening the stall door, Sarah called for her friend. Mona didn't answer. Stepping out, Sarah attempted to get to the sinks.

"You must be Sarah Watkins," a girl said in a snide tone.

Sarah jumped. Nodding, she calmly felt her way to wash her hands. Not knowing who was in with her, Sarah braced herself, knowing Lucas couldn't come to her.

"Are you and Lucas sleeping together?" the girl asked.

"Excuse me?" Sarah then realized it was the voice of that Tanya girl.

"You heard me. He has no interest in any other girl but you, or so it seems. Maybe he's gay."

"He's not gay."

"Well, then you must be keeping him somehow. How can you provide if you can't see? He deserves a girl who can see how hot he is, a girl that knows what she's got. Someone who is not going to be a burden to him. Besides, you aren't even that good looking."

"We're not sleeping together and never have. Perhaps he's into girls who are concerned with more than just sex and popularity. I'm sure Lucas wants a girl with a brain. Besides, there are no rules saying that you have to be able to see to provide for a man. I plan to wait until I am married and I am sure Lucas does, too. I know that you want him. Maybe, since he doesn't want you back, you should turn your accusing stare back at yourself. He could just think you a waste of time." Sarah didn't know where her sudden daring was coming from. The jealousy she could understand. The bravery she wasn't quite sure of.

Tanya gasped. "You little retard! Why I have half a mind to—"

"Sarah?" Mona called in, entering the bathroom. Noticing Tanya, Mona looked to her friend.

"Are you okay?" Mona asked.

Sarah nodded her response.

"We have to go," Mona informed. "The roses are going to be passed out. I'm sure Lucas got you one."

"He probably got me three," Tanya threw in.

"Oh, shut up!" Mona hissed, taking Sarah's arm. "He doesn't even know that you exist."

Sarah followed Mona back to their seats and waited. Every year the sweetheart dance was near Valentine's Day and always after a basketball game. At halftime, the varsity athletes would hand out roses to a person or persons of their choice. Since they hadn't gone last year, Lucas had brought a dozen roses to her house after the game, along with a pint of ice cream.

The announcer called for the crowd's attention. Everyone quieted and listened as she told about the flowers and the tradition. Finally, quiet music started to play. Sarah could hear the players step forward to the flowers.

Mona did a play-by-play for Sarah. "Lucas is at the flowers... He grabbed two... He's coming this way... Oh, Tanya intercepted him... She's reaching for the flowers... Ha-ha, he slapped her hand away... Here he comes and, oh, there's Josh. He has a rose for me!"

Mona was lost, running up to meet Josh. Sarah laughed at her friend who was smitten beyond all belief. Sarah heard someone come up beside her; she turned her face.

"Take my hand."

Only that voice could cause Sarah's heart to pound like it was. She smiled and took Lucas's hand. He pulled her to her feet and ran the roses across her cheeks and under her nose so she could feel and smell them. She giggled.

"Wait for me in the hall outside the locker room," Lucas whispered in her ear. He then kissed Sarah's cheek.

"I'll be there," she replied, feeling slightly faint. She heard Lucas move away, followed by Mona giggling her way back to her seat. She started to prattle on about Josh and how cute he was, how nice he was, how athletic and smart he was. Sarah only half-listened. Most of her thoughts were still on the memory of Lucas's breath on her neck as he whispered in her ear.

The second half of the game was crazy. Lucas was on fire, according to Mona. At the final buzzer, the crowd cheered and rushed the floor. They had won by a three-point shot at the buzzer from Lucas. Mona ran to Josh and left Sarah where she was. Sarah knew that she would be trampled in the chaos, so she simply stayed where she was. As it was, Sarah was bumped from all sides as people rushed by, hopping down the bleachers rather than taking the steps.

Suddenly, strong arms scooped her up and started to carry her down the steps. "Lucas, put me down," Sarah demanded.

"How did you know it was me?"

"I can smell your cologne."

"I put that on this morning. How do you still smell it? I'm sure that is not the most potent smell on me right now."

Sarah laughed. "True. You do smell just a little. Heightened sense of smell, remember? Why do you think I tell you to take it easy on the applications?" Smiling, Sarah wrapped her arms around Lucas's damp neck.

Lucas laughed, moved down the bleachers and then lowered Sarah to her feet beside Mona. He kissed her hand.

"Don't forget to wait for me," he said quietly. "It won't be worth going if you aren't there."

"Okay," Sarah replied breathlessly.

Lucas kissed her hand again and turned to go as well. Sarah turned and followed Mona to the bathroom so they could change. Once there, Sarah started to shake. She had never been to a school dance before, and she was still worried about what it would be like. Besides, not only had Lucas asked her to go with him, but he had also been more, well, intimate with his expressions lately. Could it possibly mean what Sarah wanted it to mean? Could God really bless her that fully?

"Do you think he likes me?" Sarah asked as Mona helped zip her baby-blue dress.

Mona didn't even have to ask who she was talking about. "Girl, are you nuts?" Mona laughed. "Like I said, I have seen the way he looks at you. Personally, I think he loves you but is too much of a gentleman to admit it without knowing your feelings."

"You say that like it is a bad thing." Sarah felt defensive.

"Easy, girl. It's not a bad thing. I think it is great that he isn't pressuring you into making out or having sex, that he isn't taking advantage of you. I think you two are meant for each other. I mean, come on. You were born on the same day of the same year at the same hospital only an hour apart. Trust me. You are destined to be together and, trust me, he definitely loves you."

"Well, I sure hope so," Sarah replied in hushed longing, "because I sure do love him."

Mona stared after Sarah as she felt her way to the door. It was the first time that she had admitted out loud to anyone that she loved Lucas, though Mona had always known. Smiling, Mona followed her friend out the door and led her to the locker room.

•

"Can I ask you a question, Josh?" Lucas stood leaning against his locker in the locker room in just a towel, hair still damp from his shower, water still gleaming off his taut muscles.

"What's on your mind, man?" Josh and Lucas had been friends ever since Josh had transferred four years earlier. He had arrived just after Christmas break in eighth grade. He was older than Lucas but in his class just the same.

Josh had never met anyone like Lucas. He was strong and athletic. He was also the perfect gentleman like his southern parents had raised him. He never cursed (well, almost never), went to church, and only fought to protect himself or those he loved—mainly Sarah. Josh knew that Lucas had been bred for the Army and could kill with his skills, but wouldn't hurt a fly. Josh envied Lucas's talent and maturity, physically and mentally. But during the past few months Josh had noticed a change in Lucas. He had become kind of quiet and really distracted. Josh had thought it was academic overload, but now he was not so sure.

"I know something's been eating at you lately," Josh admitted, buttoning his shirt. "What's up?"

Lucas sighed, pulling on his slacks. "It's Sarah. I think she's in love with me. I think she wants to be more than friends, and I don't know what to do."

Josh sighed. "If you don't feel the same, just let her know."

"That's the problem," Lucas hissed, harsher than he meant to. Sighing again, Lucas zipped his slacks and leaned his head on his locker door.

"I do feel the same," he groaned.

Josh looked at his friend, bewildered. "How's that a problem?"

Lucas glared sideways at his friend. "I can't protect her properly if I love her. My emotions will blind my senses, slow my reflexes, and dull my instincts. Besides, what would her father say? I can't protect *and* date the governor's daughter. That is one of the rules: don't get emotionally attached to the mission."

Josh let out an exasperated growl. "Lucas, look"—Josh grabbed his shoulders, turning him so that they faced each other—"love is one thing that you cannot command or plan for. Don't let your pride, your training, or what you believe to be your duties get in the way. Don't be such a jackass. Sarah needs you. She loves you."

Josh sprayed on a touch of cologne, patted Lucas on the back, and headed for the door. Lucas started to follow, but the coach called him back. Lucas yelled at Josh to let Sarah know he would be out soon.

●

Sarah stood outside the locker room with her back against the wall. Her right foot was tapping as the anxiety she was feeling spilled over. Mona was next to her, dancing from side to side excitedly. The door of the locker room opened, but it wasn't Lucas.

"You look really beautiful," Josh said to Mona.

Mona giggled. "Thanks. You look really good as well."

"Sarah, the coach wanted to talk to Lucas, so he told me to tell you that he would be out in a minute."

"Do you want us to wait with you?" Mona asked.

Sarah could tell by the tone in Mona's voice that she really didn't want to wait with Sarah. She probably wanted a few moments alone with Josh before going into the dance.

"No, you two go ahead. I can wait here by myself." Sarah hated to think she would be a burden to them.

It took a little bit of persuasion, but Mona and Josh finally walked off. Standing patiently, Sarah waited for Lucas. She knew that the coach had a tendency to be long-winded, especially when he was going on and on about how wonderful Lucas was. Sarah smiled. Not that she would disagree with him on that. Someone walked up beside Sarah just then, but it was not Lucas. The smell was all wrong.

"Hello, Sarah," Carl sneered.

Sarah gasped. "Get lost, Carl. Lucas will be out any minute." Sarah feared Carl more than she feared death. She was terrified to think of what he would do to her if he ever met her in a dark alley. He was constantly trying to grab at her and never missed a beat when it came to a dirty comment. Luckily, Lucas was never far behind. All he ever had to do was stand face-to-face with Carl, and Carl would back down. Carl would always hiss "Just wait until I get you alone." Now Sarah was alone.

"One minute is all I need, babe." Carl reached over and grabbed Sarah's arms and had both of her wrists locked in one of his hands before she could blink. His free hand came down over her mouth. "If only I had the chance…" Carl let his intentions hang in the arm, causing goose bumps to rise on Sarah's arms.

Sarah tried to pull away, but Carl would not let go. Sarah prayed for Lucas to come to her. Carl moved closer holding her arms above her head and pinning her to the wall. Sarah tried to squirm away. Carl used his elbows to hold her head still; he pressed his body to hers. Sarah could feel his body pressing on hers and started to panic.

Carl leaned in closer, his lips nearly to hers. "What I wouldn't give for just a few moments alone with you," he hissed, licking her cheek. He moved his hand just then, leaning in to try to kiss Sarah, but he also shifted his entire body to the angle she needed. With a snap of her hip, Sarah slammed her knee upward into Carl's groin. He cried out in surprise and pain.

"Lucas!" Sarah screamed.

Carl cursed and shoved her to the ground.

Commotion from within the locker room sounded, and seconds later the door slammed open. Lucas rushed out, and before Carl could react, Lucas slammed both of his hands into Carl's chest, shoving him backward away from Sarah. Sarah moved to the wall again and stood up out of the way. Lucas stepped to the side, putting himself between Carl and Sarah.

Carl got to his feet. He came back at Lucas full force, his fists clenched. Lucas waited and just when Carl was about to swing, Lucas lashed out with his hand, catching Carl in the throat. Carl choked and sputtered, stumbling back once more.

"Come near her again, even look at her, and it is over," Lucas sneered, taking a defensive stance once more in front of Sarah. Carl climbed to his feet.

"What gives you the authority to tell me what to do?" Carl snarled hoarsely.

"She gives me the authority," Lucas responded. "She doesn't want you around. She has said that before. Since she can't see you in order to defend herself against you, then I will."

"Just go ahead and try," Carl responded.

Sarah heard Carl rush forward again. Someone's fist came into contact with the other's face. Sarah assumed it was Lucas throwing the punch, but she couldn't be sure. A body fell to the floor.

Sarah heard someone scamper to his feet once more and move down the hall. "You are going to regret messing with my space," Carl threatened. Footsteps moved away, and then everything was quiet. A moment or two passed in silence.

Lucas glared after Carl as he moved away, his threat echoing in Lucas's mind. Turning away, Lucas faced Sarah. Her beautiful face was pinched in worry and fear. Her head was tilted as she tried to listen to what was happening now that it was quiet. Lucas was angry again, angry at what Carl had done and continued to threaten to do. Lucas couldn't let that happen.

"Lucas? Are you there?" Sarah questioned, her voice quivering.

"Yeah, I'm here. Are you okay?"

Sarah nodded, shaken, reaching to him to be held. It had happened before, incidences like this, but this was the first time Carl had ever gotten physical. Lucas was usually there to stop him first. The only part Sarah was not used to was the foreboding feeling of what would happen if Lucas couldn't come save her.

"Did he hurt you?" Lucas asked, rage still edging his voice.

Sarah shook her head. "He just held me down and tried to kiss me."

"I'll kill him," Lucas growled. He made to go after Carl, but Sarah stopped him.

"I gave him a knee to the groin. He got what was coming," Sarah said.

Lucas had to hold back a smile, despite his fury over Carl's harassment. He was glad he had taught Sarah a few basic moves of defense that she could do even though she couldn't see. She was good at the knee to the groin and was getting better at flipping a body over her back.

"Let's just go and try to enjoy the rest of the night," Sarah suggested, though she would have rather gone home. Lucas silently fumed as he led Sarah down the hall. It was a while before he spoke.

"You look really beautiful by the way," Lucas assured, stopping and wrapping his arms around Sarah. "It took the breath out of me at first."

Sarah felt herself blush not only from the compliment but also from the way Lucas had his arms around her. He hadn't done that before. He had hugged her before, sure, but he had never *held* her that way before. She pulled away and placed her hand on Lucas's cheek. "I'm sure you look equally wonderful."

"Well, ya know." Sarah felt the corners of his mouth turn up in a smile. Taking her hand, Lucas kissed her cheek, but then stopped. Sarah felt his other hand come up to the cheek he just kissed.

"I don't know what I'd do if anything ever happened to you," Lucas whispered. Sarah placed her hands on his chest; Lucas wondered if her heart was beating as fast as his. Cupping her face, Lucas gently pulled Sarah's lips to his. The feelings that rushed over him were like none he had ever felt before.

With her hands on his chest, Sarah felt Lucas's lips touch her own and lost herself in the splendor. She couldn't breathe, her head spinning. Lucas pressed his lips harder against hers, eager and loving. Sarah welcomed it, her body melting against his, making the world spin. She was sure her heart would explode.

Lucas pulled away. "I love you, Sarah," he whispered, emotion in his voice. "I have since I was ten."

"I always knew you would come to me," Sarah confessed. "I loved you before I even knew your name."

•

"Are you kidding me?" Mona squealed loudly.

Sarah felt herself blush. "No, I'm not kidding. He kissed me. And, well, he told me that he loves me."

Mona screamed out loud jumping up and down. Sarah turned to rushed footsteps on her left.

"What's the matter?" Lucas asked, his voice tense. "Are you okay, Sarah?"

Sarah felt herself blush harder. "Yes, I am fine. Mona is just—"

"You kissed her!" Mona yelled out loud. "Thank you. It is about time. I've been waiting forever for you two to get your ducks in a row."

Sarah felt a look of chagrin pass over her face. She turned to Lucas with what she hoped was an apologetic look on her face.

Lucas cleared his throat. "Well, you know…anyway…"

And with that, Lucas kissed Sarah on the forehead and walked back off.

"Well, he was redder than Santa's suit," Mona laughed.

"You shouldn't have embarrassed him that way," Sarah scolded, though she couldn't be mad. Not with all of the love she had in her heart.

She and Mona went over to a bench to sit for a while. The music was a little too loud for Sarah's taste, but she guessed that was due to her oversensitive ears. She let Lucas lead her onto the dance floor for every slow song they played. She sat out the fast ones and let Lucas goof around with his friends in celebration of their win.

As she sat, Sarah started to think about how perfectly she and Lucas seemed to fit together. They had never fought and rarely ever disagreed, except for when both of their stubborn streaks shone through at the same time. Usually that happened when Sarah wanted to do something that Lucas didn't approve of. Sarah knew that she loved Lucas. She knew that he loved her, but why would he want her? She hated the idea of forever being a burden to him as Tanya had so eloquently pointed out.

Sarah knew that she was only sixteen, but she couldn't help but think about a future with Lucas. It seemed bright to her, but what would he think? Would he tire of caring for her? *Would* she end up being a burden to him? What would happen then? What would she do without Lucas?

Sarah felt someone sit down beside her. "Lucas?"

"No, it's me," Mona replied. "Be glad you can't see right now. Tanya is throwing herself at Lucas to the point I think he may hit her. It is so disgusting."

Sarah sighed. "I think I want to leave."

Mona glanced at her friend. "Why? Aren't you having fun?"

Sarah shook her head. "It's not that, it's just, being here has made me realize that Lucas and I have no future. Why would he want to be burdened by me when he could have any girl he wants? He's only sixteen. I can't ask him to throw his life away to take care of me."

Mona nearly screamed. "Girl, when will you get it through your thick skull that he does love you? He said so, didn't he? Why do you think he takes you home every day? Why do you think that, if he can help it, he is never more than ten feet from your side? He doesn't get paid to protect you. He does it out of love and always has. He told me once that the first day he met you he never wanted to lose you. You love him too. What brought about the mood change? You were so happy."

Sarah sighed. "I don't know. Just insecure, I guess."

"Just let your love lead you, and don't worry about any-thing else."

But Sarah couldn't help worrying. She needed some air; it was so stuffy in the gymnasium. "I need to go out in the hall for a minute. Let Lucas know."

"I can get him for you so…wait, I don't see him. Hold on for a minute." Mona stood up to look through the crowd.

"I can go on my own. The door is fifteen steps to my right and the hallway dead ends to the right. I can manage. I only need a bit of air." Sarah stood, turned and walked the fifteen steps to the door, bumping a few people along the way and Mona still call-ing to her to wait. She felt the door frame and turned to the left, knowing that there were benches there to sit on. Taking ten steps along the wall, Sarah found one, turned to sit, and laid her shawl down beside her.

Only moments passed as Sarah sat and battled her feelings. She wanted to tell Lucas how she felt but did not want him to feel sorry for her. She certainly didn't want to do anything to actively push him away. A presence suddenly rose beside her, making Sarah jump. Waiting, she expected the person to say something. When silence was only heard, Sarah got to her feet. The silence around her was creepy and somehow very foreboding.

"Someone there? Lucas?"

"No," a voice hissed in her ear, "not Lucas."

Sarah gasped, felt herself spun around, and a hand slapped over her mouth. Someone else grabbed her feet; her body was lifted off the ground. Trying to scream, the muffled sound not penetrating the pounding noise from the dance, Sarah felt herself being carried away.

CHAPTER

7

Lucas took note of where Sarah was and then went back to the task at hand. "I-do-not-want-to-dance-with-you," he stated in a sarcastically slow manner like he was talking to a less intelligent person. Glaring again at the person in front of him, Lucas decided that it was an appropriate manner of speech.

Tanya pretended to pout. "Why not? I know I can make you feel like twice the man that the misfit can." She tried to press her body against his.

Lucas grabbed Tanya's shoulders and got in her face. "She is not a misfit. She is already twice the woman you will ever be and makes me want to be a better man. I love *her*, and there is nothing you can do to change my mind. Being with you would make me want to jump off a bridge."

Tanya gasped and slapped Lucas across the face. "Well, I never…"

"And you never will, so stop trying."

Lucas smirked as Tanya walked off. He hoped she would leave him alone from now on. He felt a hand on his shoulder and turned to see Mona.

"Sarah said she needs some air," Mona informed.

"Okay," Lucas replied, looking to where Sarah had been. She wasn't there anymore. "Where is she?"

Mona turned as well, sighing in frustration. "She must have gone out already. I told her to wait for you."

"She went out alone?" Lucas spun away from Mona and ran out into the hall. He looked around and then noticed Sarah's shawl on a bench; she was nowhere to be seen.

•

The cool night air brushed passed Sarah's face as her captors carried her out of the school. She tried to pay attention to her surroundings instead of struggle. The two who carried her had on dress shoes, which clicked as they covered ground across pavement. Sarah knew she was outside, but where? Her foot hit something; it made a hollow sound that Sarah recognized as the hood of a car. They were in the parking lot.

"Shh," the one holding her upper body hissed to the other.

Soon the shoes stopped clicking. Sarah could smell dirt and grass. The only grass at the school that close to the parking lot was the football field. Taking in more around her, Sarah could smell aftershave (it seemed familiar) and cigarettes. She could feel the cold band of what she assumed to be a class ring; one was on her hip, under her skirt, and the other over her mouth. Judging by the position of the bodies and hands holding her, both rings seemed to be on the right hands of her captors; middle fingers, perhaps? Sarah also caught a whiff of soap; she could not tell what kind. There was only one scent. Sarah figured that she couldn't smell the soap or aftershave on the captor holding her legs. With them moving forward, the scent would travel behind him, away from Sarah. On and on they walked for at least half an hour, moving quickly.

As they moved, Sarah was aware of the changes her surroundings took on. The air around them got damper, cooler. She could smell foliage, dirt, and leaves. Branches scratched at her skin and pulled at her skirt. All around her she heard the noises of night creatures and could smell trees. She decided that they must be in the forest behind the football field at the back of the high school.

Suddenly, her feet were put down. One of the people let her go; the other kept a hand over her mouth and wrapped the other arm around her waist. They had walked far enough that Sarah feared no one would be able to hear her scream. Shaking, Sarah waited for what was to come. Besides, there were two of them and she was blind. Sarah wasn't an idiot. She knew that there was no way for her to escape without being able to see. She wasn't sure she wanted to fight, either. Lucas had told her not to engage an enemy unless she was fairly certain she stood a chance. Sarah wasn't sure she did. She heard a key in a lock and the creak of a door. Lucas had told her rumors of an old shack where students went to smoke and have sex, among other things. He had also told her that apparently it was so overgrown with foliage that you had to know what to look for to find it; that was why the teachers hadn't discovered it yet. Its location was secret among the students.

The hand was removed from her mouth as she was shoved into the shack. It smelt of mildew and rotting leaves. Sarah stumbled, caught her balance, and started screaming; she was met with a slap in the face. The force threw her off balance. Sarah fell to the floor, scraping her arm. Before she knew what was happening, her captors had her on her back trying to hold her arms and legs held down. Sarah kept fighting, still screaming, but they were much stronger than she was. She made sure to scratch both of them as hard as she could and pull their hair. She hoped that she would be able to gather enough DNA samples for justice to be served. Lucas had taught her enough that Sarah was fairly certain she was able to fight hard enough to gather evidence. Though the harder she fought, the more terrified she was about the crime her evidence would be standing up against.

"Lucas isn't here to save you now," a guy hissed in a whisper as he pinned her to the floor. It made it impossible for Sarah to recognize the voice.

Ropes were tied around her wrists and ankles. Sarah realized what was happening, what they planned to do. She kept screaming for all she was worth, knowing in her heart that no one would hear.

"Please, don't do this," Sarah begged. "Please, no."

Sarah was met with knuckles to the face again. This time so hard that it nearly knocked her unconscious. Her skirt ripped in protest to harsh hands pulling it out of the way. Sarah pulled against the ropes holding her down, the fibers biting into her skin. She screamed again as her captors took what they came for, stole from Sarah what she would never get back.

•

"Sarah! Sarah!"

Lucas ran from room to room looking for Sarah, screaming her name. At last, horrified, he realized that she was no longer in the school. Running around the perimeter of the campus, Lucas began to panic. He loved Sarah, no doubt, and the thought of harm coming to her was more than he could handle. His breath was not coming the way it should. Hurried footsteps came up from behind him. Lucas spun, ready to fight, almost punching Josh in the face.

"Did you find her?" Mona asked running up behind Josh. She was close to hysterics. "Did you find her? Oh, heaven, help us. This is all my fault."

Lucas could feel his body shake. He pulled his cell phone from his pocket, his hand trembling so badly that he could barely dial. Lucas knew who he had to call. They were going to hate him after this. Beth picked up after two rings.

"Mrs. Watkins," Lucas voice shook just as much as his body, "this is Lucas. I am so sorry...Sarah's missing."

Jonathan and Beth arrived moments after the phone call. Within five minutes, the police were at the school. Lucas watched as they secured the scene, ending the dance and making sure that no one left. Lucas's parents showed up as well, his father taking control and his mother wrapping him up in a hug. Lucas could feel himself losing control as he paced around, watching the commotion.

His father finally walked up to him. Lucas had to look down. He hated when anything happened that made him feel like a failure, for in turn he felt as if he had failed his father.

"Lucas, this is Chief Nelson. He needs a statement from you, son." His father then shocked Lucas by coming to stand next to him, loosely laying his arm over his shoulders.

Lucas took a deep breath. He didn't want to talk. He didn't want to relive his discovery of Sarah's absence. He didn't want even more reminders of his failure. And he had failed. He had failed Sarah. He was supposed to protect her. It was his job as her friend. It was his job as the one who promised her father. It was his job as the man who loved her.

Lucas braced himself for the pain this would cause. "I was inside the dance talking with another student when Mona came to me to say that Sarah wanted to step out…"

●

Tears flowed down Sarah's face, sobs breaking from her chest. One of her captors untied the ropes holding her; one of them pulled Sarah to her feet. A fist came into contact with Sarah's stomach followed by a slap across the face. She doubled over in pain; a heavy object was brought down across her back. Sarah fell onto floor. A foot made contact with her face, another in her stomach, and another to her back. Sarah tried to protect herself, but she couldn't see which way to block from. The beating went on for what seemed like forever. Sarah felt nearly unconscious when the other guy pulled the one beating her away. There were a few heated, whispered words between the two, and then another swift kick came at Sarah's side. She was certain one of her ribs snapped. She couldn't help the scream of pain that escaped her lips. Someone lit a cigarette. The two of them walked out of the shack. Horrified, Sarah heard them lock the door from the outside as it had been before.

Climbing to her feet, Sarah stumbled to the door. She started pounding for all she was worth. "Don't leave me here!" she screamed. "Please don't leave me! Please! Help me! Someone, please help me!" Sarah threw herself against the door again and again, trying to break it down. She knew that it would do no good. She wasn't strong enough, not even to bust down the old rotted wood.

Sobs racked Sarah's body. She tried to calm herself. She felt close to hyperventilating. Thinking back, Sarah tried to recall the details. Not the details that would make her skin crawl, but the details that would help her get justice. Lucas had always told her to know everything possible about friends but even more about enemies. Leaning against the door, Sarah slide to the floor and tried to think back. One of the guys had been a smoker; the other reeked of chewing tobacco. The memory made Sarah gag. The aftershave had been the same, as had the soap. One had had facial hair, the other had not. The voices had been similar as they both had hissed at her, moaned and...

Sarah couldn't take anymore. Heaving, she leaned over, gagging and retching. She couldn't believe what had happened. She couldn't believe what had been stolen from her. What would her parents think? What would Lucas think? Sarah was gasping again, nauseated, her head was spinning. She passed out.

When she woke up, the day and time were unknown to her. She could hear birds chirping; that suggested to her that it was the morning of the next day. She had no way to tell the time, but she could feel a warm sun. Sarah was stiff and cold from the night, but she feared that heat would follow as the day wore on even though she did welcome it now. The weather had been unusually hot for February. Her mouth was dry with thirst. Her head was pounding, and her body ached. Her ribs screamed with every breath; she felt extremely dirty, in more ways than one. She knew that she was injured. She knew that she needed a doctor. However, Sarah also knew that no one knew where she was. Most people didn't even know about the shack; well, according to Lucas, they knew about it, but not where it was. Those who did know would most definitely not be at the school on a Saturday. Sarah simply prayed that Lucas would come for her.

The temperature reached unbearable levels in the shack as the day wore on. Sarah guessed that it had to be at least eighty degrees out as it had been all week. She was sweating, and her mouth was dry. Her stomach demanded nourishment; her body screamed in pain. Sarah had never been so fatigued in her entire life. It took everything that she had to continue to call for help. Slowly standing, Sarah felt the walls for a window. Her leg brushed something sharp. Sarah screamed as the object sliced through her skin. Finding a window, she forced it open, relieved to feel a slight breeze.

Slumping back down, Sarah ripped a piece of cloth from her already torn skirt to wrap around the wound on her leg. Moving her hand gently along her leg, Sarah felt the warmth of blood. Focusing on the task at hand, Sarah slowly positioned the cloth over the wound and tied it tight, wincing, and not bothering to hold back a cry of pain. At least she could stop herself from bleeding to death.

Tears started to form once more as Sarah thought about Lucas, envisioned once more the future that she dreamed for them. She had imagined marrying him for quite some time, had always envisioned them having children and living in Texas. Sarah loved Lucas more than life, but she didn't want to die. She wanted to live, to be with Lucas. Sarah knew Lucas would try to find her, but he had no idea where to look.

Despair overcame Sarah as she was once again hit with the reality of what had been stolen from her. Would Lucas look at her the same? Would he consider her unclean? Sarah had always admired Lucas and his old-fashioned qualities. He cherished women and moral standards. He was a gentleman in every sense of the word, and he treated Sarah like a lady. She now feared that things may change. Would he still care? Would he blame himself? Lucas had never been able to *not* protect her. How would he take it if she died? Would he die as well? The thought made Sarah feel ill. Fatigue suddenly overwhelmed, causing her head to spin. Sarah wasn't sure how long she would be in the shack. All she knew was that she wasn't going to survive forever.

●

Sunday morning Lucas yelled and sat up in his bed frantically glancing around, sweat on his brow and his heart pounding. His fists were balled and ready to fight the threat he felt. But it wasn't a threat to him that caused his fear. He had once again dreamed that Sarah was dead, but he would not let himself believe it. Why would anyone kill Sarah? Who would want to? Her father was a politician, but he was a good governor. Lucas took a few deep breaths, trying to gather himself, reign in his emotions. It would do him no good to be overcome with his fear, guilt, and worry. There had been no leads, no signs of what had happened to Sarah. Lucas knew that she needed to be found, and needed to be found quickly. Lucas knew that her life depended on it. Swinging out of his bed, Lucas walked into the bathroom to shower, making up his mind to go out and look for Sarah himself. He hoped that his love for her would guide him.

CHAPTER

8

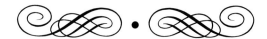

Sarah woke up and the birds were chirping again. *It must be Sunday*, Sarah thought to herself. *How much longer will I be here? Will they ever find me? Will I ever get to see Lucas again?* Sarah pulled herself into a sitting position, her head swimming. Thirst hit her like nothing else in life ever had. The hunger pain in her belly never quit, not to mention every other pain in her body.

I have to keep fighting to stay alive, Sarah told herself. *Lucas will come for me one way or the other.* Sarah felt her face and body. Her ribs screamed with each breath; one eye was nearly swollen shut. The cut on her leg burned but had stopped bleeding. Sarah knew that she was injured. Possible broken ribs and dehydration were the immediate dangers, she knew. *I have to survive. I have to pull through. Lucas will come, he loves me. Please, God, let him come for me. Let my love find me.*

Climbing to her feet, Sarah tried calling for help again. She pounded on the door of the shack, praying that it would just fall off. Not that she would be any better off. Sarah couldn't figure out what would be worse, dying of heat stroke in the shack or being eaten alive in the woods by some animal. She didn't know how much longer she would be able to keep it up, though. Sarah fought to stay conscious as long as she could. The day wore on, and the heat kept beating down on the shack. Midafternoon, Sarah's eyes drooped, and she slumped to the floor.

•

Lucas finished his lunch and then excused himself from the house and the presence of his parents, Beth and Jonathan. They insisted on sitting by the phone waiting for a ransom call, or any word at all. Climbing into his truck, Lucas headed to the school to try and sort out where Sarah might be.

The football field loomed out before Lucas as he prayed to God to help Sarah and keep her safe.

What do I need to do? Where do I need to go? I will go to the ends of the earth and give my own life if it would just bring her home safe so I might kiss her one last time. Lucas closed his eyes against the burning behind his eyelids.

I need her back with me, God. I can't live if she is dead. I don't deserve her, but my faults should not mean the end of her life.

Lucas stared up at the sky as if waiting for God to appear and show him the right direction to go. He wasn't sure how long he stood there, arms out, eyes closed. Startled, he spun when he heard a voice.

"Hoping for divine intervention?" Carl sneered, coming out from behind some bleachers. He tossed a cigarette butt to the ground.

Blood surged through Lucas's veins. He had never wanted to kill someone so badly in all his life. Lucas would bet his last dollar that Carl knew where Sarah was.

"Where is she? Where is Sarah?"

Carl laughed. "You think I know? Why would I want anything to do with that reject?" The look on his face mocked Lucas as if he really did know. "Is she hidden where even the mighty Lucas Monroe can't find her?"

Lucas advanced toward Carl; out of nowhere, Trevor came up as well. Lucas was outnumbered but knew that he could handle both of them. However, he had just had a thought come to mind. Lucas had just had a flash in his memory of something Carl had said once. Something about the perfect place to take a woman when you didn't want to be disturbed, never wanted to be found, never wanted to be heard.

"I don't want any trouble," Lucas stated. "I have to go."

Turning, he walked away from Carl and Trevor, hoping they would not try to follow him. Miraculously, they let him be. Lucas made like he was heading to his car and when he was sure that Carl and Trevor could not see him, he doubled back and headed for the trees behind the football field. Lucas was suddenly overcome with urgency. Starting to run, he made his way toward where the shack he had heard rumors about was supposed to be, about a mile away. On more than one occasion, he had heard people at school talk about an abandoned shack behind the school that was the perfect spot to misbehave because only certain people knew about it and you could only find it if you knew where it was. Lucas's only chance was to trust what he had heard.

The moss-covered oak, then go east. The old willow tree, then north. The mushroom-covered hill and just around the other side.

The shack was there. Lucas was less than twenty feet away. He felt a pull toward it, not wanting to look inside. Instinctively, Lucas knew. He ran to the door and tried to open it. The lock rattled on the handle. Bouncing around the side of the shack, Lucas took a deep breath and peered in the window. Bile rose up in his throat.

"Sarah! Sarah!"

Lucas ran back to the door and lashed out at it with his foot, pummeling it twice before the rotted wood gave way. The old door nearly tore from its hinges and gave Lucas front row to a sight that nearly tore his heart out. Sarah lay on the floor, her legs tucked under her as if she were kneeling when she passed out. Her face was bruised, one eye nearly swollen shut.

Breath came in ragged gasps as Lucas approached his love. Tears choked his throat, heart pounding in his chest. The shack spun as Lucas fell to his knees.

"Sarah," he whispered. "Please be alive. Please."

Her breathing was shallow, but her pulse was still there. That was all the encouragement that Lucas needed.

"Hold on, baby. I'm gonna get you out of here. Just hold on." Lucas scooped Sarah up like a child. Going as fast as he could without injuring her more, Lucas carried Sarah to his truck, laid her in the backseat and made the trip to the hospital as fast as possible.

•

Sarah heard Lucas's voice. She knew she was dreaming. Her body was lifted off the floor of the shack. She felt like she was flying, convinced that she was dying. She sank into darkness but then was lifted again and laid back down on something hard, flat, and moving.

The next few hours were horrible for Sarah. She felt people touching her, talking to her. She couldn't understand what they were saying. Her voice refused to respond. Her dress was removed. She lay naked on what felt like a cold, hard bed. Sharp things poked at her arms. A hand touched her leg. A male voice spoke.

Sarah's reflexes came back. Sarah kicked her legs, trying to get whoever it was away from her. Hands tried to hold her down; voices tried to speak to her. A hand gripped her midsection. Screaming, Sarah threw herself off the table landing hard on a cold floor and then righted herself. Lucas had taught her how to defend herself; she had frozen in fear once and refused to do it again. She didn't care how many there were.

A hand clasped her right arm. Sarah lashed out with her left, contacting with a face. Arms restrained her from behind. Sarah lifted her legs up and then brought them back down, using her momentum to flip her attacker over her back. Standing straight,

Sarah felt her arm being restrained and tried to pull away. A needle poked her bicep. Sarah tried to fight, but there was more than one of them holding her now. Warmth suddenly overcame her body; they had given her something to sedate her. She fell to the floor. The whole encounter she had screamed Lucas's name and had never realized.

•

Governor and Mrs. Watkins rushed through the halls of the emergency room with Paige and Owen in tow. Mona and Josh were on their way. They found Lucas sitting in the waiting room, tears still on his cheeks, and his head in his hands.

"Lucas! Oh, dear Lord. Is she alive?" Jonathan rushed to Lucas.

Lucas's breath was coming in quick gasps. "This…is all…my fault," he sobbed. "I am…so s-sorry." Lucas accepted embraces from everyone and gathered himself a little.

"I never should have left her side that night. We never should have gone to the dance. I don't know what's wrong with her. I haven't heard anything. I went to the school to try and replay the night, and I ran into Carl. Something he had said a while back made me think of this shack behind the school. I found her unconscious on the floor. I am so sorry. I don't deserve her anymore. I don't deserve her. I've failed her." Sobs overtook Lucas's whole body once more. Paige hurried to hold her son again as a doctor walked in.

"Governor Watkins," the doctor greeted, shaking Jonathan's hand.

"Is my daughter alive? What happened to her?"

The doctor nodded. "She's alive. She was raped and beaten pretty badly. She has a concussion, a bad cut on her leg, two broken ribs, and other bruises and cuts. She is also badly dehydrated which is to be expected if she was trapped all weekend with the heat we had. We collected as much DNA as we could off of her, but until she wakes back up, I'm afraid we will not be able to identify who did this."

"You won't be able to afterwards either," Lucas snapped. "She's blind."

The doctor looked surprised. "I never would have guessed. I just moved to Texas, so forgive me for not knowing, Mr. Governor. I was in the ER when they brought her in. They told me who she was but did not mention that she was blind. They may have assumed I knew. I never would have guessed because of the way she fought us in the ER."

"What?" Beth asked. "What do you mean she fought you?"

The doctor sighed. "She came to as we were examining her. She got scared and wouldn't listen to us. She was so scared I don't know if she could even hear us. Anyway, the nurses tried to restrain her, and she broke one of their noses and flipped a second over her shoulder when he tried to grab her from behind. We had to sedate her. She's resting now."

Sarah's parents looked astonished. Lucas knew that she had used moves he had taught her. Had she done it when she was raped? Was that why she had been beaten? Had his teachings caused her more harm than good? Lucas had to sit down.

The doctor shook Jonathan's hand again and prepared to leave. "The hospital will do its best to keep all of this as quiet as possible. Oh, by the way," he continued, "who is Lucas?"

"I am," Lucas responded.

"Well, you must be special to Sarah. She never stopped calling for you the entire time she fought us." The doctor nodded curtly and then left.

Lucas started to cry again. Josh and Mona showed up after that and sat with everyone else for the next couple of hours.

CHAPTER

9

Sarah felt herself wake up and her eyes open. Even though she could not see, the sounds and smells told her that she was not in the shack any longer. It wasn't blistering hot anymore. Sarah could feel cool air around her as the vents blew air. Had she been found? Was she in the hospital? The beeps and wires made Sarah assume that she was. She felt electrodes stuck to her chest, making the monitor beep in time with her heart rate. She reached over and felt the IV taped to her right arm. She was wearing a hospital gown. Sarah reached down and felt the cut on her leg was bandaged. Her skin felt cleaner.

Tears came to her eyes. Sarah prayed that Lucas was nearby. She longed to feel his touch and to smell his hair. He had always had his own scent, a mixture between his pheromones and the cologne he always wore. Where was he? Where was she? Did Lucas know where she was? Would he come for her?

A hand touched her arm. "Don't touch me!" Sarah screamed, panicking, not even thinking that they were there to help. "Leave me alone! I want Lucas! Lucas!" The hands tried to restrain her. Sarah heard a female voice but refused to listen because the voice was unfamiliar and most importantly it was not Lucas. She didn't trust anyone that she didn't know, not after what had happened.

"No, no, no! Don't touch me! Lucas, help me!" Sarah fought away and rolled out of the bed. She felt the IV tear out of her arm, pushed down whoever was in the room with her, and ran away from the person. Slipping, Sarah fell to the floor and crawled until she reached a wall and moved to a corner, prepared to defend herself again.

"Lucas!"

●

Lucas snapped his eyes open. He was the only one in the waiting room. Everyone else had gone to the cafeteria to get food. He had been dosing off but could have sworn he heard Sarah call to him. He closed his eyes and then heard her scream again. Jumping out of his seat, Lucas ran down the hall to Sarah's room. He found her backed into the corner fighting off the doctor and three nurses. He moved forward and told them to be quiet.

Sarah was screaming and breathing so hard that she had not heard anyone enter the room, but suddenly the voices stopped. Sarah still stood her ground, not knowing what was coming next. During the silence, Sarah's breathing slowed, her ears became aware of every little sound.

"Take my hand, Sarah."

Sarah cried out in relief. She slumped forward into the warmth of Lucas's embrace.

●

Lucas sat holding Sarah's hand as she slept. She had wept hysterically after he had gotten her back to bed. She hadn't spoken a word about what had happened, just cried. She had latched on to him, gripping his shirt as though she would never let go. She had cried, gasping his name, and then flinching in pain from her broken ribs. Lucas knew that the police were waiting for a statement from her. Jonathan had asked that they wait until she was a little calmer; if it were up to Lucas, she wouldn't ever have to face what happened, but he knew that she did.

Sarah moaned in her sleep, her brow furrowed. Her breathing became rapid in fear. It clenched Lucas's heart to think about what had happened to her. Her face was bruised and her leg cut, but that was nothing to what they had done to her soul. She would be forever scarred, and it was his fault. He never should have taken Sarah to the dance, especially after what had happened with Carl prior.

Lucas ground his teeth at the thought of who had done this. He was certain that it was Carl who had taken Sarah. Bile rose up in Lucas's throat as he thought about what had been done to Sarah's body; he started to shake. He couldn't believe what had happened. He wasn't worthy of Sarah anymore, couldn't protect her anymore.

Suddenly, Sarah sat bolt upright, gasping for air, reaching out for him. Lucas jumped up, wrapping his arms around her.

"It's okay, Sarah, I have you," he soothed.

She started to cry again, Lucas holding her tight, unable to think of a way to ease her pain. He tried to soothe her as best he could, but mostly he just held her as she cried. She was just beginning to calm down when Jonathan walked in with two officers.

"Honey," Jonathan started, "I have Officers Wilbur and McKinnon with me. They really need to hear from you what happened. Is that okay?"

Sarah started to tremble again. She latched on to Lucas's arm with a vice grip. "Can Lucas stay with me?"

"Of course," Jonathan said, glancing at Lucas. He doubted the boy wanted to hear the details, but he knew that Lucas would stay if it would make Sarah feel better. Lucas nodded stiffly to him once and stayed where he was, at Sarah's side.

Officer McKinnon stepped toward the bed and introduced herself. "Sarah, I am Officer McKinnon. I brought a tape recorder with me, and I would like to record your statement, if that is okay."

Sarah looked in the direction that she had last heard her father. She wasn't sure if this was okay with the whole "public life" thing.

"It's okay, Sarah," her father said. Sarah nodded her consent. She heard the click of a button, and the recorder was set on something hard, a table probably.

"Okay, Sarah," Officer McKinnon started, "just tell us what happened in your own words. Please don't leave anything out. The smallest of details may help us to get justice."

Sarah took a deep breath and squeezed Lucas's hand.

"I'm right here," he whispered.

Tears came to Sarah's eyes as she started her story. The terrifying memories of the sound and feelings that flooded her mind were coupled with fresh waves of pain that lashed at her body as she relived what had happened. She could feel Lucas cringe next to her, but she kept going.

Lucas thought for sure he was going to vomit. Hearing what had happened to Sarah in her own words coming from her own beautiful mouth in her own sweet voice was almost more than he could handle. When she got to the point about the second rapist, Lucas felt himself sway. What had they done to her? How was his failure going to affect the rest of her life? Sarah was choking on her sobs by the time her story was finished, and all Lucas could do was hold her and cry along.

●

"Lucas! Lucas!"

Someone's voice soothed her, but it was not his. Arms tried to hold her, but they were not his. It took a while for Sarah to recognize that it was her mother. Her breath was coming in gasps and wheezes, the nightmare having been terrifyingly real. She swatted at her mother's hands as she tried to hold Sarah, to comfort her.

"Lucas," she gasped again.

"Sarah, baby, it's okay," her mother soothed. "Lucas had to go home to get some rest. We made him go. He'll be back in the morning."

Sarah started to cry harder. "He's gone? He's gone! He left me! In my nightmare he left me! Why did he have to go? Why did he leave me, Mom?"

"Sarah, honey, he'll be back in the morning," Beth tried to soothe. "He isn't gone for good."

"I need him, Mom! I can't be without him. I can't handle him leaving me. I need him so much!"

Sarah's sobs racked her body. The nightmare had been so real. Lucas had been gone, and there had been nothing. Nothing left for her. No one there for her. She had been lost in the dark, calling for help, and no one was there. Sarah was having a hard time breathing. Would Lucas come back for her? Had this changed the way he felt about her? The fear brought on a new wave of hysteria.

It was almost an hour before Beth could get Sarah settled down. When she was finally asleep again, Beth stole a glance at the clock. It was close to five in the morning. She hadn't realized how much Sarah loved Lucas. Her need for him ran so much deeper than just her sight. It was a physical, emotional, and spiritual need that Beth could not comprehend. Picking up her cell phone, Beth dialed Lucas's. He answered on the first ring.

"Hello?" Anxiety edged his voice.

"Lucas, this is Beth. I need you to come back to the hospital."

A sharp intake of breath sounded on the other line. "What happened? Is she okay?"

"She woke up calling for you, and when she realized that you weren't here, well, it took me almost an hour to calm her down. I think it would be best for her if you were here if she calls for you again."

"I'm already in my truck." And he hung up.

Sarah was released from the hospital two days after being admitted. Lucas had stayed with her and hardly left. His parents had gotten him his homework. Once home, Beth brought in a tutor for Sarah whom had refused to go back to school that year. Lucas went back to school, but refused to do anything else. He wouldn't even finish out the basketball season. Luckily, the press on the situation was kept quiet. The media knew that Sarah was in the hospital, but her injuries were made out to be caused by some sort of accident.

DNA had been collected from under Sarah's fingernails and hair samples from her clothes; no fluids were left behind. The culprits had worn condoms, which eased Sarah's worry about lingering consequences to her ordeal. The police had gone to the shack, led by Lucas, and looked around for more evidence. Then, by request of Jonathan, they turned the other cheek as Lucas burned the thing down. The DNA did not match any from the police files. Sarah was asked if she could somehow make an identification from a line-up.

"I can smell them," Sarah told the police about two weeks after the attack. "If it is safe for me to get that close, I can smell the scents that linger on their bodies. I did the night of the attack. I can also use my other senses, sound and touch, that sort of thing."

On Jonathan and Lucas's suggestion, they decided to bring in different guys from Lucas's class. The police had already questioned Carl and Trevor (Jack having moved two years prior) and various other guys, but they all had a story. Lucas, convinced that it was Carl and Trevor, told the police that if they had interviewed both the guys who attacked Sarah, they had probably cooked up a story to cover for each other. So three weeks after the attack, Sarah stood in a room with Lucas and two police officers. The guys chosen for the line-up were led in and blindfolded.

Calmly as she could, Sarah allowed herself to be ushered into the line-up room and put in front of each of seven guys. With each one she sniffed, felt and listened. The first guy smelled all wrong, too expensive. The second had similar cologne but also had three rings hanging from his lip. Sarah didn't remember that. Number three didn't smell at all like tobacco when he whispered, nor did his hands smell. Number four had the right soap smell, the right cologne and facial hair. When he whispered on command to her, Sarah could smell the chewing tobacco. He even had a class ring on the middle finger of his right hand. She held number four in her mind, trying to remain calm but was shaking nonetheless. Number five, no tobacco again. Number six, wrong soap and no rings. When Sarah got to number seven, she smelled the same soap as number four. The cologne matched, he had no facial hair. Reaching down, Sarah grasped his hand, found a class ring on the middle finger of his right hand and then brought the fingers under her nose. Cigarettes. He whispered to her. Sarah could feel the color drain from her face, and she swayed on the spot.

She couldn't believe it. How had this happened? They had found the right two guys? What if she were wrong? Would the DNA match?

Lucas watched as Sarah went from person to person, shaking like a leaf. She had to be the bravest person he knew. However, he knew that if it were not for him, she may not have had to be brave at all. He had failed her. He knew who did this to her. Lucas watched as Sarah reached for Carl's hands to smell them. Bile rose up in Lucas's throat as he thought about what they had done to her. What they had done to his Sarah, his love. She looked paler than before as the officer escorted her out.

Sarah quickly was lead from the room back behind the two-way mirror.

"Can you make an identification?" the police chief asked.

Sarah nodded. "Numbers four and seven, no doubt in my mind."

Sarah heard Lucas curse and pound the table. She was lead out of the room by her mother who whispered that number four was Trevor and number seven was Carl.

CHAPTER
10

Sarah was a little anxious. Today was the first day that the therapist was coming to see her. It was at the suggestion of her doctor that Sarah agreed to the counseling. She hadn't been too sure about going out to offices and things like that. When her father had been able to find a doctor who would come to their house and was female, well, Sarah was a little more comfortable with the whole thing. She had to admit she did have some things that she felt she needed closure on that she wasn't comfortable talking with her mother about.

The doorbell rang. Sarah jumped slightly in her seat. She was sitting in the den, waiting for Dr. Withers to arrive. Dr. Jacquelyn Withers. Sarah could hear muted voices at the front door and then her mother was walking her way with someone else in tow. Sarah heard them come to the doorway of the den. She turned her head in their direction.

"Honey, this is Dr. Withers," Beth said.

Sarah heard the extra set of shoes move forward across the hardwood floors. Not heels, though; apparently Dr. Withers liked comfort. She came up beside Sarah, a little too closely. Sarah flinched slightly. The shoes stepped back. Sarah caught a scent of expensive perfume under her nose, along with peppermint.

"Hello, Sarah," Dr. Withers said. "I am Dr. Withers. You may call me Jackie. Is it all right if I sit down?"

Sarah liked her voice. She had a very soft, feathery voice. It made Sarah sleepy. She had expected her to have a sharper, more business-like voice. Sarah motioned for Jackie to sit in the chair across from her. She heard the sliding sound of dress slacks as Jackie sat down.

"So, Sarah, I know that you understand why I am here. I just wanted to make sure that you are agreeable with the sessions."

"Mom, you can go," Sarah said, speaking over her shoulder.

"Oh, okay, honey," Beth replied, moving away from the doorway.

"How did you know she was still there?" Jackie asked.

Sarah laughed. "I didn't hear her leave. And to answer your question, I am okay with it. I wasn't at first, but when my father was able to find a female doctor that was willing to come to our house, well, then I didn't mind. I wanted to, actually."

"And why is that?" Jackie asked.

Sarah sighed. "I just don't want what happened to influence who I am and who I will be. I want to face it, acknowledge it, and move on. That is what Lucas says to do with all of your fears."

"Who's Lucas?" Jackie asked.

Sarah felt herself blush. "He's, well, he's, um…"

"Your boyfriend?"

Sarah laughed. "No, well, I mean yes. But it seems funny to call him that because he is so much more than that. He's my guardian. He's my security. He's my best friend. He's pretty much everything to me."

"That must be nice to have someone like that in your life. Why don't you tell me more about you? That way, when we get to why we are here, I will have a better understanding of who you are as a person."

Sarah took a deep breath and began her story. The entire first session was spent telling Jackie about her birth, her childhood, how she and Lucas had met and everything since then. She was just getting to what happened when Jackie told her their time was up.

"I will see you next time, Sarah," Jackie said. "If you need anything until then, just let me know."

Sarah continued to have sessions with Jackie on a weekly basis for the next couple of months. They had spent two sessions talking specifically about the attack and how Sarah felt now in its wake. Sarah also was able to dig up the courage to ask her the questions that she had.

"I had a few things that I wanted to ask you," Sarah started as they began their fifth session.

"Go right ahead, Sarah," Jackie replied. "You may ask me anything."

"Well, I wanted to know..."—Sarah could feel herself blushing—"well, how will what happened affect me? You know, when I am older and get married and things like that. Will I still be able to be with a man, be a wife?"

"Well," Jackie sighed, "that is different for each rape victim that I have ever counseled. It will be up to you, Sarah. The best advice that I can give you is to detach yourself from what happened. Don't deny that it happened by any means. But don't let it control you either. If you want to have a relationship with Lucas, or whoever it might be, then you will have to decide to have that relationship. Don't let what happened dictate everything else that you do from here on out. You have to move past it and live your life."

Sarah nodded her understanding, unable to speak. Tears were budding in her eyes once more. She didn't say anything for a moment as she contemplated what Jackie was saying. Sarah knew that she was able to move past what had happened. She didn't even correlate her rape and her relationship with Lucas on the same brain wave. The only parallel identity that they shared was that it was Lucas who rescued her, as she had known it would be.

Sarah sighed. The only thing that concerned her was the way that Lucas saw her. He had been a little distant since it had happened, but Sarah guessed that was normal. He was jumpier when they were out, almost like he wanted to run with her at every little noise that he heard. But did he see *her* differently? Sarah understood him being edgier; she was as well. But what she wanted to know was whether or not he saw her in a different light, on a personal level. She knew that Jackie couldn't answer that. Sarah knew that only Lucas could answer how he felt, and Sarah was terrified to ask him.

●

The months that followed her attack were very slow for Sarah. Following the identification, Carl and Trevor were subpoenaed to give DNA tests. Their DNA was tested against what was obtained from the skin cells and hairs collected from Sarah's rape kit. The tests matched; the case went to court. The publicity turned awful. If the country did not know that the governor of Texas had a blind daughter, they did now. Everything about Sarah was brought into the story, even Lucas. He even had to testify about the continuing harassment. He was a rock, like always. Sarah wanted to vomit during her questioning. At least the entire ordeal didn't make her look bad.

The trial, thankfully, did not take long. It went to court and was handled quickly because of whom Sarah's father was. Between the DNA and testimonies, the jury found both guys guilty of rape, harassment, and kidnapping. They both were tried as adults (since they both were over eighteen) and sent to prison. Sarah was so glad when it was over. She had always told herself that Carl was all talk and would never actually hurt her. She had been wrong.

Sarah stayed home, schooled by a tutor and visited by Mona. Lucas came over nearly every day, but his attitude was so depressed and not his normal self that he wasn't much reassurance to Sarah.

She knew that he felt badly over what had happened. He had said as much. He blamed himself, even though Sarah had assured him a million times that it was not his fault.

Before she knew it, it was time for Lucas's high school graduation. Sarah made sure to put on a brave face. Lucas had told her that he didn't mind if she stayed home, so she didn't have to go out in public. Sarah considered it but immediately told herself to stop being such a coward. She had been holed up in her house for months. It was time to join the world again.

The night of the graduation ceremony, Sarah went with her parents to the school and tried to be brave. She did find herself jumping at every sudden noise, though. It got to the point that her mother put her arm around her until they were in their seats. It wasn't that Sarah was worried about someone attacking her in such a large crowd. It was just that she wasn't near Lucas. Sarah was always more jumpy when Lucas was not around, especially when she wasn't at home.

More and more people filed into the gymnasium for the ceremony. A few things happened before they got to the heart of the graduation. The principal made a speech, and then the superintendent spoke. The choir and band performed, and then it was time for the speeches. The salutatorian went first and then it was time for Lucas's speech. Sarah had never been more proud of Lucas. When the principal announced his name and informed that he was the youngest valedictorian in the school's history, Sarah wanted to stand up and scream. However, she maintained her dignity and just clapped along with everyone else.

As the clapping died down, Sarah could hear that Lucas was up at the podium. He cleared his throat, and Sarah's heart soared. She knew it was silly, but she felt instantly better just knowing that he was nearby. There was a quiet rustle of papers and then a soft bump as Lucas adjusted the microphone.

"What is commencement?" Lucas started. "According to the dictionary, to commence is to begin. That is what we are doing now. We are leaving our old lives, what we used to know, and beginning a bright new time. Some of us had an easy time getting here. Some of us have had a harder time. Either path that we have been given, the important thing is that we made it." His classmates cheered. Lucas cleared his throat and continued.

"What is success? It is defined as the favorable outcome to one's endeavors. To some, it is money. To some, it is fame. Others push to reach certain goals, certain levels of knowledge or accomplishment. It can be a job. It can be marriage and family. It can be the military. Whatever our goals, we are told that to be successful, we have to reach those goals, go beyond them, even. However, I don't agree. I believe that someone can be just as successful if he or she has the courage to pursue those goals. Chase those dreams. Don't stand down. Don't give up. Do not let what might get in your way succeed. *You* succeed. Push through the hard times. Hold on to your dreams and don't let adversity stand in your way." Lucas paused as everyone clapped and then started again.

"What is adversity? We are told that it is a bad thing, that it is marked by misfortune and distress. Again, I disagree. I think that adversity should be viewed on a lighter note. I believe it should be viewed as a stepping stone to becoming the strongest individual that you can be. I believe that it should be looked at as a way to push forward and succeed. It should be embraced and welcomed as a way to become the best person that you ever could be. It is what drives us forward. It is what pushes us to go on. It is what God puts in our way to enable us to live more like him." Lucas had to pause again while everyone clapped.

"I want to thank God for the adversity that he gives us so that we may be the best we can be. I want to thank all of the parents and other guardians for helping us get there, helping us on our paths. Most of all, I want to thank those who have inspired us, my own source especially. We are who we are because of you. We are where we are because of you. We are better. We are stronger. Thank you for the love. Thank you for the support. Thank you for being there when you were needed. Thank you for allowing us a place in your hearts and a memory for the future. And above all, thank you for showing us what it is to be a true hero and a true source of inspiration. It is because of you that we, myself included, are able to overcome adversity, succeed in our goals, and commence into a brighter future."

The gymnasium erupted in applause. Sarah got to her feet (not caring if anyone else was, but she had a feeling they were) and clapped for all she was worth, tears pouring down her face. When the applause died down after a few minutes, the principal got back up to the podium, announced that the diplomas would be handed out now, and the ceremony continued.

CHAPTER
11

The summer that followed was busy. Sarah was in her parents' company as they traveled the country. Her father was planning to run for president in two years; his campaign was already in motion. Sarah hoped that her blindness and the attack would not put a damper on her father's chances. She knew that it had always been his desire to go as far as the presidency. He was younger than most candidates, and presidents for that matter, but Sarah also knew that he was a prime candidate and a favorite among the possible nominees.

Sarah hadn't had much time to see Lucas, and it was killing her. They talked on the phone about every other night, but Sarah could tell that Lucas was still not himself. He had gotten a job at the rec center helping teach younger kids martial arts. It was where Lucas himself received training. Sarah tried to get him to talk to her, but he would quickly change the subject away from anything too painful. He wanted to talk about the future, both his and hers. Sarah didn't know what was so exciting about two more years of high school. She knew Lucas was still planning to go to the military prep school in Austin but hoped that he did not have to leave before she got to see him.

When Sarah did get to see him, like when she talked to him, he wasn't himself. He was distant and jumpy. Sarah tried to ask him about his odd behavior, but all he would tell her was that he had a lot on his mind. Sarah's heart ached for him. She knew that he blamed himself about what happened, though he didn't need to. He was constantly talking about how he had failed her, how he wasn't good enough for her anymore and how she would be better off without him. It terrified Sarah to think about being without Lucas, and she prayed that he would not leave her.

•

Lucas was in his room when there was a knock on his door. He gave his consent for entrance and was surprised when both of his parents walked through the door. They came in and sat on his bed. His father looked at him in such a way that meant he was to be part of the conversation, so Lucas dropped the book in his hands and swiveled in his chair to look at the two of them.

"I have been offered a position in Washington, and I have accepted," his father started. "Your mother and I wanted to give you an option. I have already looked into a military prep school for you in Washington—"

"You want me to leave Sarah?" Lucas blurted, nearly coming out of his chair.

"Please, hear me out, son," his father scolded for the interruption. "I looked into Washington for you, but I also have not declined your acceptance here either. We were going to leave it up to you. You may either move with us to Washington or stay here, with Sarah."

After Lucas's heart had restarted, he had to think about it. He loved Sarah with every fiber of his soul, but did she still love him the same? *Would* she be better without him? Lucas knew that it hadn't been totally his fault in regard to what had happened. He felt responsible, but mostly he felt so undeniably angry and guilty that he could hardly look at or talk to Sarah without feeling sick. It wasn't anything against her. It really wasn't. He had never loved her more. She was so strong, and so brave to go through what she had been through. And to top it all off, she didn't blame him for any of it. That fact alone made Lucas feel even guiltier.

He blamed himself, though. Lucas didn't know if he could stick around and be with Sarah when he was feeling this way. Would he ever be able to give himself to her totally? They had just started to declare themselves to one another and then the worst had happened. Sarah seemed to be moving past it fairly well, but could he? It wasn't that he saw Sarah in a different light. If anything, he was even fonder of her, loved her even more. But was that enough? Would it be enough for her to have just his love? She needed so much more from the man in her life, and Lucas just didn't know if he had it in him any longer to be that man. Not when he knew the guilt would eat him alive every second they were together.

His mother sighed, as if knowing her son's thoughts. "I hope you won't let the incident make your decision for you. Sarah loves you, and you love her. She needs you now more than ever."

"I failed her, Mom," Lucas whispered. "I don't deserve her anymore."

"Lucas, you didn't fail anybody," Paige soothed. "You found her. You saved her. You love her. Make your choice based on that fact alone." She kissed his forehead as she rose and walked out with his father.

He did love Sarah, but what was best for her? Was staying with her the best thing? Or was leaving the best thing for her? If leaving was the best thing for her, was he strong enough to do just that?

●

Sarah arrived back home with her family one week before school was supposed to start again. Lucas was due to leave for the military prep academy the following week as well. The afternoon that they arrived home, Sarah was up in her room putting her clothes and things away when she heard the doorbell ring. Someone (her father, judging by the heaviness of the steps) moved to answer the door. A few moments later, her father called up the stairs.

"Sarah, Lucas is here."

Sarah's heart skipped a beat. She wanted desperately to be near Lucas, to feel his hand in hers and to hear his sweet voice beside her. Sarah quickly threw the things in her arms onto her bed and hurried down the stairs. She could smell Lucas's cologne before she was even close, the warm breeze blowing in through the screen door.

"Hey Hercules," she greeted, once she was through the living room.

"Hi, Sarah," Lucas replied, sounding a little depressed. Nothing like himself. Sarah's heart clenched in fear.

"Can we sit and talk for a moment?"

"Sure," Sarah replied, a little nervous.

Lucas opened the screen door, took her hand, stiffer than usual and not nearly as warm as he normally was, and led Sarah to the porch swing. They sat in silence for a few minutes. Sarah could sense that Lucas was upset. His leg was bouncing repeatedly, nearly moving the entire swing. He was tapping his finger on the arm, his nail clicking against the wood. His anxiety was making Sarah nervous, and afraid.

"You haven't been yourself all summer," Sarah commented. "I'm sorry I was gone so much, but you know I had no choice." Sarah paused. "Do you look at me differently since, well, since what happened?"

Lucas sighed. He looked over at Sarah. That was a mistake. She was so beautiful. How was he ever going to do this? He knew what he had to do, what he had decided was the right choice for Sarah. But would he be strong enough to do it?

"I don't look at you differently," Lucas informed. "I blame myself, though. I failed you."

Sarah could hear the tears in his voice. "You didn't fail me. I should not have gone out into the hallway by myself. There was nothing you could have done! You have been there for me since we were ten. No one could have helped me because no one knew where I was. But it was you that found me, Lucas. That was all I prayed for. You kept me alive. It wasn't your fault, it wasn't any-one's fault but mine and the monsters that attacked me. I should not have gone out without you."

There was a moment of silence. "I'm going to miss you," Lucas whispered as if his mind was not on what she had just said.

"What do you mean? You're allowed to visit on the weekends from the prep school, right?"

"Yes, but I won't be able to visit coming from Washington, DC. We're moving. My father got promoted. We're leaving tonight."

The news hit Sarah like a bolt of lightning. She couldn't breathe. It had to be a joke, some cruel, sick, twisted joke. She waited a breath for Lucas to shout "April Fools'" or something, but the silence stretched on. It wasn't a joke. Sarah's throat threatened to close off, tears clogging her voice. Her body started to tremble.

"Why…why didn't you tell me? We won't ever see each other. I can't live without you. I love you."

"I love you too, that is why I have to go. I am going to attend the military prep school there." Lucas's voice was a dead monotone.

"No! If you love me, then that is why you have to stay. Go to school here. I need you!"

Lucas stood. "You can have an assistant assigned to you."

"You are not my assistant, Lucas! I love you! You…you are so much more to me than that." Sarah got to her feet and reached out to Lucas. "Please…don't go." She grabbed his shoulders and held on. "Please…please…don't leave me."

"I have to. You will be better without me, I promise."

"Who says?" Sarah was mad. Him and his pride. "Who says I will be better without you? You are my life, Lucas. I can't live without you."

"I am sorry," Lucas whispered, his voice thick. "I have to go. I have to let you get on with your life."

Sarah was trying to remain calm. "Is there someone else?"

Lucas felt like he had been slapped. "There will never be anyone but you, Sarah."

"Then, why are you going?"

"Because I have to. It's not you, it's a battle inside my heart. I love you, Sarah, but I just don't think I can keep you safe anymore. It was my fault, and now I have to pay for my mistakes."

"You're punishing yourself?" Sarah couldn't believe it. She grabbed handfuls of his shirt in her fists that were still on his shoulders. "You're punishing yourself by ending our relationship? Can't you stay as my boyfriend? What about me? Am I supposed to be punished too?"

"No. I don't mean to hurt you more with my decision. It is just something I have to do." Lucas gently took Sarah's wrists and pulled himself free. She stood still, her arms falling to her sides in shock.

Sarah heard Lucas turn to go. "Look at me," she demanded.

Lucas stopped. "I can't."

Tears welled up in Sarah's eyes. "Look at me!"

"I can't!"

"Why not?"

Lucas whipped around. "Because I blame myself for that scar on your cheek! I blame myself for the scar on your leg! I blame myself for the scars on your soul! I can't protect you if I love you, and damn my love for you, Sarah! I love you with every fiber of my being! I can't stay as your guard because of my love for you, and I can't stay as your boyfriend because I will be too worried about your safety to be able to give you my whole heart. You deserve someone who can give you his whole heart. I have to make sure you are safe because I love you, and I can't keep you safe if I love you."

"Yes, you can. It will make you protect me better."

"No, I can't. I'm sorry, my love." Lucas kissed Sarah's cheek and walked down the steps.

"Lucas, wait! Take my hand."

Lucas paused, and then silently continued.

"Lucas, please, take my hand!"

A door slammed; the truck's engine started.

Sarah felt through the air for Lucas's hand. For the first time in six years, it was not there. Sarah felt as if she was splitting in two. Pain ravaged her body like she had never felt before. She couldn't breathe. Her heart felt as if it had stopped. Her soul had been ripped from her body. After all that had happened, now this. Sobs racked her body. She shuffled forward to try to get to the steps of the porch. She made it down the first one but then slipped on the second, falling to the dirt.

Lucas saw her fall. He had to stop himself from running to her. Tears fell from his eyes, and he let the pain of leaving Sarah have him. Lucas hoped that he was doing the right thing. It felt to him the only thing he had left to do. He had failed her, and even though he was being proud, he knew he did not deserve her and had to leave. The guilt would eat away at him, and he would never be able to give her all of himself. He could hear Sarah yelling at him.

"Lucas, don't do this! Please! You are letting your pride make your decisions for you. If you leave, I will never forgive you! You are being stupid! You will regret this one day! Please don't leave me!" Sarah heard the truck pulling away. Sobs wrenched her body. "Lucas! No, please, come back to me! Please, take my hand! Lucas!"

CHAPTER

12

FOUR YEARS LATER

Lucas stood in his old room at his parents' house in Virginia. He knew he should be happy, but in truth he was miserable. He had completed his training and was now an Army sergeant, having been honored with promotion nine months ago; it was his life's dream come true. However, now as he prepared to leave for yet another secret mission in some secret place that would only end in death, Lucas felt terrible. He had come home on leave after being stabbed in the leg (surgery had been required to repair the damage inflicted from the wound and from Lucas continuing to fight with the knife there) and was departing after dinner that very night. Sighing, Lucas grabbed his bag and headed down the stairs to dinner.

It was a subdued affair, the dinner that night. His mother was on the brink of tears at every moment, and even his father was on the edge. Lucas knew that the intensity of the war he was in made them very nervous for his life. It didn't help any that he was their only child, their miracle. Lucas sure did hope President Watkins ended their involvement soon.

Lucas's heart skipped a beat. Thinking about President Watkins made Lucas think about his daughter, Sarah. Lucas still loved her. He wasn't sure, even to this day, what it was he had been thinking when leaving her. He wanted to talk to her, to see her, to hold her once more. She had said that she would never forgive him. He didn't doubt it. Lucas's food was stuck in his throat; it always closed off when he thought about Sarah. As if reading his mind, his mother spoke.

"I saw Sarah on TV today," Paige stated. "She was at the children's hospital talking with children that were injured and are now going to have a lifelong disability. She looked good."

Lucas stared at his plate. His mother knew that he hated to talk about Sarah. She knew that he kicked himself every day for leaving her.

"Did she look happy?" he asked, not looking at his mother.

Paige shrugged. "She always smiles when she knows she's on TV."

"Have you, um, spoken to President or Mrs. Watkins lately?" Lucas hoped that his forced casual tone would pass as real. He felt both his parents' eyes on him.

"I called Jonathan shortly after he was elected to offer my congratulations. However, with this bloody war, I daresay he is far too busy for catch-up-on-old-times phone calls." Owen sighed. "He mentioned concern over the war, said that Sarah had adjusted well, but was sad."

Lucas's head snapped up. His father was giving him a don't-you-dare-ask-why-she's-sad-because-you-know-why look. Lucas looked back down at his plate, no longer hungry.

After dinner, Lucas said good-bye to his mother and father, jumped in his taxi, and started to mentally prepare himself for battle once more. Reaching in the pocket of his jacket, Lucas pulled out his only picture of Sarah that he had. It was now over four years old, but from what he had seen in magazines and on TV, she hadn't changed much. She was still beautiful.

Lucas closed his eyes and tried to remember what it was like having Sarah's hand in his, remembering the kiss they shared the night of the dance. That memory shot through him like a knife. He still had nightmares about the night Sarah was raped. He still felt the terror he had felt that night; he still felt the hatred over those who had done that to her.

Lucas sighed, leaning his head back against the seat. He missed Sarah so much that it actually hurt. Her memory was the only thing that sustained him through most of the missions that he had been sent to. He wanted to talk to her, to write to her, but what would he say? Sorry for being so insensitive, prideful, and stupid? Well, that sounded good to Lucas, but would she even respond? Would she acknowledge his existence?

Lucas paid the driver and slowly walked through the gates of his base, showing his ID to the night guard. Once in his room, Lucas didn't even bother to change; he had to be up and dressed by 0400 to fly out anyway, which was only five hours away. Lying down, Lucas unwillingly reflected back upon the last day he had seen Sarah. It had been the hardest thing in the world for him to leave her sobbing on the ground like he had, calling out to him. He had cried the entire way home. His time in military school had been lonely for him; everyone there was his age but still in high school. Lucas had to go to the local community college for his classes since all the classes offered he had already taken. He was mainly there for the training anyway.

After two years there, his father had been transferred to Virginia, and Lucas had enlisted. He had left DC before Sarah had come to the White House. Now he was off to war again. Sarah's tear-stained face entered his memory again. What had he been thinking? She had been on the ground, begging him to take her hand and come back to her. Why had he left? Sarah's voice still rang in his ears.

"No, please, come back to me! Please, take my hand! Lucas!"

●

"Lucas!"

Sarah sat up in her bed. Her unseeing eyes were still closed, her right hand extended out in front of her. She had once again been dreaming of the last day she had seen Lucas. Her cheeks were wet with tears and her nightshirt soaked with sweat. Four years had passed since she had last seen him, but it felt like yesterday. Sarah could still remember the smell of his cologne, the sound of his voice, and the way his hand used to feel in hers. She was now graduated from high school, in college studying music and her father was President of the United States. Mona had moved to DC with Sarah and had found her own apartment. However, she had almost never been there, finally just moving in with Sarah as her "personal assistant."

Sarah refused to talk about Lucas. She had not even mentioned his name out loud in four years. Sarah knew that he had done well in the military prep school and he was now a sergeant in the Army having advanced unnaturally fast. Sarah would have been proud, but in truth, she was terrified. Her father had been sworn into presidency deep in the middle of a war in Africa, something that their country should never have gotten involved in. For the past two years, her father had been working to end their involvement. His success was close at hand, but Sarah was still scared. She knew that Lucas was over there somewhere on highly dangerous missions. She wondered if he thought about her like she did him.

Sarah couldn't go back to sleep. Heading downstairs to the kitchen for a glass of milk, she found Mona there having a midnight ice cream. She worked nightshift at her job, so on her nights off, she had a hard time sleeping.

"You are so predictable," Sarah laughed. "I should have known that you would be down here."

"How did you know it was me?" Mona asked, her voice thick.

"Who else would it be?" Sarah chuckled. "Besides, I smell fudge sauce. Are you reading a romance novel as well?"

Mona sniffed. "Yes. Bradley just rescued Mary Ann from almost certain death. Why can't real love be like that? I want a love that makes me feel safe at all times. I would love to feel protected and watched over. Ya know, like with you and Lucas." Mona bit her tongue after she realized what she had said.

"It is nice," Sarah whispered. "I wish I could forget him." Sarah could feel Mona's eyes appraising her.

"Well, maybe you'll meet a new man," Mona said, though she knew no one would ever hold up to Lucas in Sarah's eyes. She doubted Sarah even had it in her to love anyone else. "Maybe he might even be blind."

"I don't know if I want a blind man," Sarah confessed. "How would we be able to do anything? How would we be able to travel? Who would describe scenery for me? But then again, what man would ever want a blind woman?"

"Maybe you should write Lucas. I'm sure he misses you."

Sarah scoffed. "If he does miss me, it is only because he still feels ridiculously guilty. Him and his stupid pride. He would not listen to me when I told him that he didn't fail me. That night was just as much my fault as his. I don't even blame him. I do still love him, though."

Sarah stopped herself. Usually, she never even spoke Lucas's name, let alone confess out loud that she still loved him, though she knew that she wasn't fooling anybody. What worried Sarah the most was that the war would kill him before her father ended it, before she could see him again. She missed him so badly that it was like a giant part of her was missing. What would she do if he were to die? Sarah couldn't even stomach the thought.

"Write to him," Mona encouraged.

Sarah shook her head. "He has to know that I love him still. If he wants me, he can find me. That's final." Standing, Sarah shot a look Mona's way and went back to her room. Tears came once more in Lucas's name as Sarah cried herself to sleep.

The first week of her third year of college went poorly for Sarah. Her fellow students kept asking her when the war was going to end. She had to keep telling them that she did not know, and even if she did, she could not release any information. She was plagued with stories about family members and friends that were over there fighting. Each story about bombs and injuries was like a fresh lash at Sarah's wounds.

Her Secret Service men had changed again. This time it was two older guys. Sarah wanted Mike and Barb back. She had felt safe with them. These two didn't seem to think Sarah was in danger unless someone was actually beating her.

Her only solace was in her schooling, in her music. It had been her gateway to healing when Lucas had left her. Her parents had even bought her a brand new piano. Sarah had begun to compose her own music, learning as she went. Once they moved to DC and Sarah started studying at college, then things really started to open up for her. She was able to learn more about writing music, reading it better as a blind person and even how to teach others. Sarah had even taken up the major of teaching music.

It wasn't until her third week that things started to look up; well, they took on the potential for looking up. Rounding the corner to head to the library, Sarah ran into someone. She fell to the ground, her backpack thumping down beside her. Sarah held up her hand out of habit, to tell her service that she didn't need help. She really didn't need to, though. Neither one of them moved. Sarah rolled her eyes and grabbed for her backpack.

"I am so sorry," a male voice apologized. "I didn't see you."

"That is not a very good joke," Sarah laughed.

"Oh, it wasn't. I'm not blind." His abrupt statement took Sarah off guard, like he wanted to make it perfectly clear that he was fully functioning.

"Oh, okay," Sarah replied.

"Let me help you up. Take my hand."

Sarah's breath caught in her throat. She knew that it was not Lucas, but someone else using the words she knew him for rubbed Sarah the wrong way. Still, she took the man's hand.

"Thank you," she replied.

"Oh, dear God, I almost maimed the First Daughter. I didn't recognize you right away with your hair down. You always seem to have it pulled back at public functions. I like it pulled back better, if you don't mind my saying so."

Sarah was a little taken aback. She never would have guessed that a guy she had just met would tell her how he preferred her to wear her hair. Maybe he was just nervous. That would make sense for him to be nervous. Sarah was used to people becoming jittery when she was around. It really had been going on all her life. It was always from who her father was or due to the fact that she was blind. Sarah hoped that he was just nervous. She couldn't imagine someone being that pompous naturally.

"Well, thank you, I guess," Sarah stammered.

"My name is Henry St. Paul." He shook Sarah's hand. "My father is Professor St. Paul in arithmetic. I hope I am not delaying you from anything important."

"I was just on my way to the library..." Sarah started.

"I suppose the importance of that would depend on what you were going there for," Henry stated, chuckling at himself. "Well, I would like to invite you to have coffee with me. To formally apologize for running you over. Besides, I can assure you that time with me is more pleasantly spent than hitting the books." Henry laughed again.

Sarah was a little unnerved by Henry's apparent overconfidence and intense personality, but it had been so long since she had been with someone other than Mona or her parents. Sarah was suddenly longing for a date. Well, not a date, really. Just something different. Maybe it would help her to forget Lucas. Sarah doubted it, but she was desperate.

"Sure, why not."

Once in the cafeteria, Sarah was amazed to find it easy to talk to Henry, even if he did like to talk about himself. She learned that he studied to be a lawyer at Harvard. His inspiration had come from his grandfather. He had already had job offers. Henry said he had developed a great passion for law by helping his grandfather and hearing the power he had in court. Sarah was beginning to think that maybe he was just self-centered. He hadn't asked her a single thing about herself.

Henry then went from talking about himself to asking Sarah about her father. Well, not her father, really, just different things about the presidency. Some of it Sarah couldn't answer and when she told Henry such, Sarah could have sworn that he sighed impatiently but she couldn't be sure. When Henry did finally get around to asking Sarah about herself, it was short-lived. She had just begun to tell him about growing up in Texas when he told her that he had to get to a meeting.

"I had a good time, though," Henry said as Sarah heard him stand and zip his jacket. "I would love to take you to dinner. Tomorrow night? I'm sure there aren't any pressing matters at hand that you have to be to."

Sarah ruffled a little. Like she had no other life? She was just dying to go out with this guy? Sarah sighed. Well, what would it hurt? She hadn't been out to dinner with anyone but her parents in who-knew-how-long.

"Sure, tomorrow night would be fine."

"Great," Henry said. "I will be there at six. I will make the reservation at six thirty, so make sure you are ready to go. Oh, and don't forget to give my name to the guards. I need to be able to get through the gates."

With that, Henry left. Sarah sat for a few moments after that, simply trying to come to terms with what had just happened.

That night at dinner, Sarah was a little reluctant to inform her parents about her date with Henry. They had become surprisingly overprotective since Lucas left. Sarah realized that they must have relied on him more than she had known. Now every new friend or acquaintance Sarah made had to endure a background check.

Finally, she found the courage to bring it up. "I met someone today," she started. "His name is Henry St. Paul, Daddy, if you want to run a check on him."

Jonathan laughed. "Does he go to school with you?"

Sarah shook her head. "He went to Harvard. He studied law. He just started his internship at Bleaker and Stagg. We actually, physically, ran into each other today. Afterwards we had coffee. He asked me to dinner for tomorrow night." Sarah held her breath to see how her parents would react. She could almost hear their surprised looks, could nearly sense them stumble over their shock.

"Well, that's wonderful, dear," her mother cooed. "I hope that he turns out to be a good friend for you."

"Is that what you want?" her father asked, not bothering to hide his skepticism.

"Jonathan," Beth scolded.

Sarah took a deep breath. She didn't *want* to be with anyone but Lucas. But she also knew that pining after someone for the rest of her life wouldn't be healthy either. It had been four years. He clearly was out of her life for good. That thought nearly drove Sarah to tears.

"I need to move on, Daddy. It's been four years. I don't think anything is going to go back to the way it was any time soon."

Sarah heard her father sigh. "If that's what you want."

That night, Sarah lay in bed considering what her mother meant. She knew that her mother hoped for her to find love. Mona and her parents knew how much losing Lucas had affected Sarah. She hadn't bothered trying to hide her despair. There was no point in trying to live life when all reasons were gone. The first two weeks after he had left were terrible. Her parents almost had her hospitalized.

The past four years had been filled with longing and fear for Sarah. She woke up more times than not crying and screaming Lucas's name as she had in the hospital. She still had dreams about her attack and nightmares about the day Lucas left her life. It felt more like he had died then just left town. It was that permanent feeling in Sarah's heart. She missed him with every fiber of her soul, every ounce of her being. But she also knew that it would take an act of God to bring them back together, especially with him in the dreaded war that he was in.

Maybe Henry will be a good friend, Sarah considered. *He seems nice enough. If not a boyfriend, then at least someone to talk to.* After all, he had seemed interested in her. Maybe he didn't care if she was blind.

Two weeks later, Sarah was in her room getting ready for dinner. Henry was coming over to meet her parents, upon his insistence. He had wanted to meet them after just two dates, but Sarah had said no, making up some meeting that her father was going to be out of town for. Sarah wasn't sure how she felt about him meeting them. Henry seemed to be moving rather quickly. Sarah wasn't sure she was quite ready for that.

Sighing, Sarah moved out of her room and down the stairs. She knew that Henry would arrive soon. She wanted to be ready when he arrived. Henry was very punctual, a perfectionist even. He got very impatient with Sarah when she made him wait or if things weren't the way he thought they should be. It was upsetting for Sarah because she always had to do things over, and she was consistently too slow for him.

Sarah made it down the stairs and waited by the front door for Henry to arrive. When the doorbell finally did ring, Sarah opened the door right away. She stepped aside so that Henry could enter.

"Hi," Henry greeted. "Is dinner running on time? It should be, with a kitchen staff like this place has."

Sarah groaned inwardly. "As far as I know, dinner is running on schedule. My parents are waiting for us in the den."

"Well, let's go then," Henry stated, taking Sarah's arm roughly by the elbow. "They've been waiting for you your whole life. No need to keep them waiting longer."

Sarah cringed but led Henry toward the den. As they got closer, Sarah started to notice Henry change. His walk became lighter. He hooked her arm through his in a gentler, more gentlemanly way. He also closed the distance between them. Sarah could nearly feel the brownnosing coming on. They walked into the den, and Sarah heard her parents get to their feet.

"Mom, Dad, this is Henry St. Paul. Henry, these are my parents." Sarah felt Henry move away from her to shake her parents' hands.

"It is a pleasure to meet you, President Watkins. Mrs. Watkins," Henry replied. Sarah felt her mouth threaten to fall open. The tone of Henry's voice was smoother and kinder than she had ever heard it. She wouldn't have known that it was the same person talking had she not been in the situation that she was in now.

"Thank you, Henry. Come and have a seat. Dinner is to be served shortly," her mother said.

Further shocking Sarah (brownnosing, she was sure), Henry gently took her hand and made a show of leading her to the couch. He assisted her in sitting down and seemed to act like he was making sure she was situated before sitting himself down. He then proceeded to talk with her parents, and *not* totally about himself. Thirty minutes later when dinner was called, Henry had talked with her father about golf, music, and the Caribbean; he had talked with her mother about music as well, even discussing the opera. It did not go unnoticed to Sarah, however, that she was not actively included in the conversations. When she did speak, Henry was quick to cut her off the moment she stopped for breath.

During the meal, it got even worse. Henry started to talk about himself, gaining velocity the more questions her parents asked him. He was very tactful about it, making sure not to hog the limelight too much. He told her parents about his childhood and where he grew up. By the time Henry left, he had gained the approval of both of her parents. However, Sarah wasn't totally convinced that he had *her* approval yet. Maybe she was just being too critical. Was she unconsciously comparing Henry to Lucas? That would be like trying to compare apples to oranges. Or better yet, apples to carrots. They weren't even in the same class to be compared. That was how different Lucas and Henry were. The only thing that Sarah was unsure of was whether or not she could be satisfied with a carrot. Or was her appetite always going to be toward apples?

By the time midterms came and went, Sarah was still seeing Henry. She wasn't sure why she kept seeing him. She liked him, sure, when he was being nice. He was still impatient, still a perfectionist. He also had shown what a short temper he had. He hadn't hit Sarah, but she wouldn't put it past him. Henry was also pretty possessive and controlling. He didn't like when he went more than a day without talking to her. He didn't approve most of her friends.

He was usually telling Sarah how much help she needed, what a burden she was to everyone because she was blind. He also made sure that he let her know how much she needed him. Sarah hadn't ever thought that she needed anyone, but maybe she had. Had she relied too much on Lucas when they were younger? Was that one of the reasons that he left? Sarah thought about breaking it off with Henry, but every time he seemed to sense that she was thinking that way, he would do something nice. It would make Sarah rethink her decision.

However, there was something about him that set Sarah on edge. It wasn't enough for anyone to notice from the outside, but it was enough to bother Sarah. It was like she couldn't be herself, but he wasn't quite trying to change her. He would insult her jokingly but always with an underlying harshness to it. He was always perfect around other people, though. Sarah found herself wishing that when they were together in private, he would be the same as he was when in public. Sarah just figured out that since being with Lucas had been so easy, it should be that easy with someone else. How wrong she was.

CHAPTER
13

Lucas was crouched rather uncomfortably on his haunches, waiting. Sweat ran down his back. The camouflage paint of his face was really starting to irritate him. They had received a tip on the location of a group of rebel spies. They were supposedly shacked up in the village that lay not even one hundred yards from where Lucas and his men were hiding. Whether the spies were there by invitation or force was yet to be determined. Lucas just hoped that they had not converted the children. There was nothing he hated more than the sight of a young child with a gun in his hand.

Lucas motioned for his men to follow him silently into the village. Slowly, deftly, they made their way to the outer rims. Just then, a young woman came out from the other side of a house. She spotted Lucas. He locked eyes with her, slowly motioning with his index finger for her to be quiet. She held up all ten fingers, flashing them three times, and then ducked under a lean-to. Lucas took it to mean that there were thirty of them. He had twenty men. Good enough.

Swiftly and silently, Lucas and his men moved from one small wooden house to another looking for captives, or spies. Suddenly, shots rang out. Yells came from his men. Lucas hurried to their aide. The rebels, having unwisely shacked up all in the same area, were now cornered in their own, brilliant hiding spot. The sound of gunfire rang through the trees like a round of morbid church bells. The sound of bodies falling to the ground was everywhere, death cries filling the air.

A wall was broken down, followed by several rebels climbing out and running into the trees. Lucas ordered his men not to follow. Then he noticed one of the rebels holding the woman from before hostage. He was yelling and gesturing with his gun, aiming first at her and then at Lucas. The woman was crying; a little boy yelled and cried from the doorway of one of the houses. Lucas understood what he was saying; he was crying for his mother.

"Put the gun down and let her go!" Lucas demanded, though he knew full well that the man did not understand English.

The rebel pointed the gun at the woman's head, and then waved it at Lucas; Lucas took the shot. The rebel's hand came apart. The woman ducked. Lucas put a round through his head.

After the three-mile hike back to base, one of his men turned on the radio. Lucas's stomach clenched painfully as he heard President Watkins's voice. Hearing his voice made him think of Sarah. The images of the woman from the village pleading with him to help her made him think of Sarah even more. His team was at ease, joking and laughing with one another, celebrating their victory, though none of them took it lightly. They all knew what it cost for them to be there, the missions they went on. Lucas hated it. He loved being in the Army, but he didn't agree with the war they were fighting. He hoped President Watkins was able to get them out soon. Lucas cringed inwardly as his thoughts about President Watkins brought on even more memories of Sarah to the surface.

●

Lucas lay in his bed trying to get some rest. The mission they had been sent on had been a success that day, but they had lost some men as well. It had been yet another ambush on the rebels in yet another village. This one had been bloody. Between the battles he had been fighting and his thoughts of Sarah, Lucas was finding it hard to sleep.

Reaching under his pillow, Lucas pulled out his picture of her. He had heard President Watkins give another speech on the radio begging for peace. He had gotten his peace too. Lucas smiled as the thought about finally going home. President Watkins was going to be signing the order to withdraw troops next week. All they had to do was lay low until then. President Watkins had been very excited about finally being able to "bring the boys home" as he had put it. Lucas was relieved. He had enlisted right in the middle of the war, and President Watkins had been working since his election to end their involvement. It had been nearly three years in the making, but now the final signing and the final withdrawal of troops was close at hand. Of course, Lucas would have to be among the soldiers last to be taken out. He hadn't mentioned anything about Sarah, not that Lucas had expected him to. Lucas sighed, staring at the face that had sustained him for so long in light of his fear and misery.

Lucas was thrilled about going home. He hadn't been home in nearly a year. He wanted so much to see Sarah. Possibly after he was home for good, he could try and talk to her. Tucking the picture under his pillow again, Lucas shut off his lamp and tried to sleep. Sarah's face swam clear as day behind his eyelids causing him to doze off with a smile on his face.

Suddenly, she was gone. She was screaming his name, pleading for him to help her. Her face was bruised, her leg bleeding. She was in the shack; Lucas could see her through the window, a faceless figure was on top of her. That faceless figure turned into Carl, who turned into a member of the army he was fighting. The rebel pulled a knife and plunged it into Sarah's heart. She screamed in agony, calling for him to help her. Lucas couldn't move, couldn't help her. Someone was holding his arm, holding him down.

Lucas yelled in fury, lashing out with his fist at the opponent who was holding him down. There was a cry of pain; lamps came on. Lucas grabbed his gun, his aim steady, though his entire body shook.

"Lucas, man, calm down," someone said. It was the man on the floor. His nose was bleeding, and as Lucas's head cleared, he noticed that the man he hit was not the enemy but his bunkmate, Frankie McGee.

Frankie stood up slowly, still looking at Lucas as if he had lost his mind. "You all right, man? You were fighting something bad in your sleep. I tried to wake you up, and you hit me."

Lucas shook his head like a dog trying to clear water from its ears. "I'm sorry, Frankie," Lucas sighed. "I was having a bad dream."

Frankie came closer to Lucas's bed while everyone else settled back down. Nightmares were nothing new. Lucas pinched the bridge of his nose, a headache pulsing behind his eyes like always after he dreamed about Sarah.

"Who's Sarah?' Frankie asked in hushed tones. "You say her name in your sleep at least once a week. Is that who your nightmares are about?"

Lucas sighed, wiping the sweat from his forehead. He nodded. "She's my old, well, girlfriend, I guess you could say." Lucas pulled out the picture from under his pillow. He handed the picture to Frankie, who whistled out loud, then gave Lucas a skeptical look.

"This is Sarah Watkins, the First Daughter," Frankie said.

Lucas nodded. "I know that. I've known her since we were ten. I saved her from some bullies right after her father became governor of Texas. After that, I kind of became her bodyguard so she didn't have to have a grown-up around her all the time. Her parents had wanted her to have an assistant, not just because she was blind or the governor's daughter. Mostly a combination of both. Sarah hadn't liked the idea."

"I can't believe you actually dated the First Daughter," Frankie stated, chuckling.

"She wasn't the First Daughter at the time."

"So what happened? Shouldn't you have a nice cushy desk job?"

Lucas rolled his eyes. "We sort of fell apart," he replied. "Something happened that I felt responsible for. I wasn't there when she needed me the most, so I left."

"Was it your fault?"

Lucas sighed. "She didn't blame me, but I blamed myself. Plus, my family was moving to DC at the time. I know I could have stayed and gone to school there, but, I don't know. If I could do it over again, I wouldn't have left her. I guess I still care for her."

Frankie laughed. "Lucas, dude, you're having dreams about the chick. I really think you probably do still care. Why don't you write to her?"

"I'm sure she hates me. Besides, it's been nearly five years and, I don't know, look at her. You think she doesn't have a million guys after her, anyway?"

"Yeah, but she blind."

"What does that have to do with anything?" Lucas snapped.

Frankie held up his hands in defeat. "I didn't mean anything by it, Lucas. I'm just saying that not everyone can look pass a disability. I heard she's a sweet girl and all, but let's face it not every guy can –"

But what it was that not every guy could do, Lucas never heard. A great resounding explosion sounded and Lucas was blown off his bunk. Slammed backwards, Lucas hit the opposite wall of where his bed was, debris falling all around him. His head slammed into the wall, crumpling him to the floor. Trying to get his bearings back, Lucas attempted to get to his feet. He stumbled slightly and then hit the floor again as gunfire sounded from every angle around them; they were under attack. Two of his men went down.

"Get to the weapons bunker!" Lucas screamed. "Get your-selves armed and open fire!" Lucas stumbled over to where his bed had been, and, miraculously, pulled out his own guns and his belt with his blades on it, ducking once more as bullets ripped through the air.

After slinging his weapons onto his body, Lucas quickly started helping pull his men free from the rubble. Once everyone but the two dead was accounted for, Lucas directed his men up to the watch tower, guns and night-vision binoculars in hand. Climbing up the three-story tower, Lucas heard one of his men take a hit, but barked at the others to keep moving. There were other soldiers on the compound to help with the fighting, but Lucas and his men were trained snipers; the tower was where they needed to be to help the best way that they knew how.

Once at the top, Lucas put on his night vision binoculars and started firing. He picked off a few of the rebels on the ground. The bursts of fire and bullets burned his eyes but Lucas kept fir-ing. He could hear more gunfire from below, but from their sta-tion in the tower, Lucas's men were free to fire down, but blocked relatively well from enemy fire below. Well, almost.

Lucas screamed in pain as a bullet tore through the muscle in his left thigh. He fell back, yelling at his men to keep firing. Quickly, Lucas ripped a strip of material off his shirt, tied it as tightly as he could around his leg and then got back up to keep firing. More explosions sounded. Lucas looked down and noticed that their weapons bunker had been set on fire. His fellow sol-diers on the ground needed help, some screaming, trapped in the burning building.

"Let's go!" Lucas shouted. "There are soldiers dying down there. We have to go help."

Lucas led his group back down the ladder. Once on the ground, they spread out to help with the fighting. Lucas couldn't believe that this was happening. His men were dying when they were only a few days from going home. Was he ever going to see Sarah again?

Lucas's guns were empty; dodging bullets, Lucas ran to the aide of some soldiers that had been trapped in a burning building. Rebel forces surrounded the building, shooting and stabbing any that tried to escape the growing flames. Lucas pulled both his knives from his belt and charged the enemy. Catching one guy in the back and another in the throat, Lucas fought his way to the door of the building. Grabbing the automatic weapon off one of the fallen enemy, Lucas opened fire into the group of rebel fighters, spraying them with bullets, sending the ones not hit running for cover. Taking advantage of the lack of rebel forces, Lucas slammed his body into the locked door of the burning building.

Screams of pain sounded from inside. Lucas slammed his body into the door again; it gave way. Lucas nearly fell into the fire.

"Move!" he shouted to the soldiers in the building. Some were trapped, some injured. Lucas started helping those who needed help. Pulling them out, one by one, Lucas finally was able to get them all out. The enemy was on the run. Lucas hurried back to the tower. As fast as he could Lucas climbed the ladder, grabbed his night vision binoculars and began to fire at the retreating enemy.

There was another explosion. The tower shook. Lucas looked down just in time to see two of the legs holding up the tower start to crumble. Grabbing the nearest support beam, Lucas held on as the tower collapsed from under him, sending him crashing to the ground thirty feet below.

CHAPTER
14

Two weeks before final exams, Sarah was in the library studying. Actually, she wasn't getting much done. Sarah was contemplating her relationship with Henry. She was starting to wonder why she stayed with him. She wasn't that happy with him. He wasn't very nice to her. He wasn't what Sarah thought a boyfriend should be.

Sarah sighed. She missed Lucas with every breath that she took. What she wouldn't give to feel his hand in hers, hear his voice again. Sarah tipped her head as she heard her agents shift in their seats. She could faintly hear something coming over their ear pieces. Suddenly, they stood abruptly and came to her side. One of them started to pack up her books and the other helped her to her feet. Together they escorted her out of the room without a word. Out the front door of the library was a limo waiting for them. Sarah sat in silent confusion all the way back to the White House. They didn't say anything; Sarah knew better than to ask. Most of the time they couldn't give her any details any way. It hadn't happened fast enough for Sarah to think it was a security thing. They must have gotten word to get her home ASAP. Sarah's heart clenched in fear. Any number of horrible ideas ran through her head in regards to what could have happened. Once back to the White House, Sarah was led to her room and left there.

Her aide bustled in moments later and started asking Sarah what she wanted to wear.

"What is going on?" Sarah demanded.

"There was an attack early this morning. I was just told to get you ready for a press conference on the matter and the early signing of the final papers to pull out the last of America's troops and end our involvement in the war. That's all I know." She helped Sarah slip into a new dress.

Sarah's thoughts immediately went to Lucas. Where was he? Was he okay? Was he near the attack? Sarah's aide left, telling her that her mother would be in to get her when they were ready. Sarah sat on her bed and waited. It was times like this that she really hated being blind. When her father had been elected, he had told her for her safety to stay where she was put unless escorted. The door opened. Sarah lifted her head. She caught a whiff of her mother's perfume. She heard her sigh.

"Sarah, I need to tell you something." Beth knelt in front of her daughter. "The attack that took place was on a military compound." Beth paused, not wanting to finish her thought. "It was an Army compound, honey."

Sarah's blood ran cold; she couldn't breathe. "Was it Lucas? Mom, was it Lucas's base?"

Beth nodded though her daughter couldn't see. She did not want to say the words. "Yes, sweetheart, the base hit was the one Lucas's battalion was thought to be assigned to. They were supposed to be there awaiting discharge."

A moan of despair escaped Sarah's throat. "Is he okay? Mom, you have to tell me. I need to know if he is alive."

"We don't know yet, sweetheart. It only just happened and they haven't – located everyone yet."

Sarah felt her world stand still. The next two hours passed agonizingly slow. She stood as her father gave his speech, fighting the urge to scream out loud. During the signing of the papers Sarah sat next to her mother and tried to smile as if she were happy; luckily the graveness of the reason for the rush on the signing allowed for an excuse for Sarah to look sad. Finally, the formalities were over. Sarah went to her room to change and then back to find her parents.

"How is Lucas?" Sarah asked, barging in without announcing herself.

Beth stood and embraced her daughter. "We don't know yet. Lucas's battalion *was* sent to that compound to await discharge home, along with many others. That much we are sure of. I just got off the phone with Paige. She and Owen don't know much more than we do at this point, but due to Owen's station with the FBI, he was able to determine that Lucas's group was definitely there."

Sarah broke down. "Oh, Mom, what if he's dead? What am I going to do without him? I can't lose him again! I can't, Mom, I can't!"

Mona was hugging her. "Sarah, hun, calm down. We don't know that he was injured."

Sarah gripped her friend for all she was worth. "I can't believe that this is happening. What if…what if…oh, I'm gonna be sick," Sarah gasped. Mona helped her to the bathroom.

Beth felt helpless. "Can you call someone?" she asked her husband.

Jonathan nodded. "I'll make some calls. I daresay I'm just as worried about the boy as his own father has to be."

"See what you can find out," Beth said. "I hope Lucas is okay. He left her once and it nearly killed her. I'm terrified to think what his death would do to her."

Sarah went to lie down in bed after losing the entire contents of her stomach. Mona had asked if Sarah wanted her to stay, but Sarah had told her to go. She couldn't believe what had happened. Lucas had been only days away from coming home for good and then this. What was she to do without him? How could she handle losing him for good this time? They hadn't been together for years, but Sarah had never given up hope of being with him again. But, what if he had been killed? She'd never even see him again. The pain was incredible. Sobs choked the breath from her body.

"Lucas...come back to me."

•

Lucas's eyes popped open. Where was he? What happened? Lucas tried to move, only to scream in pain. His left arm was pinned, as were both his legs. Memories came back to him. The attack, the fire, the tower falling and now Lucas was trapped under the debris. He tried to move again, only to be in more pain. He tried to yell for help.

"Hey!" he called, his voice hoarse. "Hey! Help me!"

"Lucas! Lucas, is that you?" It was Frankie.

"Frankie, I'm trapped. Help me!"

"I'll be right back, Lucas. I'm gonna need more help."

Lucas heard Frankie run off, tripping over something and cussing in his haste. Early morning daylight was peeking through the cracks in the wood covering him. Lucas thought about Sarah. Where was she? Did she know about the attack? Surely President Watkins would be informed. The signing of the papers may even be pushed up a few days.

Pain suddenly shot through Lucas. He screamed in agony. Frankie was calling to him.

"Lucas, man, you okay?"

"Oh, I'm just dandy," Lucas groaned. "What are you doing up there?"

Frankie was barking orders at someone else. "We're trying to get you out, Lucas. However, it's not going to be easy. You have the whole tower on top of you right now. If we hurt you too bad, yell."

Lucas tried not to scream too much as the weight of the wood on him shifted to press down on his legs more. More than once, though, the pressure on his wounded body was too much, causing him to cry out in agony. Lucas also noticed that there was a good amount of blood running from his scalp and even pooling under his right leg. After an agonizing hour, the last bit of the wood was taken off. Lucas was nearly unconscious again.

"Lucas, man, hang on. Stay with us," Frankie was saying.

Lucas could hear people talking all around him, screaming at each other to get the medics. Something was tied tightly around the bleeding wound on his leg. His heart felt like it was going a million miles per minute; he felt very weak. His hands and feet were numb; his head was spinning. He felt very sleepy. Lucas was vaguely aware of the sound of chopper blade through the air. He was loaded up and passed out.

Suddenly, Lucas noticed he was in a hospital. He was being rolled side to side. Pain shot through him but he wasn't conscious enough to tell anyone. He was being poked with needles and felt as though braces were being placed everywhere. His uniform was cut off him.

Suddenly, someone moved his legs causing him to scream out in pain. That brought him around enough to talk.

"Sergeant Monroe? Lucas? Lucas, can you hear me?" the doctor asked.

"Yes," Lucas replied barely above a whisper.

"Where do you hurt?"

Lucas groaned. "I think…a better question…would be…where I don't hurt."

The doctor chuckled. "Okay, well, we're gonna do the best we can to get you stable enough to go home. Just stay with us."

As the doctors worked on him, Lucas's thoughts went back to Sarah. Her face came to memory and Lucas smiled. He wondered if she was worried about him. He wondered if she still cared. The doctor was telling Lucas that he needed surgery to stop some internal bleeding and set his broken legs and arm. Lucas couldn't respond, so he focused his groggy thoughts on Sarah.

"Lucas, come back to me."

Lucas jumped, startled at hearing Sarah call to him. He tried to open his eyes and look around, but they wouldn't work. Lucas couldn't move. He could feel himself slipping of the edge of reality. He could still hear what the doctor was saying, but Lucas couldn't talk. He couldn't tell them that he needed Sarah. He had to tell them how much he needed her.

The doctor was yelling to his team, "...to OR STAT or he won't make it...four units of blood...no, no we have to go now... there's no time. Damn, we're losing him..."

Everything went black.

●

Sarah didn't sleep well that night. She kept having nightmares about Lucas's bloody body and his funeral. She rolled over around nine and decided anymore sleep was a lost cause. Just as she was zipping her pants her door flew open.

"Miss Watkins, Miss Watkins," her aide rushed, "your father is on the phone with Mr. Monroe at this very moment. Your mother told me to come and get you."

Sarah couldn't breathe as she let her aide lead her down the steps. She nearly tripped twice in her haste. What if Lucas was dead? What if he was fatally wounded and only had hours to live? Would she ever see him again? Would she ever hear his voice again? Without waiting to be announced, Sarah burst into the Oval Office.

"What is it?" she demanded. "Is it Lucas? Is he alive?" She held out both of her hands, waiting for someone, anyone, to give her news.

Sarah felt her mother's arms around her. "He's alive, honey. He's alive."

Sarah's legs felt weak; she gripped her mother for support. Sarah had been so certain that she was going to be told that Lucas was dead. It was almost surreal to hear that he was alive.

It took Sarah a moment to realize what her mother was saying. She had to sit down. Sarah started to back toward the couch she knew was behind her. Her mother helped guide her and Sarah was shocked to find someone else already on the couch. Sarah's gut clenched as she caught a whiff of Henry's cologne, but her mother was speaking, so she listened to her.

"Lucas was injured in the fighting during the attack, but he is going to be fine. He and his troops fought bravely. He was in a lookout tower when it collapsed, trapping him under it. He was pulled out and taken to hospital. His left arm was broken as were both his legs. He had to have surgery to set the bones and stop internal bleeding. Not to mention he had a bleeding artery in his leg. He very nearly died, but the doctors say he is going to pull through. Paige and Owen were told he should be stable enough for transfer to a hospital here in about ten days."

Sarah breathed a huge sigh of relief. He was coming home; Lucas was coming home. Sarah could feel all the fear and worry melt off her face. But then she felt Henry stiffen next to her. Sarah tried to cover for her relief.

"Mr. and Mrs. Monroe must be so relieved," Sarah commented, her voice trembling. "They have to be very worried." Sarah felt Henry take her arm, gripping far too tightly to be considered a reassuring gesture. She flinched.

"Yes, I daresay they are quite worried. Your father spoke with Owen just now, so I think I will go and call Paige myself, offer what comfort I can. I can't imagine what they are going through. Their only child…"

Sarah heard her mother walk off and then a door open and close. Henry pulled her to her feet holding her by both upper arms.

"Who's Lucas?" He asked, his voice cold.

"He's just an old friend," Sarah replied, unwilling to let Henry know just how close she and Lucas had been. "I only wanted to know if he was okay."

"You seemed quite concerned," Henry stated.

"Well, he was like my best friend when I was younger. Our families were very close. We've lost touch with him in the service and myself the First Daughter, but I'm still allowed to be concerned about him as my friend, aren't I?"

"Well, as long as that's all it was. I won't have any woman of mine pining over some other guy, I don't care how brave he is." Henry's voice was cold enough to make Sarah shiver.

•

Lucas opened his eyes as he felt the altitude of the plane change. Soon, the medical team was prepping him to be transferred from the plane to an ambulance. It had been a week since the attack and Lucas was barely feeling back to normal. Finally, the medic wheeled him off the airplane into his mother's waiting arms.

"Oh, Lucas," Paige sobbed. "We thought we had lost you. We thought you were never going to come home."

"I'm home now, Mom," Lucas replied, smiling up at her from his place on the stretcher. He was really tired and extremely sore, but glad to be home, glad to be alive.

His father reached down to shake Lucas's hand, then as if throwing caution to the wind, bent down and hugged him, sniffing loudly.

"I'm proud of you, son," Owen stated, a little choked up. "You've served your country well."

"Thanks Dad," Lucas replied.

The medic wheeled Lucas to the ambulance, lifted him in, gave a salute and then turned to go. Paige and Owen got in their car to follow their son to the hospital. Lucas stayed in the hospital for a few days after that, followed by six more weeks in a wheelchair while his legs healed. On the first day of his therapy, Lucas almost cried.

"I can't believe how stiff my legs are," he growled. "I will never be back to normal."

"I don't allow my patients to say never," Janet, his therapist scolded. "You will be back to normal in no time."

Lucas hoped so. He wanted to see Sarah so bad that it hurt, but he wanted to be fully functioning when he did so.

The following weeks were some of the longest in Lucas's life. Had he not been so determined to get better so that he could see Sarah again, Lucas probably would have given up. He felt as though he had been given a second chance. God had spared his life and Lucas was dead set to use his second chance to ask Sarah for her forgiveness, possibly even rekindle their relationship.

"Don't push too hard," Janet scolded for the millionth time.

"I'm fine," Lucas huffed, pressing the leg machine again and again. His muscles were screaming in protest, but Lucas was not going to stop. He had too much at stake. When he was done with his reps, he swung his legs around and sat up off the machine.

"Is it just stubbornness driving you forward, or do you have some ulterior motive for getting better?" Janet asked.

"I have to get better," Lucas informed, taking a swig of water. "I have to be better when I see Sarah again."

Janet raised an eyebrow. "Who's Sarah?" she asked. "I never knew that you had a woman in your life."

Lucas sighed, running a hand through his damp hair. "She's not really *in* my life," Lucas said. "It's sort of a long story; an unbelievable story."

Janet grinned. "Well, you do have another half hour to your session. Talk while you work."

Lucas glanced up at Janet, nodded and then limped over to the weight bench.

●

Sarah's felt as though life was passing in confusing blocks of time. On one hand, she was excited that her father had been reelected for a second term; his dream come true. That gave her a lot of joy. She had finished her exams, anxious for a break and even more anxious to finish her final semester. Christmas passed with a trip back to Texas. Mona traveled with them so that she could see her family. Those were all happy things. Sarah still found herself worrying about Lucas, though. She had only gotten bits and pieces of a "Lucas report" after that initial one; that all important report stating that he was still alive. He had made it back to the United States and, according to a call from Paige Monroe two months prior, had undergone six months of healing and therapy to regain full use of his legs. He had been awarded the Distinguished Service Cross and had been honorably discharged from the Army. It had been eight months since the attack.

The black cloud in Sarah's life actually was Henry. She had become so intensely nervous around him that Sarah didn't get any enjoyment out of their relationship at all. She wanted to end it, but wasn't sure how. Not to mention every time Henry suspected she might be considering ending their relationship, he was sure to tell her, rather harshly, that she would never find anyone else to take care of her. He tried to convince her that she needed someone to watch over her, but Sarah didn't totally believe that. She wanted to have someone in her life because she loved them, not because he bullied her into believing that she couldn't go on without him.

Soon, it was time for the Inauguration. Following was a black tie dinner at the White House in honor of Sarah's father. Everything passed smoothly and before she knew it, Sarah found herself in an evening gown with hundreds of guests around her that she did not know. Henry had joined her, much to her dismay. He couldn't pass up the chance to rub elbows with everyone and been seen among such a crowd.

Around ten o'clock, Henry dismissed himself to the restroom. After he left, Sarah heard the unmistakable laugh of Paige Monroe. Her heart jumped; she hadn't known they would be coming. She was to the left of where Sarah sat.

"Mrs. Monroe?" Sarah called getting to her feet.

"Sarah!" Mrs. Monroe squealed, pulling Sarah into a hug. "I have been trying to find you all night. It is so good to see you my dear. I have not seen you since you were sixteen. It must be going on six years now. How are you?"

"I'm doing well," Sarah replied, holding down the desire to ask about Lucas. How was he doing? Where was he? Had he come with them? "I am about to start my final semester at the college. I'm studying music."

"Sarah! How are you?" Mr. Monroe asked, hurrying over to them and embracing Sarah.

"I'm doing well. How are you enjoying that promotion Dad said you received?"

"I love it. I have contacts with the new secret service assigned to your family. They are good men. It's good to be back in Washington. We just arrived not two weeks ago. How are you enjoying college?"

"I'm enjoying it very much." Sarah heard someone come up behind her and then felt Henry's firm grip on her elbow.

"I don't believe I have met your friends, Sarah," he said in his fake-friendly voice. He gripped Sarah's elbow tighter. She had to resist flinching.

"Henry, this is Mr. Owen Monroe and his wife, Paige. They are old friends of the family. This is my boyfriend, Henry."

"Oh, you're the hero's parents," Henry commented. Sarah recognized his my-manhood-is-bigger-than-yours voice. She cringed.

"Excuse me?" Owen asked.

"Sarah told me your son, Lucas was it, was injured in the war. That he was awarded a medal for his bravery and everything. It must be nice to have a hero for a son."

Sarah could nearly feel the tension in the air. She knew that Henry was insulting Paige and Owen. She was insulted and Lucas wasn't her son. Henry proceeded to talk himself up, informing Paige and Owen about his internship and everything. Sarah had to fight rolling her eyes. She would have walked away had Henry not had ahold of her elbow, still. She thought she would burst for sure if she did not hear about Lucas soon. It had only been two months since she had heard anything, but Sarah still thought she would die. Her parents never mentioned Lucas unless Sarah brought it up. Her pride kept her from asking and the little she had heard in the last eight months since the attack was what her parents said in her presence before catching themselves.

Suddenly, a familiar scent entered Sarah's nose. Her body locked down in shock, in surprise, in anticipation. Memories flooded her mind, her heart pounding. She was suddenly sixteen again, sitting on her front porch. That single scent caused such a reaction for Sarah that she nearly fainted; it caused her to want to scream, laugh and cry all at once. It was the scent of a cologne that she had not smelled in six years. Sarah turned in the direction it was coming from, her body starting to tremble.

"Hello, Sarah," Lucas greeted his voice soft and hesitant.

Sarah thought for sure that she would faint. The very sound, smell and presence of him made her weak. She took a deep breath to compose herself. She would not appear weak, would not let it show how much his very existence affected her.

"Hello, Lucas," she greeted back. "How have you been?"

"I'm well, thank you. You look wonderful. How have you been?"

"I'm fine (Henry pinched the back of her arm). Lucas, this is Henry. Henry, this is Lucas Monroe."

"Oh, the hero," Henry practically sneered.

"What was that?" Lucas asked.

"So, Henry, you were saying about your internship…" Paige interjected, trying to diffuse the situation.

Sarah knew why she did it too. The tone to Lucas's voice suggested that he was feeling challenged or threatened. She knew that his eyebrows would be slammed together, his fists clenched.

"Well, as I was saying, before I was interrupted,"— Lucas scuffed — "was that I expect to be offered the job any day. They say that I am the quickest intern that they have ever hired. They expect me to go far in my career. Why, they even say that…"

Sarah couldn't take it anymore. Not only was she sick of hearing Henry talk about himself, but she could also feel Lucas's eyes on her. It was unnerving for her to have him this close again. She couldn't think straight, she couldn't breathe. Most of all, she couldn't stand that he was within reach, and wasn't hers to touch.

"Excuse me," Sarah muttered.

She turned to leave pulling her arm out of Henry's grasp. Trying to make her way through the crowd, someone bumped into her and knocked her down. Five separate voices started to apologize to her, trying to help her up.

"Sarah!" Lucas called, coming to her side, pushing everyone else away. "Take my hand."

"I'm fine," Sarah hissed. Lucas huffed and bent to grab her hand anyway.

Tears came to Sarah's eyes as she let Lucas pull her to her feet. The feeling of his hand in hers was all too familiar. Straightening herself, Sarah tried to be brave.

"Thank you for your assistance, Lucas. I really must go."

"I haven't gone a day without thinking about you," Lucas confessed, stopping Sarah before she could leave. Sarah was acutely aware of all the other people around, but she didn't care.

"Don't start, Lucas. I have a…well, I'm with someone. And you had your chance. It took a long time for me to get over what you did. I still don't understand it. I haven't been able to decide whether or not I still hold feelings for you. We had a connection, Lucas, and that is not something I can break easily. You must not have felt the same or you would not have done what you did."

"I told you why I did it."

"What happened was not your fault, you stubborn mule . No one blamed you, least of all me. The entire time I was going through that ordeal all I did was pray for you to find me. I loved you, Lucas…and I still do."

Sarah could hear Lucas's breath coming in short puffs. She couldn't handle it anymore. Spinning on her heels, tears running down her face, Sarah made her way out of the banquet hall and through the house. Finally, she gave up.

"Max?" Sarah called to one of her bodyguards. "Are you there?"

"Yes, ma'am, I'm here," Max replied. He had been told to always follow Sarah but to only assist her if she asked. Since she had only been to the banquet hall a handful of times Sarah was not sure how to get back to her room from there.

"I'm lost. I wish to go to my room please." Sarah felt Max take her arm and lead her through the house. Once in her room, Sarah asked Max to give her regards to Henry and tell him that she would call him later. More tears poured down her cheeks the minute the door to her room shut.

The next morning after breakfast, Henry showed up unannounced and took Sarah out back to the gardens. They didn't go for a leisurely walk, either. No, he grabbed her elbow and nearly dragged her out there.

"I'm sorry about last night," Sarah apologized once they had stopped walking. "I got a headache and went to lie down."

"Are you sure it wasn't your confessions that made your head ache?" Henry hissed, his voice cold as ice.

"What confessions?" Sarah asked, though her instincts told her what he was talking about.

"You know what I mean," Henry spat pulling her to him. "I heard your little conversation with the war hero last night. I just wanted to let you know, *dear*, that you are not to have anything to do with him anymore. I don't care how brave he is. I don't care how handsome and muscular he is. I don't even care about his medals. You are mine and mine alone. I *will not* have any woman of mine salivating over some other guy."

"Excuse me, but you don't have the authority to tell me who I may and may not be friends with," Sarah spat back.

He squeezed her arms even tighter, pulling her to him even more. His voice was low, more dangerous than Sarah had ever heard it.

"Listen here, I do have the authority. You are mine and no one else's. No one else will want you. You need me to survive. You are not to have anything else to do with him or his family. Do you understand me, Sarah?"

All Sarah could do was nod, fear having stolen her voice.

•

Much to Sarah's dismay, Owen and Paige began to come over again as frequently as they had in Texas now that they lived in Washington, DC, once more. Both families now had more time to get together since they lived closer together and schedules were less chaotic. They were even invited to the White House for dinner to celebrate Lucas and Sarah's birthdays. The night of the party, Henry showed up at the door.

"I thought you couldn't make it," Sarah questioned.

"I altered my plans so that I could come," Henry replied coldly, pushing past Sarah.

Sarah knew that the only reason he altered his plans was so that he could keep an eye on her. Ever since the day after the Inauguration dinner, Henry had changed, had worsened. It was like he had thought that he was the first guy Sarah had ever been interested in, and now that he knew he wasn't, he was jealous. It had steadily gotten worse; now it had become somewhat ridiculous. He didn't even like when Owen and Paige visited. She hadn't said anything to anyone, but Henry's jealousy was beginning to scare her. His temper had gone from moderate to raging. Sarah had been starting to watch what she said. Paige had let it slip that Sarah and Lucas had been in love. Now Henry wouldn't let Sarah mention Paige and Owen, let alone anything about Lucas.

Once the Monroe's arrived, Sarah thought that she would suffocate with all of the tension. Not only was there tension between

Lucas and Sarah that everyone could feel, but there was also tension between Sarah and Henry, and Henry and Lucas. Henry would pinch her leg painfully every time she spoke to Lucas, so Sarah kept quiet mostly, listening to her father tell Owen about a problem the German president was having that he was asking for help with.

"Apparently this crime boss, this Adolf Krause, is quite the threat. He has an extensive militia following and they are big on weapons and drugs. The German president is pretty much at his limit on resources to capture him. He has asked for my help," her father was saying.

"What is it that you plan to do?" Owen asked.

Jonathan sighed. "I have had several phone meetings with him. I do believe that I may have to involve the military, maybe even the CIA."

Owen nodded his understanding, asking no further questions because he seemed to realized that Jonathan had said about all he could on the subject.

Sarah's father soon asked Lucas what he had been up to which sent Lucas on a rampage of stories. He told them of his time in military school ("top in his class," Owen added). He told them stories about the war and his missions, as much as he could anyway. They made Sarah's heart stop. She hated to think about Lucas in battle and lying in the hospital. He also mentioned that he graduated from college while in military school and was now done with the police academy. He was starting with the city precinct in a month. He also hoped to join the Secret Service. By the end of Lucas's speech, Sarah knew that Mr. Monroe was swelling with pride.

"My colleagues say that give him another year and he may be ready for the service," he commented.

"That's great," Jonathan commented. "You would be a great asset."

"Thank you, sir," Lucas replied.

"Why don't we go have our coffee and dessert in the sitting room?" Beth suggested. "We'll be more comfortable."

Sarah heard her parents get to their feet, along with Owen and Paige. Sarah started to get up, but Henry grabbed her leg and squeezed it painfully. She stayed where she was.

"Sarah, are you coming?" her mother asked.

"Oh, I'll be along in a moment."

"Lucas?" Owen asked.

"Right behind you, Dad. Just give me a sec."

Sarah could hear the tension in Lucas's voice. Henry's hand was still gripping her leg. Sarah had the strangest notion that the two men might be staring each other down. She heard the other four hesitate and then leave.

"You know, hero, brute strength will only get you so far in life," Henry commented darkly.

"So will brains," Lucas fired back. "Being Einstein won't stop you from being at the rough end of a good beating."

"Is that how you graduated? Did you beat up your teachers?"

Lucas laughed humorlessly. "I'll have you know I graduated high school, valedictorian, when I was sixteen. Just ask Sarah."

Sarah's head snapped up. She was worried about what Lucas's mention of them knowing each other would lead Henry to do. As she had suspected, his hand came up to grab the back of her arm roughly. He pulled her to her feet.

"I don't need to ask Sarah. And I wouldn't either. She's not yours anymore." Henry pulled Sarah back, nearly making her trip over her chair.

"Sarah!" Lucas called. Sarah heard the tension in his voice. He was worried about her. "Let her go," he demanded. "You can't treat her like that."

"Who says?"

"I say. I'll stop you too. Just give me the chance."

"You lost your chance when you ran off to be hero, soldier boy," Henry hissed.

Sarah heard Lucas's sharp intake of breath, pain coloring every inch of that one simple act. Sarah was tired of all of the testosterone. She yanked her arm out of Henry's grasp.

"Oh, knock it off, both of you," she spat, turning on her heels and storming off.

As quickly as she could, Sarah led herself out of the dining room and through the front door, informing Max to stay inside. The cold air blasted her skin, turning her tears to ice. Moments later, she heard someone behind her. She hoped it was Lucas, but of course it wasn't.

"You don't speak to me like that," Henry demanded coldly, grabbing her arm and spinning her toward him. "And I don't like you speaking to the hero. I don't like him near you, or his parents near you."

Sarah couldn't handle the ridiculousness anymore. "Why are you so jealous? I told you we were just friends back in the day."

"I think that you were more than that, and I expect the truth. Paige said you were in love. You told me you have never been with anyone before, but I can feel the sexual tension between you two. I can see the way that he looks at you."

"You're being foolish," Sarah scuffed. "Nothing ever went on between Lucas and me. We were friends and had just started to date when he left. We were never together physically. Of course not."

"Do you love him?"

"I did."

"Do you still love him?"

Sarah could hear the anger in Henry's voice. It was starting to tremble. His temper was starting to build. Sarah knew that she should just placate him and tell him what he wanted to hear, but she couldn't.

"He was my best friend for quite a while. I will always have a place for him in my heart."

"That is not what I asked," Henry hissed, grabbing Sarah by her arms again. He pulled her to him. "Do you still love him?"

Sarah was shaking. "Let me go."

"Answer my question!"

"Let me go!"

"Answer the question, woman!"

"I love all my friends in their own ways, so, yes in a way I guess—"

Henry's hand came swiftly across Sarah's cheek, knocking her to the ground. He grabbed her arm and pulled her back up.

"I will not have any woman of mine—"

Suddenly, Henry's grip was lost. Sarah lost her balance and fell back down. She could hear the sound of physical struggle, a grunt of pain and a low voice as it hissed nearby.

"If I didn't have so much restraint over myself, you would be dead right now," Lucas seethed. "Let me assure you, though, that if you come near her again, I will end your life. So help me God, I will break you in half. Do you understand me?"

Sarah heard Lucas shove Henry away; he attempted to come back at Lucas. There were more hurried footsteps coming from different directions. There was a crack of a fist against a face, a body hit the ground, and then Henry (cussing up a storm) was assisted off the premises by the Secret Service. Lucas's footsteps were soft as they came back to where Sarah was sitting on the ground.

"Take my hand," he whispered.

Sarah was trembling. She had not felt this way since the night of that retched dance. Reaching out, she once again felt the strength and comfort of Lucas's hand. He gently lifted her to her feet.

"Lucas," Sarah whispered.

"It's okay, Sarah," Lucas responded. "I'm right here."

Tears started to stream down Sarah's face. It was all too much. Not only had her worst fears been confirmed in Henry, but Lucas was back in her life. It was like being in heaven and hell all in one day. A sob broke from her lips as she reached for Lucas, reached for his strength, reached for his love. Silently, he scooped his arm under her legs and cradled her like a child. Walking back to the house, Lucas carried Sarah up to her room and laid her in bed. He made to leave, but she gasped, sat up, and reached out to him. Lucas took her hand, pulled up a chair, and sat with her until she fell asleep.

When Sarah was finally asleep, Lucas made his way back down the stairs. He had seen the whole event happen. That low-life had hit her, and Lucas had run out there as fast as he could. He should have followed the bastard right out of the door, but he had hung back, not wanting to overstep his boundaries. Lucas was sure he would have killed him had Sarah not been so close by. Her guards hadn't been looking; they were going to get an earful. Everyone waited for him in a sitting room. They had clearly been informed that something had happened.

"How is she?" Beth asked.

"What happened?" Jonathan demanded.

"Henry hit her," Lucas informed them, turning to Max. "I would advise you not to take your eyes off her again."

"I'm sorry, sir," Max apologized to Jonathan.

"From what I understood, they were arguing about mine and Sarah's relationship. He didn't like the fact that we had been together. She made him angry, and he hit her." Lucas gave Jonathan and Beth an apologetic look.

Everyone was silent for a moment.

"She still loves you," Beth blurted. "I've never said anything, but for the past six years, she's been waking up from dreams in the middle of the night calling for you just like she did in the hospital. She thinks you don't love her."

Tears were in Lucas's eyes. "I do still love her. I've loved her since the first day I saw her huddled on the ground. I only did what I did because I blamed myself for what happened to her. I felt like I no longer deserved her." Lucas slumped into a chair. "I felt so unbelievably guilty. I couldn't protect her then, so how could I in the future?"

"You did again tonight," Paige added, laying a hand on her son's shoulder.

Tears fell from Lucas's cheeks as he thought of all the nights he had lay awake missing Sarah. The long, cold nights in the Army, all he thought about was Sarah. The love he felt for her had kept him warm during the night. It kept him courageous in battle.

"She never blamed you, Lucas," Jonathan assured. "No one did. If anything, Sarah blamed herself. She knew that she should have stayed within your sight, especially with the past problems she had had."

Lucas turned, glanced up the stairs, and then back at Beth and Jonathan. "Would you mind if I sat with her tonight?" he asked. "I would like to be there this time if she calls to me."

Beth nodded her head with tears in her eyes. She had always wanted Sarah to find love; she had always secretly hoped it would still be with Lucas.

●

The shack was hot and then ice-cold. Sarah could hear laughter, harsh laughter. She could feel the bonds cutting into her wrists. A pain shot through her. A hot sting came across her face. Bodies were all around her. She could not breathe. Pressure came down on top of her. The pain…there was so much pain. Sarah wanted Lucas. She needed him to help her.

"Lucas," she whispered, calling to him from mostly her heart. "Lucas."

"Lucas!" Sarah screamed, sitting up in bed.

Strong arms wrapped around her body. Sarah gasped, shocked to her inner core to feel arms around her. She nearly pushed them away, until she recognized their strength.

"Shh, I'm here, Sarah," Lucas soothed. "You're safe."

"You're here," Sarah sobbed. "You're really here." She took his hand and crawled onto his lap. "I am so tired of the dreams, Lucas. I can't get it out of my head. I'm back in the shack, and you don't come. I call and call, and you never come."

"I'm here now," Lucas replied. "I will never leave you again. I promise."

"Do you swear?" Sarah asked. "I need you, Lucas. I need you so much. Please don't ever leave me again."

Lucas's heart clenched. How had he ever left her? "I swear, Sarah. Where you go, I will go. If you bleed, I will bleed. If you are sad, I will make you happy. If you are hurt, I will ease your pain. If you are lost, I will find you. I love you, Sarah. I have ever since I first saw you. I promise that I will die before I ever let anything happen to you again."

Sarah couldn't believe it. Could it be true? Did she really have Lucas back after all these years? After all this time? Sarah lifted her face toward Lucas's.

"I love you, Lucas. Kiss me."

Lucas gently cupped Sarah's face in his hands. Leaning in, he kissed her lips so softly Sarah was not sure that they had touched at all. Laying her back down, Lucas pulled his chair closer to the bed and held Sarah's hand until she fell back asleep.

CHAPTER
15

The next morning, Lucas was gone when Sarah woke up. Max, however, was stationed right outside her door. He said that Lucas threatened to have him fired if he ever left Sarah's side when he was not around. Sarah laughed and moved down the stairs to the dining room. The kitchen staff brought her breakfast, and her mother soon joined her. Sarah looked up as she heard her mother's steps.

"Do I have a bruise?" Sarah asked.

Beth gently inspected her daughter's face. "I think you are going to be fine. I have never seen Lucas so mad."

Sarah smiled. "He still loves me," she bragged.

"I know, dear."

Sarah paused before speaking again. "Did he spend the *entire* night here?" she asked, color rising up on her cheeks.

Beth chuckled. "Yes, he did. He said that he wanted to be there for you if you called to him."

"Was that okay with you and Dad?"

"Lucas asked permission. Besides, I know how honorable of a man he is."

That made Sarah blush harder. "Where did he go? Did you see him this morning?"

Beth smiled. "He had to go to work."

"I have to call Mona at Jenny's," Sarah exclaimed. "She will be so excited."

Sarah got to her feet and wandered out of the dining room. She met her father in the hall, gave him a kiss, and then hummed her way up the stairs, her father chuckling his own way to breakfast.

The following weeks to come seemed to pass in slow motion for Sarah, but a very good, savor-every-second kind of slow motion. She treasured every moment that she had with Lucas, even picking up calling him Hercules again from time to time. School proceeded rather normally; Sarah was overly thankful that she didn't have to take Professor St. Paul's course. She didn't hear from Henry anymore nor did he even try to make contact. He tried one time, but thankfully Lucas had been there. Sarah hadn't asked what had transpired between the two of them, but Lucas's fist had been a little swollen afterward. Lucas made sure he came to see her at least once a day; when he had the day off, it was two or three times a day, usually just staying all day long. Sarah had never been happier.

The semester came to an end with Sarah's graduation following. They didn't make a big deal about it. They simply had a dinner at the White House with Owen, Paige, and Lucas, of course. Mona came as well.

A few weeks later, Jonathan needed to go to Europe. The German president was requesting his presence at a trial and a few press events and also honoring him for his services. Jonathan had managed to aid the German government in the capture of the crime lord, Adolf Krause. Something about the CIA and military joining forces, surprise attacks and infiltration of militia forces. Sarah wasn't quite sure what had all gone on. She didn't usually pay too close attention to her father's business, especially now that Lucas wasn't in the Army anymore. She did, however, ask to stay behind.

"I need the whole family there," her father said. "However, I would be willing to let Lucas join us if he could get the time off work. Max has been wanting some time off. And to tell you the truth"—Jonathan leaned in closer to his daughter—"I feel better about your safety with Lucas around."

Sarah smiled. Calling to Max, Sarah grabbed her sweater and asked him to take her to Lucas's apartment. On the drive over, Sarah tried to imagine what a vacation of sorts to Germany would be like with Lucas at her side. He was so much better at describing the scenery than her mother. Or maybe she just liked to have him there more. They arrived shortly at the building Lucas lived in. Max buzzed him for Sarah.

"Who is it?" Lucas asked.

"It's me, Hercules," Sarah responded.

"Oh, wait, I'll be down to get you."

Seconds later Sarah could hear Lucas's footsteps pounding down the stairs. He opened the front door and told Max he could wait outside. Max laughed.

"The elevator is broken, again," Lucas informed her. "The steps can be tricky so let me help you."

Sarah laughed. "You are just looking for a reason to hold my hand."

"Well, maybe."

They made it up the stairs and to Lucas's apartment. He opened the door for her and then helped her over to the couch.

"Can I get you anything, tea or coffee?" Lucas offered.

"No, thanks, I'm fine. I just came to see you."

Sarah felt Lucas sit down beside her. She shifted a little so that she was facing him more. He held her hand in one of his and touched her face with the other. Sarah couldn't help but lean in to his touch.

"You are so beautiful," he commented. "So what brings you to me? Is it safe for you to be here? I could have come over, you know."

"Can you take two weeks off work?"

Lucas nearly choked. "Why?"

"I want you to come to Germany with us. My father has already invited you saying that Max has wanted time off for a while now and that he feels safer with you around than Max."

"I can't afford to go to Germany."

Sarah laughed. "You would come as my personal guard. My father can pay for it."

Lucas paused. It was an enticing offer. "Well, I have always wanted to travel leisurely. And I do have enough in the bank to cover for missed wages."

"Oh, thank you!" Sarah squealed, jumping into his arms. She threw them off balance, tumbling them to the floor. Sarah laughed; Lucas panicked, quickly helping Sarah back up.

"Are you okay?" Lucas asked.

"I am perfectly capable of handling a fall off the couch. I did it many times when I was younger. What do you think I did before you came into my life?"

"You don't have to worry about that anymore now, do you?" Lucas smiled even though he knew she could not see him. Leaning in, he gently kissed her lips. Wrapping her arms around his neck, Sarah kissed him back with more intensity.

"I love you," she whispered.

"I love you more."

Two weeks later, Sarah found herself on Air Force One headed to Germany. Lucas was currently around the corner standing at attention, Sarah was sure, in front of her father's desk. Sarah listened as her father lectured him.

"Now, Lucas, I want Sarah to have a good time, but not too good of a time, if you know what I mean."

"Yes, sir." Lucas smiled.

"I need her to attend all of the public viewings with you in tow. You are her bodyguard for the next two weeks. Be professional at the public events, and you may act like her boyfriend elsewhere, but do not let your guard down at any time."

"Yes, sir."

"Above all, just let her have a good time. That is why I invited you along. I knew that with Max around, she would be miserable. She would also have missed you terribly."

"And I her, sir."

Lucas shook Jonathan's hand and came back out of the office. He chuckled at the amused look on Sarah's face as he led her back to her seat on one of the couches and sat next to her.

"Did my father give you a well-rounded lecture on how to care for me?"

Lucas laughed. "I think he forgets that I have been looking out for you for twelve years."

"It wasn't a consistent twelve years, though," Sarah sighed.

"It should have been," Lucas replied. Regret echoed in his voice. "I promise never to leave you again. I regret doing so before. It killed me because I never stopped loving you and I knew that it was my own fault I wasn't with you. I feared that the war would take me before I could see you again and apologize." He took Sarah's hand, kissing the back of it. "You kept me alive through my entire time serving. You were, and are, my only life source."

"I feared that as well," Sarah whispered reaching up to touch Lucas's face. "I never stopped loving you and prayed you would come back to me."

"I'm here now and never leaving again."

Sarah smiled and laid her head on Lucas's shoulder. She was happy and felt safe for the first time in years. Words could not describe how she felt having Lucas back in her life. Sighing contently, Sarah shifted to lay her head down on Lucas's lap. He chuckled softly and started to stroke her hair. She was asleep in minutes.

Sarah woke up as the plane started its descent. The change in the altitude made her ears pop and startled her awake. She sat up from her place lying across Lucas's lap. Sarah held his hand as the plane touched down onto the runway. She assumed that landing in an airplane was unnerving enough for normal people, but it was terrifying for her, not being able to see and all. There was a crowd of people waiting for them to land, or so Lucas said. Sarah knew that Krause had been a major crime threat in all of Germany. The entire country was grateful to her father for his assistance. Sarah also knew that all involved were concerned about the remaining threat from the man's followers.

The crowd cheered as she and her family stepped out of the plane. Sarah reached for Lucas's hand, gripping it tightly. She could hear the size of the crowd. Sarah heard her father speak to some men in German. She caught most of it; her German was a little rusty. Lucas did not let go of her hand until they were seated next to each other in the limo. Even then he laid his arm around her shoulders, so he wasn't too far away. A short drive to the hotel followed.

The limo pulled up to a stop in front of the hotel. Sarah heard the driver put the vehicle into park and open his door. Lucas shifted next to her, anxious.

"What's the matter?" Sarah asked, reaching for his hand.

"I'm just nervous," Lucas confessed. "I need to figure out how to be your boyfriend and security at the same time. The last time that I tried it, well, it didn't turn out so hot."

Sarah sighed. "I told you before, that was not your fault. I don't want to think about that right now. This time around, I will not leave your side. I promise to do anything that you tell me. Oh, did I mention that I'm not going to leave your side?"

Lucas laughed. He was beside himself with joy at having Sarah once more. He knew that he would never be able to leave her again, not unless she told him to go. Even then, Lucas was sure that he would beg her to take him back before he actually left her alone.

The chauffer opened the door to the limo. Lucas climbed out, turned, and reached back in to take Sarah's hand. She smiled, as she always did, when he took her hand. Lucas loved the smile she saved for him. It was a smile that let him know how much she loved him. It also had a way of reminding him how much he had hurt her, and how desperate he was to never do it again.

Sarah allowed Lucas to guide her through the rotating doors of the hotel. She was glad that he was there to help her through. She had followed her mother through a revolving door once. Sarah had gotten stuck going around and around, never knowing when she was supposed to get out. Sarah had made five whole rotations before her mother had rescued her. They both had laughed for quite some time following that little mishap.

They walked through the doors, Lucas's hand in hers. Sarah heard her father being greeted by the manager of the hotel. As her father spoke to the man, Sarah let her ears wander around the room. She heard many voices, some echoing as if the room was very large.

"What does it look like?" she asked Lucas.

Lucas laughed. "Well, the ceilings are high, golden, with sky-lights. The lobby is painted white, accented in gold, of course, with maroon curtains and furniture. The front desk looks like it may be made out of cherry wood. It's accented in gold as well." Lucas couldn't hide the laugh in his voice.

"What's so funny?" Sarah asked.

"It's a little overdone, if you know what I mean. They are *try-ing* to look fancy," Lucas whispered in her ear.

The feel of his breath on her neck sent shivers up Sarah's spine. She loved having him back to her, having him this close.

Suddenly, excited voices were yelling from all points around Sarah. She felt Lucas tensed and wrapped his arms around her. Sarah could hear her father in front of them talking to the crowd, his voice tense as well. Sarah caught a little of the conversation. They were glad for his help. They were overjoyed that they would be rid of the bad man.

A hand suddenly grabbed Sarah's arm. She gasped. Lucas pulled her even tighter to him, his vise grip ever present on her waist. A voice was babbling next to Sarah; she was fairly certain that the person just wanted a handshake. Sarah held out her hand. It was shook enthusiastically by more than one other hand. The bodies pressing her from all sides were making Sarah very nervous. The tension she felt in Lucas was not helping matters at all. She could feel the anxiety he felt over the crowd rolling off of him. Adrenaline seemed to rush through every fiber in his body, his muscles tense and ready to take action.

"Please get me out of here," Sarah whispered, the anxiety in her voice evident even to her.

That was all Lucas needed to hear. The crowds had been pressing in to them. He wasn't sure which way to watch to keep an eye on the ones closest to Sarah. They had all been very much too close. Wrapping his arm more securely around her, Lucas practically dragged her through the crowd to her parents. After a quick word with Jonathan, Lucas was able to duck out and get Sarah to the private elevators.

Sarah didn't feel Lucas relax until she heard the elevator doors shut. It was only then that she was able to settle down as well. She wasn't sure why the crowd had made her so nervous, but it had.

"Are you okay?" Lucas asked.

Sarah nodded. "Yes, I am fine. I'm not sure why I was so nervous. It was just something about the whole situation that bothered me. I didn't know who was in the crowd."

Lucas shuddered internally. "Neither did I. I'm glad that you asked me to get you away. I would have felt paranoid if I had done it on my own. Don't ever feel afraid to let me know how you feel, what you need."

"You are all I need," Sarah cooed, pulling Lucas tighter to her side. "As long as I have you, I don't need anything else."

Her words made Lucas's heart soar.

Once settled into the presidential suite, Sarah lay down on the couch with her head on Lucas's lap. He caressed her hair with one hand and held her hand with the other. They tried to decide what to do while they were there. Sarah knew that she was obligated to make an appearance at the trial, the honorary dinner/ dance, press conferences, and dinner with the German president. However, her father had told her that this was all. Sarah was excited that the rest of the time was for her and Lucas alone. Two days after their arrival, the First Family attended the final part of the trial for the crime lord. Sarah tried to pay attention to what the judge was saying. Lucas was not making it any easier. He had promised Jonathan that during public appearances, he would take only the role of Sarah's bodyguard. Lucas had taken a seat behind Sarah and her parents, trying to appear as a bodyguard. He was afraid that if he sat beside Sarah, he wouldn't be able to keep from putting his arms around her or kissing her cheek. Sarah wasn't letting him too far, though. She had her right hand twisted behind her to hold on to his.

Lucas laughed as Sarah's hand twitched in his. He was sitting in his seat, looking professional on the outside, but really he was tracing little circles on Sarah's palm. Lucas knew that she loved that. Her parents were next to her, so they weren't any wiser to what he was doing. Sarah knew what he was doing, though. Every now and then she would shoot a small smile over her shoulder, meant only for him.

Lucas leaned on right next to her ear. "I love you," he whispered. The smile on Sarah's face was blinding. She turned her face toward him.

Suddenly, the front doors of the courtroom slammed open. Gunfire rang through the air, as did profanity and loud shouting. Sarah screamed, as did the entire courtroom. She heard Lucas jumped to his feet.

Lucas grabbed Sarah's hand and pulled her to her feet. She could hear yelling, gunfire, and the sound of people dying. She knew that the service men would care for her parents; they were already gone from her side. Lucas pulled her through the crowd and toward an exit. He tried for the same exit that Sarah's parents had been pulled to, but there were too many people. Lucas cussed and started to lead her in another direction.

Suddenly, Sarah was grabbed, and her hand was torn from Lucas's. She screamed. Lucas called her name, but then it sounded to Sarah like he had taken a hit. There were so many sounds of physical fighting that Sarah didn't know what was going on, or where Lucas was.

"Lucas! Lucas!"

Sarah struggled as much as she could. She didn't know who had her or what had happened to Lucas. Sarah could hear the man screaming to his fellow men and understood his words. The man holding her was a follower of Krause and knew she was the American president's daughter. He was rejoicing his success. He was after her!

Lucas punched the guy who held him in the face. A swift knee to the head took that opposition down. Lucas turned to get back to Sarah when he was suddenly tackled from behind. His head slapped the hard wooden floor, a cut opening above his left eye.

Lucas growled in pain. He could hear Sarah yelling his name. Pushing up from the floor, Lucas was able to get his arms and legs underneath him. He arched his body enough to toss his captors to the side. A fist contacted with Lucas's jaw. His head snapped to the side. A foot came quick, aimed for his stomach. Lucas caught the foot, twisted it to the side, and sent the attacker to the floor. The other caught him from behind. Lucas flipped him over his back, kicked him in the face, and then turned back to help Sarah. The man who had her was gripping her by the arms, Sarah wiggling wildly to try and get free. Lucas ran forward to help her.

Sarah's captor suddenly let go. Sarah could hear Lucas yelling and cussing at the man, the sound of physical fighting sounded from behind her. Arms grabbed her again and scooped her up. Sarah screamed. Lucas called out to her. Two men held Sarah this time, one on each arm. Sarah wrenched one arm free and lashed out with her fist, knocking one of the men in the face. This man fell back, and the other was pulled away. Sarah fell to the floor. More fighting nearby. Bodies crashed into Sarah, repeatedly knocking her down. Screams sounded all around. Sarah had no idea where Lucas was or who was around her.

"Lucas!" Sarah cried. She screamed as someone lifted her off the ground.

"It's okay, baby, I got you."

Sarah could hear the yelling and cursing in English and German. She wrapped her arms around Lucas's neck and held on tight in case Lucas lost his grip on her body. She held on as Lucas fought his way through the crowd, kicking and punching. Sarah finally felt the cool breeze of outside on her face as Lucas hurried her to one of the limos. She didn't even let go once they were in and on the way back to the hotel. Finally, Sarah felt Lucas carry her into the hotel through a private entrance and up to the suite. Her parents frantically greeted them. Sarah was relieved that they were okay. Only when she knew she was in her room and on her bed did she loosen her grip on Lucas.

"Are you all right?" he asked, pushing her back to inspect her for injuries.

"I'm fine," Sarah responded, a little shaky. She wrapped her arms around Lucas again. "Are you okay?" Sarah reached up with her hands to feel Lucas's face. Blood was dripping from his nose, his eye was swollen slightly, his forehead bleeding. "Lucas, you need medical attention."

Lucas laughed. "I'm fine. This is nothing. I once fought for five hours with a knife blade in my leg."

"Oh, don't tell me that." Sarah got tears in her eyes. "I was so scared. I heard the man yell to the other men. They were after me."

"What!"

"I heard him say, 'I have what we came for. I have what we came for.'"

Lucas couldn't believe it. He held in his shock while Sarah snuggled back up into his lap. She continued to tremble for a while, silent tears running down her face. Her grip on his arm never let go until she calmed down and had dozed off. Once she seemed to be sleeping well, Lucas got up, laid her down, and went into the bathroom. After washing the blood off his face and knuckles, he put a bandage on his cut eye and hurried to talk to Jonathan.

Lucas found Jonathan in the common room of the suite, on the phone. He waited until Jonathan offered a chair and then sat across from him, waiting for his turn and watching his face. Jonathan's forehead was creased in concern; he was speaking in rapid German. Lucas had no idea what he was saying, but had he wagered a guess, he was sure what the conversation was about.

Jonathan heaved a huge sigh as he hung up his phone. He pinched the bridge of his nose in frustration. When he turned to look at Lucas, he had moisture in his eyes.

"Thank you for what you did today, Lucas," Jonathan started. "When I heard that gunfire and the service men pulled Beth and me out the back door, the only thing that kept me from worrying about Sarah was knowing that she was with you."

"I did my best, sir," Lucas replied.

"You brought her back safely. That is what matters."

Lucas bit his lip. "Sarah told me that one of the Germans that grabbed her started yelling to his fellows that he had what they came for. I'm not sure if they were really after her or not, but I wouldn't doubt it."

Jonathan felt as if is heart had stopped. "I wouldn't put it past them to go after her to get to me. Rumor has it, Krause's follow-ers are not happy with me, not happy at all. Lucas, I need you to pull double time while we are here. I can't let anything happen to Sarah. She depends on you, as do I. I need you to protect her."

"You can count on me, sir," Lucas promised.

Getting to his feet, Lucas shook Jonathan's hand and walked back toward Sarah's room. After checking on her, making sure she seemed comfortable and the window was locked (even though they were fifteen floors up), he then moved to his room. After changing, Lucas crawled into bed, unnerved by the day's events and even more unnerved by what could possibly transpire. He had to stay on his toes and keep Sarah safe, no matter what.

The following morning, Sarah found out from her father that the invasion *was* done by some of the man's followers. She also learned that they killed three people and injured many more. Luckily, Krause had not escaped, and the followers had either been killed or captured. She knew that they were severely angry at her father. Krause would not have been nailed down if her father had not interfered. He had personally aided in the capture by going through connections with the CIA and the military. Sarah didn't know all the details. She wasn't sure she cared to know. Her father demanded that she would not leave the hotel room or even go down the hall without Lucas. He also told Lucas not to let Sarah out of his sight. Even with the incident haunting them and Sarah seemingly a target for revenge, the First Family proceeded with the events they had planned.

Sarah sat beside her parents at the press conference that day following the trial. The reporters were firing questions at her father faster than he could answer them. They seemed to be from two different points of view. One side of the room was happy about what her father had done; the other half thought him an interfering fool.

"Mr. President, what do you intend to do to keep Krause in jail? What about the threat of his followers that are still at large?" a reporter asked in broken English.

"I plan to work closely with the German president and the military to..."

Sarah let her mind wander while her father spoke. She knew that Lucas was standing behind her and to her right. She could smell his cologne. It made her feel safe having him so close by. Even in the middle of all the trouble, Sarah felt safer than she had in a long time.

Yelling voices brought her out of her reverence. She flinched as a fist came down on a table, sounding like a gunshot. She felt Lucas's hand on her shoulder, heard him step closer to her. The press leader called for order. A long time passed after that before Lucas removed his hand from its protective stance on her shoulder, and he never did step back to his original position.

The honorary dinner stayed on schedule. It was held at the mansion where the German president lived. The banquet hall was extravagant and under heavy guard. Lucas was on edge all night, not sure if he was supposed to be a guard, a date, or both. Sarah tried to settle his nerves, but he still grabbed her hand ready to run at every loud noise.

After dinner was complete, the German president made a speech thanking President Watkins for his friendship, wisdom, and courage. A plaque was presented, and then pictures were taken. Sarah and her mother were asked to join. Lucas led Sarah to the stage and helped her up. He then stepped out of the way, waiting to escort her back to their seats. Finally, the dancing was to begin. Sarah ordered Lucas to switch to date mode and dance with her. He did as he was told, even sneaking a few soft kisses as the night went on.

It was later than Sarah had hoped when her parents were finally ready to go. Her eyes were almost closed as she sat with her head on Lucas's shoulder when Beth came over and told them it was time to leave. Sarah repositioned her head on Lucas's shoulder once again in the limo. She didn't even stir when he carried her to her room and laid her in her bed.

Lucas closed the closet door as softly as he could, making sure Sarah's shawl did not get caught in the hinges. She was lying on top of the covers on her bed. He didn't have the heart to wake her up to change. Grabbing an extra blanket, Lucas covered her where she lay. Smiling softly, Sarah murmured that she loved him and rolled to her side. Lucas's throat constricted.

She was so beautiful. He loved her with every beat of his heart. He would do anything for her. He would die for her. Stroking her cheek gently with the back of his hand, Lucas whispered his love and let himself out. He went into his room, set his gun on his dresser, changed out of his tuxedo, and sat on the end of his bed. He felt a little too keyed up to sleep. Lucas lay back, feet still on the floor. All he could think about was Sarah. She slept peacefully in the room next to his, so why did he feel like she was miles away? Why did he feel the need to sit by her side? Why did he feel like she was going to vanish? He couldn't let that happen. He needed her. He needed her to survive.

A scream. Lucas sat straight up. He had fallen asleep where he had lay down, his feet hanging off the end of the bed.

"Lucas! Lucas, help me!"

Lucas jumped to his feet, grabbed his gun, and blasted into Sarah's room. She was sitting up, sobbing hysterically; one arm was wrapped around her midsection, the other was extended, fingers waving in the air and waiting for him to take her hand. Lucas quickly scanned the room, looking for an intruder but unable to find anyone. She must have had a nightmare. He set his gun down and quickly moved to her side.

"Sarah, honey, it's okay. I'm right here," Lucas soothed. "I'm right here and I'll never leave you."

Jonathan and Beth came running through the door just then. They caught sight of Lucas comforting Sarah, and they both visibly sighed in relief. Guilt shot through Lucas as he remembered what Beth had said about Sarah's nightmares while he wasn't in her life. Apparently, they weren't quite used to him being back.

Lucas rocked Sarah back and forth until she was quiet and sleeping once more. He wasn't even sure if she had ever woken up completely. Even after her breathing evened out, he stayed by her side, holding her hand.

The next two days were wet with rain, postponing Sarah and Lucas's plans. Sarah didn't mind, though. She and Lucas simply sat in the hotel room renting German movies in pay-per-view; Sarah interpreted, of course, as best as she could. When she couldn't decipher what the actors were saying, Lucas would make up his own dialogue, causing them both to laugh.

The sun finally peeked through the clouds bringing Lucas and Sarah out of the hotel. Every place they went, Lucas made sure to find something for Sarah to taste, smell, or touch. The sounds of the city surrounded her. Lucas promised the experience would not be hindered by her inability to see.

They spent an afternoon in a market. Lucas had Sarah tasting things unlike any she had ever tried before. He said that it was a good thing that she was blind because had she been able to see what the dish looked like, she probably would not have touched it. They visited a petting farm. Lucas picked up a baby chick and ran its downy body next to Sarah's face. She smacked him when he fell over laughing at her for squealing when a calf licked her hand. Lucas even surprised them all with tickets to a symphony. The music affected Sarah greatly. The final piece was one composed in such a way that the music filled the listener with hope; it made Sarah think of her and Lucas's relationship. She cried.

One evening, they were invited to an opera by the German president and his wife. Lucas described the settings to Sarah who cried over the music again. He even took her to dinner at a little outdoor bistro, making sure she knew which constellations they were sitting under.

While together, Sarah and Lucas played tourist as well. Lucas took her to every attraction he could find and made sure to describe it well enough so that she could get a mental image of what it looked like, well, the best she could anyway. For the most part, the time they spent in the city was quiet. Every so often someone would recognize Sarah; Lucas would switch to guard duty. Most of the time the people just wanted Sarah to thank her father for his assistance. Some of the people wanted to know if Sarah knew what they were going to do to ensure that Krause did not escape.

Sarah tried to be gracious. She tried to explain to the curious people that she did not really know what her father had planned but that he was doing all he could. There was one group of young people who wanted pictures with Sarah. She wasn't too sure about it, but agreed. Everything went fine until one of the young men, while shaking Sarah's hand, decided to be bold and kiss her cheeks. Sarah was too shocked to say anything; all she could do was gasp. Lucas, on the other hand, jumped forward and yanked the guy away.

"Watch it," he growled. There was a little scuffling sound like the guy was trying to fight Lucas off, but did not succeed. He stormed off, cussing Lucas out in German.

Sarah couldn't help but giggle. She knew that what Lucas had done had been from more of a boyfriend perspective than a bodyguard. She couldn't help but be a little flattered at his moment of jealousy.

Two days before they were set to leave, the First Family was expected at two more press conferences. Lucas switched to guard mode, even going as far as to inform President Watkins of his uncertainty of the location.

"I just don't think that it is a good idea to have the conferences outdoors and both in the same location, sir."

President Watkins sighed. "I appreciate your concern, Lucas, and you have done a superb job watching Sarah, but the president has assured me safety, so I have to go with that."

Lucas was still on edge. He knew that hanging in one place for too long was the easiest way to get ambushed. He stuck to Sarah like flypaper all through the first conference. It was only halfway through the second that he began to relax. Maybe he was paranoid.

On their last day out, however, they ran into a problem. Sarah and Lucas had just finished lunch and were strolling in the park when Lucas tensed up and grabbed Sarah's hand.

"What's wrong?" Sarah whispered.

"Don't be scared, but we're being followed," Lucas replied, tension in his voice. "Just stay calm and do as I say." Lucas appraised his surroundings, taking in everything; the location of other people, hiding spots, safety zones. They were, unfortunately, in a rather open, unoccupied area. He had to get Sarah away from the threat; he had to make sure that she was safe.

Sarah knew that listening to Lucas could mean the difference between life and death. They kept walking on the course they had been on in the park. Lucas kept a hold of her hand. Suddenly, he stopped, pulling her close to him. Sarah could hear a lot of footsteps, like people were surrounding them. Bullets were clicked into chambers. Men shouted in German.

"What are they saying?" Lucas whispered in Sarah's ear.

Sarah was shaking. "They said to surrender me or face your death."

"Yeah, like that'll happen. This is what I need you to do, baby. When I say so, hit the dirt and crawl to your immediate left. Move fast. They're armed." Sarah could hear the men coming closer, still shouting. "Keep crawling," Lucas continued, "until you reach a bench. It is bolted to the cement walk, so hold on for dear life, and if someone other than me grabs you, kick as hard as you can. Hit the button on your watch too. There are six of them, and I don't know how long I will be able to hold them off. I love you, baby. Go."

Sarah dropped to her knees and felt Lucas flip over her. The sounds that followed Sarah could never get used to. Listening to physical fighting had to be worse than watching it, not to mention the gunshots that rang through the air. Sarah found the bench Lucas had spoken of and pushed the emergency button that had been installed on her watch. Sarah knew that help was only moments away. Grasping with all her might, Sarah tried to block out the sounds of the fight. She feared for Lucas. How long could he last against men with guns? Did he even have his?

Lucas flipped himself over Sarah, landing crouched, ready to defend his love. The men advanced, drawing their weapons up preparing to fire. There were six of them; Lucas knew that he was outnumbered, but he had to protect Sarah. Dodging around, Lucas attacked, surprising the men and knocking two of them out before they realized what had happened. He grabbed the third, wrestling his gun from him, whipping his arm around as he fired to catch one of his companions in the chest. Lucas then used the guy's body to block a shot aimed at him; he tossed the body aside. Lucas then pulled his own gun.

Another of the guys jumped at Lucas. Lucas tried to fire his gun, but he was barreled to the ground, his gun bouncing away. Lucas took a hit to the jaw and slammed his own fist back into the face of his attacker. They wrestled for a few minutes until Lucas was able to knock him out. Another came from behind, wrapping his arms around Lucas and pinning his arms to his side. One of the others came at Lucas with a knife. He moved to stab Lucas in the stomach. Lucas swung his right leg up and was able to kick the man in the head, but not before the knife grazed the skin of his abdomen.

Sarah heard Lucas yell in pain. Fighting the urge to go to him, Sarah tightened her grip on the bench. A hand grabbed her ankle. Screaming, Sarah kicked as hard as she could with the other foot. She kept kicking at the person who held her. Fear seized her as someone else began to pry her hands free from the bench leg.

"Lucas! Lucas, help me!"

Sarah tried to fight free, but the men were too strong. They pulled her from the bench and lifted her into the air. Twisting and turning, she finally felt her legs fall to the ground. Righting herself, Sarah bent her legs and flipped the person holding her arms to the ground.

"Sarah, spin kick, left leg!" Lucas yelled, distracted enough to miss blocking the punch aimed at his stomach.

Sarah followed his orders and felt her foot contact a face. She heard Lucas fight free of his captors and run to her. He wasn't quick enough.

"Sarah, block!" Lucas screamed, but not soon enough. Before Sarah could get her arms up to her face, a fist backhanded the side of her head. Sirens were suddenly blaring through the air, coming closer.

"Dirty, rotten American," a man hissed in German. "Your father will regret what he did."

Lucas finally reached the men around Sarah. He had just started to fight when the other guards arrived. The Germans took off at a run, leaving the two dead behind; Lucas waved the service onward, pointing them toward the fleeing Germans. He then walked over to Sarah.

"It's just me, babe," he assured as he picked her up and carried her to the car.

Sarah was shaking. "I think I have had enough vacation," she stated.

Lucas couldn't help but laugh.

The flight home passed too quickly for Sarah's liking. She and Lucas lay on one of the couches together, talking. Lucas admitted to his reluctance about going back to reality, wishing he could just get paid to be with her. Sarah told him he might as well go back to work because she had to start work in two weeks.

"I worry about you at work," Lucas confessed. "I know that Max is good at his job, but I don't really trust anyone to protect you but myself. I especially worry when you go to the bathroom. Neither Max nor I can follow you in there."

"I really think that I'll be safe using the bathroom, Hercules," Sarah laughed. "I believe, sir, at times you are too protective."

Lucas smiled. "Well, you are the president's daughter and the woman I love, so with all due respect, miss, I don't think I'm protective enough."

"Are you going to start guarding me while I shower?"

Lucas raised an eyebrow, knowing Sarah was being coy. "Now there's an idea. However, I do believe your father would not agree with that arrangement."

Sarah laughed and kissed Lucas. She could not believe how much she loved him.

CHAPTER

16

Sarah sat in silence while the car took her to the blind college once more. She had been hired as the new music teacher. As they drove, Sarah's foot tapped nervously. She had spoken to her new boss, Linda Grey (who had been her dean before), on the phone. Linda had told her to just come in and she would explain Sarah's position to her. Once at the college, Sarah was ushered into Mrs. Grey's office.

"Hello, Sarah, it is good to see you again," Linda greeted, taking Sarah's hand.

"It's nice to see you, Mrs. Grey."

"Please, call me Linda. You are allowed, now that you aren't a student anymore. Please, have a seat. The chair is to your left."

Sarah sat and waited for instruction.

"So you come highly recommended," Linda complimented, laughing.

"Thank you," Sarah chuckled. Linda had offered Sarah the job even before Sarah had graduated due to Sarah being at the top of her class.

Linda smiled and continued, "Now, basically, what I have in mind for you, to start, is teaching our beginning courses that meet twice a week. It would be one day a week for theory, composition, and reading music and the other day would be for practice and application. We have quite a few students interested in the music program and what better way for the blind to learn music than to be taught by a blind musician?"

"I'm happy I can help," Sarah replied.

"Now we have to decide how to handle things. I know that it could be difficult for you to come from the White House every day. The president called me and told me about what happened in Germany. Also, there was an Officer Monroe that called as well, concerned over your security."

Sarah felt herself blush, and Linda laughed quietly before continuing. "I think that, given the state of things, you could work from home, for the most part. You would need to come in for classes, of course, but the rest of your work may be done from home. We can make the children have homework due weekly, instead of delivering it to your office daily like with the other teachers. Any extra tutelage that students need will have to be done on one of the two days that you are already here. Does that sound okay to you?"

Sarah smiled. She liked the idea of working from home. She knew that everyone was worried about her vulnerability as First Daughter, not to mention she was blind. If it were up to Lucas, Sarah knew that he would lock her in the house and throw away the key. Sarah thanked Linda for her kindness and gathered everything she would need to work from home. She knew that Lucas would be thrilled that she only had to go in two days a week. He still trusted no one but himself to watch over her.

The relationship between Sarah and Lucas soon grew beyond what it had been. Mona was also in love. She had met a man named Derek, so the four of them were double-dating at least twice a month. Lucas, however, came over every day, even if it was just to say goodnight. It had gotten to the point that the guards at the front gate knew him by sight and name and even recognized his car coming up the drive. They had told Lucas that he didn't have to stop and show ID; they could just open the gate when they saw him coming. Lucas wouldn't hear of it. He informed them that someone bad could have a car just like his and pretend to be him. So everyday Lucas showed his ID, and sometimes it was two or three times a day.

Lucas marveled over the relationship between Sarah and himself as well. It was to the point that a little less than a year after getting back with Sarah, Lucas found himself sitting outside the Oval Office waiting for President Watkins to be available for their meeting. Lucas knew that Sarah was at work; that was the way he wanted it. He wanted to speak with Jonathan alone.

Just then the door opened and one of the aides informed Lucas that he could come in. He stood, followed her through the outer offices, and then through the door leading to the Oval Office. Lucas thought he might puke.

"Hey, Lucas," Jonathan greeted, extending his hand.

"Good morning, sir," Lucas replied, shaking Jonathan's hand. Jonathan indicated for him to sit, so Lucas did, his spine straight like it always was when he was nervous, or under scrutiny, or just about any other time.

"So to what do I owe this visit?" Jonathan asked. "You really didn't have to make an official meeting, Lucas. You could have just stopped by. You are practically family."

Lucas swallowed convulsively. War had been less nerve-racking than what he was about to do. Lucas cleared his throat.

"Well, that is sort of what I wanted to talk with you about, sir. I didn't want us to be interrupted."

Jonathan looked as though he was trying to fight a smile. "Well, you have my full attention. What is it that you would like to discuss?"

"Well, sir, it's about Sarah, and myself of course. I, well, I wanted to ask you – " Lucas had to pause, clear his throat again, and then continued, "I wanted to ask you for Sarah's hand in marriage."

Jonathan appraised Lucas stoically for a moment and then got to his feet. Lucas stood as well. Jonathan walked around his desk and came to stand in front of Lucas. It hit Lucas just then that he had just asked the president for his daughter's hand in marriage. Oh, great, he was getting demoted.

Just then, Jonathan smiled and pulled Lucas into an enormous hug. "Of course, Lucas. Of course you have my blessings. Nothing would make Beth and I happier than to know that Sarah will be looked after once we are gone." Jonathan sounded as though he might cry.

Lucas felt a little emotional himself. "Thank you, sir. I will do my best to take care of her."

"I know you will, Lucas. I know that you will."

By the time it was Sarah and Lucas's birthdays again, Sarah couldn't imagine life being any sweeter. She was absolutely in love with her job and what she felt for Lucas was so much more than love that Sarah couldn't put a name to it. The night of their birthdays, Lucas came over for dinner with his parents. Mona and Derek were also invited. Sarah noticed that Lucas seemed on edge but in a different way than his usual protective nature. He seemed nervous, but more like an actor-before-performance nervous than his usual there-are-too-many-people-for-my-jumped-up-Army-self-to-be-calm kind of nervous.

Dinner was wonderful, thanks to the class-A chefs on the White House staff. They all talked and laughed, Derek entertaining them all with his impersonations that he had become famous for. Owen and Jonathan talked business until the rest of them told them to knock it off. As they waited for the dessert, Lucas stood to make a toast.

"I want to thank you all for coming tonight," Lucas began. "I also want to wish a happy birthday to myself and my love, Sarah." Everyone clapped. "Sarah, can you stand for me, please?" Sarah stood, a little concerned over the fact that Lucas's voice cracked.

Lucas continued, "I want you to know how much I love you. My feelings for you have magnified this past year since we reconciled. I almost lost you once because of my stupidity. I want to make sure it never happens again. Take my hand, Sarah."

Sarah felt Lucas take her left hand, his voice trembling slightly, and continued, "I will love you forever, to the end of my last breath." Lucas had to pause and take a deep breath. "Sarah, will you be my wife?"

Everyone gasped. The coolness of a ring slipped over Sarah's finger. Tears choked her voice. She couldn't believe it. Was this really happening? Was she really, *finally*, wearing a ring on her finger from Lucas? Taking a deep breath, she reached for Lucas's face.

"I thought you'd never ask."

After dessert was through, everyone gathered in a sitting room to discuss the wedding.

"When do you want to get married?" Lucas asked Sarah.

"Today, tomorrow, yesterday…now? I want something small and quiet. How about the first weekend in April?"

Sarah's mother nearly choked on her coffee. "You want it to be that soon?"

"Well," Sarah considered, "yes. I can't see the festivities, and knowing Lucas, he'd prefer to elope. Why not just find a priest, call a few relatives, and have the wedding and dinner here?"

"That's fine with me," Lucas informed. "As long as I get to marry you, we could do it in the street for all I care." Everyone laughed.

The planning commenced and over the next eight weeks, Sarah, her mother, and Mona planned the wedding. Sarah wasn't sure how extravagant she wanted to get. She couldn't see the details of anything, so she had to rely on her mother and Mona to describe the lace on her dress and the candy flowers on the cake. She tasted cake and punches; she was introduced to food that she had never tasted before. They would certainly eat well. She also smelled flowers and listened to piano sonatas to be played. Grandparents, aunts, uncles and cousins were coming in for the celebration. Sarah and Lucas had decided to write their own vows. A priest was found, the meal finalized, and the honeymoon scheduled.

Lucas had managed to reserve a cabin on a private lake in Jamaica, though he wasn't telling Sarah where they were going. They were going to spend ten days there, no one around but themselves. She had always wanted to go to the Caribbean, so Lucas was going to surprise her, with help from Jonathan of course.

The night before the wedding, Mona came over to have a girl's night. Popcorn popped, soda poured, and music on, Sarah finally found the courage to ask Mona the question that had been burning at her for months.

"What's sex like?" Sarah blurted.

Mona nearly spit her soda. "You and Lucas have never had sex?"

"Of course not. I would have told you if we had. Besides, after what happened, I don't think that Lucas would have even asked. He says he respects me too much. I always planned to wait for Lucas, I mean marriage, anyway."

Mona laughed. "Didn't he ever have anyone else? Not even in the military?"

"Thankfully, no."

Mona squealed. "You mean he's still a virgin!"

Sarah laughed. "You don't have to say it like it is a disease. He simply wanted to wait for the right woman."

"In other words, he was waiting for you."

Sarah smiled. "I'm really nervous, though. What is it like?"

Mona sat back and thought. "I can't really describe it. It may be uncomfortable at first, but then it's pretty great. It's like the warmth of a first kiss, but magnified. I imagine that with your extreme sense of touch it will be even better. Honestly, though, I think the experience is different for different people. With as much love as Lucas and you share, I'm sure the love making won't be a problem. The more emotion involved, the better the sex."

Sarah laughed. She knew that she wanted to share that moment with Lucas. She also knew that he was counting the minutes until the wedding night. As nervous as she was, Sarah knew that Lucas had never had anything but her best interests at heart. She knew that she would be safe.

"Can I ask you a question?" Mona chirped.

"Sure, go ahead." Sarah noticed an edge in Mona's voice.

"Do you ever think about the night of the attack? I hate to bring it up now, but you have never spoken about it. I just want to make sure that the memories won't get in the way of intimacy with Lucas."

Sarah took a deep breath. "To tell you the truth, I don't remember much. Jackie, my counselor, told me that memory shutout was my way of dealing with it. I actually don't even link intimacy with Lucas to what happened. I kind of look at it as a bad dream. I don't deny it happened on any part, but I don't dwell on it either. Jackie told me that as long as I don't deny what happened, I can deal with the memory however I want."

Mona smiled. "Sounds like you have everything under control."

●

Sarah practically shook as the music played and her father walked her to where Lucas stood, waiting for her to be his bride.

"I'm so proud of you," Jonathan whispered in a thick voice. "I have hoped you'd marry Lucas since the day I first met him. I prayed and prayed that you would find someone to care for you and love you, especially after your mother and I are gone. You look so beautiful. Lucas looks pretty good too."

Sarah knew he did. Tears came to her eyes as the reality hit her once more that she was about to finally become Lucas's wife. She couldn't believe it. After all these years. After all of the fear and worry and pain. He was about to belong to her forever, and she to him. Sarah could barely contain herself. It took all of her restraint to not run down the aisle and dive into his arms. Had she been able to see, Sarah just might have. Finally, they reach the end of the aisle.

"Who gives this woman to this man?" the priest asked.

"Her mother and I." Jonathan gave his daughter away, tears in his eyes. He shook Lucas's hand.

"There is no one else I would want her to marry," Jonathan assured.

"Thank you, sir," Lucas replied, his voice breaking.

Jonathan turned to sit beside his wife, who was already crying. He still remembered the day that Sarah was born, the day that he and Beth were told that their daughter was blind. He had been so scared for her. Thousands of questions about what her future would hold had flooded his mind. And then Lucas had arrived in their lives. Jonathan knew that Lucas would care for Sarah and protect her to his death. That thought alone allowed Jonathan to let his daughter go.

"And now," the priest stated, "Sarah and Lucas will recite the vows they have written for each other. Sarah, you may go first."

Sarah took a deep breath. She had managed, with difficulty, to sum up her love in a short speech. She had finished it three weeks prior and memorized it. She was still nervous about speaking in front of all the people.

"Lucas," Sarah started, her voice clouded by tears. She had to clear her throat before continuing. "I love you with all my heart. I never want to be away from you, and I never want to be without you. You have been my guardian since I was ten. I owe my life to you and accept my security from you. You are my life, my love, my everlasting protector. I promise to love you until I die, love you as I have for the past thirteen years. I love you eternally, and becoming your wife is my proudest moment." Tears were on Sarah's cheeks when she had finished. She heard Lucas take a deep breath before starting to speak.

"Sarah, I have spent my life wanting to be part of something bigger than myself. I searched and searched for years and what I wanted was in front of me the entire time. My love for you is the biggest and greatest thing that I have ever encountered. I have been stubborn and proud in the past. That mistake almost cost me your love forever. I promise it will never happen again. Where you go, I will go. If you bleed, I will bleed. If you are sad, I will make you happy. If you are hurt, I will ease your pain. If you are lost, I will find you. I love you Sarah and I promise to love and protect you until the day I die."

Lucas's voice cracked at the end of his speech. Sarah was choked up. She couldn't believe Lucas had used the same words in his vows as he had used the night of their reconciliation. It was the sweetest and most romantic thing he could have ever done for her. The priest continued the ceremony. Sarah lost control of her tears as they were introduced as Mr. and Mrs. Lucas Monroe.

CHAPTER

17

Sarah's eyes opened as she felt the pressure in the plane change as it started to descend. She moved slightly away from her position curled against Lucas's chest, her feet tucked under her in the spacious first-class seat. Her toes were a little tingly. Sarah laughed.

"What's so funny?" Lucas questioned.

"Oh, nothing," Sarah replied. "My feet are just asleep, and it feels weird."

Lucas chuckled. "They put on the seatbelt sign," he told her, taking one of her feet in his hands and rubbing it gently. Sarah fumbled around for her seatbelt and was finally able to get it latched.

They touched down, and Sarah was starting to get really curious about where they were. Lucas wouldn't tell her. He had said that he wanted her to be surprised. Sarah heard the door to the plane open and people started to get to their feet. Lucas followed suit, pulling their bags from the overhead compartment. Sarah got to her feet, holding out her hand for him to take it. Sure enough, she felt his strong grip, and he began to guide her off the plane. They moved through the tunnel that would take them into the airport. As they waited for their luggage, Sarah stretched her hearing to try and figure out where she was.

Lucas chuckled next to her. "Have you figured it out yet?"

Sarah frowned. "Well, I smell coconut oil and the air is pretty humid. So we are definitely south. I am hearing too many languages to be able to decipher which is native."

A sliding door suddenly opened and Sarah was hit with a breeze from outside. It was like nothing she had ever smelled before. She could hear birds chirping, but none that she recognized. The air was warm, moist, and smelled briny.

"I'm guessing we are near an ocean," Sarah stated.

Lucas just chuckled again as the conveyer belt for the luggage started to move. He stepped forward and, before long, had pulled their bags free from the mass. Sarah was starting to wonder what was in her luggage. Her mother and Mona had packed for her so that she wouldn't be tipped off as to where they were going. Grabbing a luggage trolley, Lucas guided it, and Sarah, outside to where taxis and limos picked up their patrons. Without a word, Lucas led Sarah to a vehicle and helped her in.

Sarah was immediately aware that she was in a limo. Nothing else had leather bench seats in the back. She slid to the other side and rolled down the window. She could hear people talking all around her, horns honking, and the squeak of luggage wheels. Just as she heard Lucas sliding in next to her, Sarah heard some music, not to mention words that let her know where they were.

"We're in Jamaica, aren't we?" she asked, untapped excitement in her voice.

Lucas smiled. "You figured it out faster than I thought you would. We are on our way to a private cottage, on a private beach, courtesy of your father, of course."

"I don't care who it is courtesy of," Sarah replied, "as long as you are there with me." She scooted over closer to Lucas, tipping her head so that he could kiss her lips.

After a short drive, they arrived. Lucas led Sarah inside and had her wait while he carried in the bags and put them in the bedroom. His footsteps were soft and unsure as he made his way back to where Sarah waited for him. Sarah felt her body start to tremble as she was suddenly, violently, aware of what was going on.

She was alone with Lucas in a private cottage on a private beach, and it was their wedding night. A feeling resembling fear mixed with embarrassment assaulted Sarah's very soul. She could smell Lucas's cologne as he stepped even closer. Sarah tried to take comfort in the fact that Lucas had never been with anyone either. And he loved her, as she did him.

Sarah reached out to him, and he willingly came to her. She wrapped her arms around him, shocked to find that he was shaking slightly as well. He just held her for a few moments, neither one of them willing to push the other. Lucas leaned down and kissed Sarah's neck, sending shocks of lightning down her spine and straight to her heart.

Suddenly, Sarah wasn't scared anymore. This was her husband, her Lucas, who held her in his arms. How long had she dreamed of being his wife? How long had she loved him? How long had she been waiting to be his legally, morally, and as fully as possible? She knew that Lucas was being cautious because of what had happened. He didn't want to push her too far, make her uncomfortable or scared. Sarah was anything but scared. There was a slow fire starting to burn its way through her body, a fire she instinctively knew that only Lucas could extinguish. Sarah pressed herself closer to him, letting go of her fears and letting her desires take control. She ran her hands down his back to the waistband of his jeans. In a swift tug, she pulled his shirt loose and trailed her fingers up the bare skin of his back. Sarah heard Lucas's breath catch, and then he shuddered next to her, his own desires coming forth as well.

Sarah tried to remain calm as she ran her fingers over Lucas's body. She removed his shirt, her hands shaking as she worked the buttons. Using her sensitive fingers, she tried to obtain as much of a picture of him as she could. Her touch went from his stomach, up his chest, and to his face. Then around to his back again, rippling over the muscles he still kept toned. She had never been around him with his shirt off before, and the heat coming from his bare skin was nearly making Sarah dizzy. As she stood with her hands on Lucas's bare back, Sarah was glad they had waited. She guessed that some of the magic would not be there had they not.

Lucas had his hands on her waist as Sarah pulled him closer. She reached up with her arms to sling them around his neck. Lucas lifted her up, Sarah wrapping her legs around his body. She cupped his face in her hands, finding his lips with hers and softly molding to him.

She pulled away, pressing her cheek to his, and whispered, "I am ready to be your wife, Lucas."

Lucas took a deep breath and then turned his face so he could kiss her again. And kiss her he did. He had never kissed her that way before, had never given that much of himself to her. Sarah suddenly realized how much he had been holding back, how much he had been restraining in his attempt to be a real man, and she was grateful for it. But she certainly didn't want him to hold back any longer. Lucas carried her into the bedroom, Sarah wrapped around him as closely as possible. He carried her to the bed, climbed up on it while she was still in his arms, and laid her down, his body pressing hers. Sarah's heart started to pound.

Lucas gently unbuttoned Sarah's blouse and helped her remove it. He then slowly slid the skirt from her hips. Sarah could feel the look on insecure uncertainty cloud her face. She didn't even know what she looked like. How was she to know if he liked what he saw? Lucas moved slowly up to her, his face pressing against hers.

"You are the most beautiful thing that I have ever laid eyes on," he whispered, tears in his voice.

Sarah had to take a few deep breaths before she could speak. "I love you, Lucas."

"As I love you."

Sarah heard the rest of Lucas's clothes hit the floor and he was soon helping her remove what was left of hers as well. Gently, Lucas laid Sarah back down, his body hovering over hers. He softly moved to press right down on top of her, his lips tracing along her neck and jawline.

Fire shot through Sarah like she couldn't have imagined. The feel of Lucas's bare skin next to hers was the most wonderfully erotic thing she had ever encountered. Her fingers caressed his body, running up and down his back, around to his chest and anywhere else she could reach. As he kissed her lips once more, Sarah wrapped her legs up around Lucas's body, willing him to claim her as his. He did so, causing Sarah's breath to catch from the sheer pleasure of what he made her feel. Lucas sighed coarsely against the skin of Sarah's neck as he, too, felt the weight of what they were sharing.

Lucas rolled them over suddenly and sat up, bringing Sarah closer to him and wrapping his arms around her body even more. Time stood still as Sarah loved her husband, as she became his for the rest of time. He was her life, her love and her rock. She knew from then on that she would be forever changed, never to go back to the girl she was, and that was okay with her. As long as she could keep Lucas right there in her arms.

The following morning, Sarah felt her eyes open. She already had a smile on her face. Stretching, Sarah couldn't believe how happy she felt. Being with Lucas the night before had been everything she had ever dreamed of. Sarah's smile got even bigger when she thought of the way Lucas had held her, how he had made her feel, how he had…well, maybe she needed a reminder.

Sarah rolled over, reaching for Lucas. She found just the sheets. Sarah flailed her hand back and forth, trying to find Lucas, expecting to hear him chuckle at her. She scooted her body farther to the side of the bed, locating the edge. Lucas was not there. Sarah sat up, moving from one end of the bed to the other.

"Lucas?" She didn't hear him respond.

Slowly, Sarah set her feet on the floor on the right side of the bed. She had no idea what the room looked like, so she would have to move slowly. Shuffling her feet, Sarah tried to find a door, or something. All she found was a wall, her shin bumping one of their suitcases. Thankfully, her robe was lying on top. Lucas must have set it out for her. Sarah would have hated to walk around the cottage naked; although the action could produce interesting results.

"Lucas?" Sarah called a little louder.

She turned to her left and moved forward, only to slam into something, probably a dresser. There was a crash as something fell to the floor, shattering into pieces right in front of where Sarah stood. She felt something wet hit her feet; it must have been a vase of flowers. Sarah could smell roses now that she wasn't preoccupied. She couldn't reach the bed anymore either, and without knowing where the glass (or whatever it was) flew to, she didn't dare try to get back. Great, just great. Sarah didn't dare move in fear of cutting her foot, or breaking something else.

She scoffed at herself, tears of frustration pricking her eyes. "Lucas!"

●

Lucas trotted to a stop, catching his breath. Looking out to the ocean, he thought about how nice it would be to be able to do his daily run on the beach every day. Sarah would never leave her family, though, nor would he. He stretched and then headed back to the cabin. He was just getting into view of the front porch when he heard Sarah scream his name; she was using too much emotion to just be calling for him. Sprinting the rest of the way, Lucas threw open the front door, wrenched his gun from its holder on the table and rushed to the bedroom.

"Sarah! What's wrong?"

Lucas threw open the door, scanning the room with his gun raised and found Sarah in her robe leaning up against the far side of the dresser.

"Where were you?" she asked. "I've been calling you forever!"

"I'm sorry, baby," Lucas apologized. "I was out running. What happened?"

Sarah sighed. "I woke up, and you weren't here. So I got up and tried to get to the door. I ran into—what is this, the dresser? Anyway, I heard something fall and shatter. I didn't know if it was glass or what, so I had to stay where I was. I didn't want to cut my foot."

Lucas could tell she was close to tears. Moving around the broken vase and scattered flowers, Lucas scooped his wife up and carried her out to the couch.

"Stay here while I clean up the glass. I'll be right back."

Sarah sat, fuming, while she heard Lucas grabbing a broom. She felt like such a fool. She hadn't really had a problem with doing things for herself in the past, so why should now be any different? Was she relying on Lucas too much? Would he get tired of caring for her? The thought of Lucas leaving her again gave Sarah a tight, panicky feeling in her chest. By the time Lucas came out of the room, Sarah had herself in a small state of anxiety. She could feel the tears flowing down her face.

"Baby, what's wrong? Are you hurt?" Lucas came and sat at Sarah's side.

"I hate feeling helpless!" Sarah cried. "I'm sorry I'm such a burden to you. I just didn't know where to go or what else I would break."

"Sarah," Lucas scolded, "you are not, nor have you ever been, a burden to me. You never will be. I love you. I'm sorry I left you, but I thought I would let you sleep. It didn't even occur to me that if you were to wake up before I got back that you didn't know the layout of the cabin. I meant to show you last night, but, well, I got distracted." Lucas let out a low chuckle, one that implied he had a dirty little secret.

Sarah smiled at the memory, wiping away her tears, finally in control of her minor meltdown. She couldn't believe what a wonderful man she had married. She was surely blessed.

"Lucas," Sarah whispered, her voice husky with emotion, "I need to be distracted right now."

Lucas chuckled again, swooped Sarah into his arms, and went back to the bedroom.

It was afternoon before Lucas finally got around to showing Sarah around the cabin. He blamed the lateness on her, though. After they ate a late lunch, Lucas convinced Sarah to go swimming. She wasn't sure at first, given the fact that she wasn't able to see waves coming at her, not to mention the water around her. However, Lucas promised to keep her safe, and he did. He kept her out of the reach of waves; he even helped her swim some. But then they both got distracted when Sarah was in Lucas's arms and wrapped around his body. Lucas began to kiss her, and given the fact they were on a private beach, well, Sarah didn't care much about swimming after that.

As their time passed, Lucas was able to convince Sarah to swim almost daily. They spent time in town tasting everything they came in contact with. During the day they were out and about, they played tourist, finding anything and everything to entertain themselves with. The nights, however, were Sarah's favorite times. The time that she had with Lucas as her husband was more than she could even ask for. More than she could ever have dreamed.

CHAPTER
18

When they got back to Washington, DC, Sarah discovered one more surprise waiting for her. Lucas shut the engine of the car off and told Sarah that she was home. Sarah didn't remember going through the gate.

"Where are we?" Sarah asked.

Lucas smiled. He should have known that he couldn't pull one past Sarah. "Well, honey, we're *home*." Lucas waited for it to sink in.

"Are you serious, Lucas? Really, babe? Our own house?" Sarah squealed and jumped out of her door. Lucas scrambled to help her before she fell or something.

"Oh, Lucas, what does it look like? Is it really ours?"

Lucas laughed. "Yes, it's ours. *Our* house is white with blue shutters and a porch that wraps around from the front all the way to the back. It is two stories, has a basement, and comes fully equipped with a baby grand and all."

Sarah squealed again, jumped into Lucas's arms and tumbled them both to the ground.

•

Things went somewhat back to normal. Sarah and Lucas were both required at press events now. It had been about eight weeks since the wedding when Sarah felt something stir inside her. Nerves, anxiety, and curiosity. She had missed a period. Sarah remembered when she had started her cycle and the trouble she and her mother had trying to figure out how Sarah could take care of her own hygiene. Over time, Sarah had learned to read her body and could usually tell within two days when she would be starting. Then it was a combination of feel, smell, and well, she had figured it out after a while.

So one afternoon, only nine weeks into her marriage, Sarah went up into her room and dialed Mona's number. She answered after the second ring.

"Hey, hun, what's up?" Mona asked after Sarah had greeted her.

"I need you to bring me a pregnancy test and sneak it in past Lucas."

There was silence at the other end, until—

"Are you SERIOUS? REALLY?" And then Mona screamed out loud.

Thirty minutes later, Mona came barreling up the stairs to Sarah's bedroom. Sarah had sent Lucas out for groceries to buy them some time to get the test done. Sarah was a little upset that Mona would find out before Lucas, but she wanted to surprise him. She was positive that she was pregnant. Her period was two weeks late and Sarah had never been that late before.

"Here you go," Mona said, out of breath. "You need to take it out of the package, hold it by the end that has the grips on it and pee on the other end. It might have a cap on it, so take that off first."

Sarah could feel the bemused look on her face. Mona giggled. "Do you want me to help you?"

That sounded embarrassing. "No, I think I will be okay. Just wait here so that you can see what it says for me."

Mona opened the bathroom door for Sarah, but then they both heard Lucas's car in the driveway.

"Never mind," Sarah said.

Mona backed out of the bathroom. "Pee on it and then count to sixty, like a minute. I will tell Lucas that you are using the bathroom and then coming down to buy you some time. Call me later." And Mona was gone.

Sarah locked the door in case Lucas decided to come right up and moved to the toilet with the little box in her hands. She pulled out the test, ripped the wrapper off of it, and located the cap and the end with the grips like Mona had said. Sitting down, Sarah did as instructed, amazed that it was easier than she had anticipated. She reached over to set it on the counter and counted to ninety, just to be safe. Sarah climbed to her feet.

"Lucas!" she yelled, a little more intensely than intended.

Something crashed downstairs as it always did when Sarah called to her husband with urgency. She wondered vaguely what he had broken or dropped. Sarah heard him pounding up the stairs and try to open the door.

"Sarah, open the door. Are you all right? Sarah!"

"Sit down," Sarah commanded.

Lucas rolled his eyes and took a breath. Sarah was always doing silly little things to surprise him, which usually involved scaring him to death first. He wondered what she had planned this time. Sarah walked out of the bathroom with her hands behind her back.

"I need you to see something for me. I need to know what it says."

Lucas didn't know what to think. The look on Sarah's face was one he had never seen before. It was beyond happiness; she was glowing, but she was crying as well. Sarah extended one hand with something clasped in it and a box in the other. Lucas took a closer look, realized what it was and what it said; all he could do was cry. He was going to be a daddy.

•

The doctor told Sarah that she was eight weeks pregnant. Everything seemed fine. The heartbeat was strong. Sarah was healthy. That evening after the doctor confirmed the pregnancy, as luck would have it, Sarah and Lucas went to the White House to have dinner with Sarah's parents. It was Jonathan's birthday. Lucas had invited his parents, along with Mona and Derek (Mona's boyfriend for a while now, whom she often referred to as "the one"). Sarah was not sure exactly how the parents would react. She was planning to inform her father by giving him a birthday card with a copy of her ultrasound picture in it.

The dinner went nicely. Sarah's hands shook slightly. Lucas kept squeezing her leg and kissing her cheek. Sarah knew that he was elated, dying to yell the news to one and all. Finally, dessert was served and presents passed. Beth presented her husband with a new set of golf clubs followed with a new golf bag from Paige and Owen. Golf balls and club sleeves were given by Mona and Derek.

Sarah stood and slowly made her own way to her father's chair. "Happy birthday, Daddy," she whispered, tears in her voice. She kissed his cheek and handed him a single card, her hand shaking.

Jonathan looked at his daughter, concerned over her emotion. Slowly, he opened the envelope; out came a homemade card. Smiling, Jonathan remembered the crooked cards she used to make him when she was younger. On the front the card read,

For this day that you were born
I send a wish your way.

On the inside was written,

I wish all the love that one can get
For you are a grandfather *today.*

Jonathan stared at the ultrasound picture taped under the words. Tears made their way to his eyes. He looked at his daughter, his baby girl. Standing, he embraced her, crying freely.

Concerned, Beth grabbed the card, read it, and screamed. She showed everyone else the card. The cheers and hugs lasted for ten minutes. Nothing matched, however, the embrace between father and daughter.

•

The pregnancy went smoothly for Sarah. She didn't have morning sickness. She didn't gain a lot of weight and was able to keep working. The only thing that really got in the way was the belly. Sarah was forever bumping it into things because she couldn't see it sticking out, so she couldn't tell how much extra room to allow herself. Sarah finally started walking with one hand out in front of her belly, sort of like a cane for her belly. She and Lucas had decided not to find out the sex of the baby. Wyatt James was the name they agreed on if it was a boy and Skylar Ann if it was a girl.

Sarah knew that Lucas was ecstatic about the baby. He told everyone that he saw and was constantly bringing new things home for the little one. Not to mention, their parents were overjoyed. Sarah was sure that they hadn't been certain about being blessed with grandchildren. She and Lucas were both only children, and she was blind. That had to have put some doubts in the minds of their parents as to whether or not they would ever see a grandchild.

Before long, it was reaching the end of Sarah's pregnancy. She went to the doctor for her thirty-six-week checkup and was relieved to hear that everything looked fine. Sarah was concerned that she had been feeling some contractions lately, but the doctor said not to worry. She said that it was normal. Afterward, Lucas surprised Sarah with a trip to the symphony.

"That was amazing," Sarah gushed after the show. "It was even better than normal. I think the baby liked it too. He or she didn't stop moving the entire time. I have to use the bathroom before we leave."

"There's a closed sign," Lucas informed.

"It's okay," a woman said with a heavy accent. She was in a janitorial uniform. "I am almost done, and I would hate to see an expecting woman wait."

"I'll be right back," Sarah told Lucas.

Sarah felt her way through the bathroom. She finished what she came to do and walked out to the sinks. As she washed her hands, Sarah felt someone come up behind her. She startled slightly.

"Aren't you Sarah Watkins, uh, Monroe?" the janitor asked. Sarah recognized her voice.

Sarah nodded.

"I thought so," the woman continued. "That must be your husband out there. I saw pictures of your wedding. It was nice. Now you're expecting. That's great. The president is going to be a grandpa."

Sarah felt the woman close behind her. She was too close for Sarah's comfort. Something in the woman's voice made her nervous; it was almost mocking.

"My parents are very excited," Sarah informed. "Please excuse me, I must return to my husband."

"I'm sorry, sweetheart, but I don't think so."

The woman pushed Sarah backward into the arms of someone she did not know was even there. Sarah prepared to scream, but the person slapped a hand over her mouth. A third person could be heard behind them. He spoke in whispered German telling the man who had her and the woman to bring Sarah to the window; another man was to take care of her husband.

Sarah feared for Lucas. She thrashed around and was horrified when someone grabbed her feet as well, lifting them off the floor. Twisting her head, she was finally able to bite the hand over her mouth.

"Lucas, help me!" she screamed.

•

Lucas stood waiting for his wife. It seemed that the day she had conceived she peed every five minutes. Lucas actually found it cute. Her belly was adorable. He only wished that she could see it herself. Everything seemed to take longer for Sarah to do, and this time was no exception. She was taking even longer than usual. He was just about to check on her when she heard her scream for him.

Lucas ran to the door only to find it locked. Suddenly, someone grabbed his shoulder. Spinning, Lucas was met with a punch in the jaw. Stumbling back, Lucas regained his balance, prepared to fight. The attacker came at him with a knife. Ducking, Lucas smoothly knocked the knife out of the man's hand. He then grabbed the guy, punched him in the stomach and kneed him in the face, knocking him to the floor.

Lucas threw his body into the door. It flew open just in time for Lucas to see the janitor climb out the window. Lucas could hear Sarah screaming. Running to the window, Lucas saw the woman climb in a black moving van with a picture of Saturn on the backdoors. Lucas pulled himself through just as the van took off.

"Sarah!"

Lucas could hear her screaming his name. He pulled out his phone and dialed 911 as he ran after the van. He was able to give his name, his location, and the Florida plate numbers of the van before someone leaned out of the van and shot a gun. One of the bullets grazed Lucas's shoulder just enough to knock him down.

"Sarah!"

He had failed her again.

●

Sarah screamed as a gun was fired. One of the men said something about the husband being down. Sarah wanted to vomit. Was Lucas hurt? Was he dead? A sob broke through her lips as they sped around a corner, nearly toppling her over. Sarah turned quiet as her abductors talked around her. They spoke in German, clearly unaware that she could understand them. Sarah had a feeling that it was an advantage for her if they didn't know she spoke their language. They spoke of the Florida Keys, a boat, and a hideout in Cuba. They also kept praising their leader, the man President Watkins had put in jail, none other than Adolf Krause.

CHAPTER
19

Lucas could not look at President Watkins as he hurried toward the ambulance Lucas was in. The bullet had only grazed the shoulder, so Lucas only needed a few stitches. But Lucas refused to go to the hospital, so they just bandaged him up. Beth hurried over to him, embracing her son-in-law.

"I am so sorry," Lucas cried. "She only went to the bathroom. I never thought I would have to follow her in there. I've failed her again."

"No, Lucas, hush," Beth soothed. "You have not failed Sarah, now or ever. She wouldn't have let you follow her to the bathroom anyway. You did the best you could. She's going to be okay." Beth sounded more confident than she felt. She knew Sarah was a survivor, but what would the stress of abduction do to her while very pregnant and closer to her due date every minute.

Lucas was getting down off the back of the ambulance when his father and mother showed up. Paige hugged her son and cried with him as Owen barked orders; after all, he was a chief in the FBI. Lucas hated the fact that he had to tell them all that Sarah didn't have her watch on, the one Jonathan had made for her with a GPS locator in it. She hadn't wanted to wear it while dressed up. They all told him not to worry about it, but Lucas couldn't help but feel guilty. He should have made her wear it. Owen reviewed the statement his son had given, noticing Lucas had mentioned the woman having a German accent. Hurrying over to the president, Owen presented him with an idea.

"Mr. President," Owen called. "I think I may have an idea who took Sarah."

Jonathan turned. "If you have any ideas at all, old friend, please let me know."

Owen showed Jonathan the report. "Lucas said that the woman posed as the janitor had a hand in taking her and also had a German accent. What if the people who took her are part of Krause's mafia?"

Jonathan nearly vomited. He had never imagined that his actions nearly two years prior could come back to haunt him now. It did make sense though; they couldn't get to Sarah while she was in Germany, so they had devised a plan to get her on American soil. That was why it had taken so long for them to take action. Not only was he worried for his daughter's safety, but now he had his unborn grandchild to be concerned about. After evidence was gathered, Jonathan went with his wife and Lucas to FBI headquarters. Once there, everyone tried to decide what to do next. Every unit was on alert for the van. There had been no ransom note and no call with demands. Basically, it was a waiting game.

●

Sarah had fallen asleep; stirring, she woke up and was famished. Lying still, Sarah tried to listen to the conversations of her captors. They spoke of it being four in the morning, the day after they had taken her. Also, they were in North Carolina already and stopping to eat in two hours. They then began to argue on whether or not to feed Sarah. The woman stuck up for her saying that she was pregnant and if not fed could lose the baby and be in danger herself. Sarah may die. The men, clearly ignorant to pregnancy, agreed to two meals a day. Sarah nearly cried in relief. At least the baby would not starve.

Two hours later, the van jerked to a stop. The woman could be heard ordering fast-food in a drive-through. Before they pulled ahead to the pickup window, someone put a blanket over Sarah. The woman told her to lie still and not make a sound or she would die. Sarah knew that they couldn't kill her yet. She had already decided that they took her to try and barter for the freedom of their leader. However, Sarah was not going to take any chances. She may if it was just her, but now she had her baby to think of.

Food in hand, the van lurched back onto the road. The woman climbed in the back, pulling the blanket off Sarah. Helping her sit up, the woman untied Sarah's hands and put the food in her lap.

"Thank you," Sarah whispered, taking the food.

"I'm a mother too," the woman replied quietly. "I remember what it is like, hungry all the time. Besides, our war is with your father and our government, not you or your unborn. I will try and make this as easy as possible on you."

Sarah nodded her understanding. She had always known that being the president's daughter made her an easy target, easier than the president himself, anyway. Sarah ate quietly. The greasy food did not sit well with her, but she was not about to complain. Sarah hated this feeling of helplessness. She had never once in her life felt like she couldn't do what others did just because she was blind. She had always given things her best shot anyway. Now Sarah couldn't even see the faces of her captors. She had no idea where they were going or how long they would have her. Lucas was her only hope. Sarah knew that the FBI and the Secret Service would do whatever the kidnappers wanted. However, Sarah knew that Lucas would come for her, even if he had to walk.

●

Lucas was frustrated. Everyone seemed to be just sitting around waiting for the abductors to call. No one had seen the van leave the city at all. For all he knew his wife and unborn child were dead. With his father leading the FBI, Lucas knew that they would do everything they could to get Sarah back. Listening quietly, Lucas caught on that they knew the plates on the van were phony, but that it was from Florida due to the fact that the phony plate had been stolen from another car registered in Florida while the owner had been at work.

"Why can't we go get her?" Lucas asked. "If you know where the van came from, don't you think they may take it back?"

"Lucas, we can't just barge down there without any idea of what these people want or where they are in Florida. We have to know more before we can plan anything," Owen stated. "Please go get some rest, son. I will call you if we hear something."

Lucas could never figure out why people in these situations were told to get some rest. As if he could sleep at a time like this.

•

Hours seemed like days to Sarah. They finally arrived in Florida; Sarah had no concept of what time or day it was. In the quiet of the night, she was ushered out of the van into a car. After a short drive, she was taken out of the car and onto a boat. Sarah could feel the rocking under her feet; she could hear the water beating against the hull. Thirty minutes after the boat had departed, Sarah's captors seemed to relax. She knew that they must be close to international waters by now. Champagne was opened. She heard them praising Krause some more.

After the champagne was finished, Sarah was led to the lower deck and locked in a room. Walking the perimeter, Sarah tried to get a feel for where she was. There were no windows, only one door and no furniture except a couch and a small table. The cushions stunk like mildew on the ancient sofa, but fatigue took over Sarah. She kicked off her shoes and soon found herself lying down to sleep.

The jolt of the boat slowing woke Sarah up and nearly threw her to the floor. On the upper deck, rushed footsteps could be heard. Sarah had a feeling that there were now more than three. Joyous shouts could be heard, along with the opening of more champagne. After a while, footsteps stomped down the stairs, and the door to her room opened. Sarah stood, not sure who was there.

"Time to go," an unfamiliar male voice said. He grabbed Sarah's arm and led her up the stairs.

Sarah tried to keep up as best as she could. She stepped off the boat, her feet squishing in sand. Her shoes had gotten left behind on the boat. They must be on a beach. Being held by the arm, Sarah was led into the woods, or so she expected due to the smell of nature all around her. Sarah could feel leaves and twigs under her feet. She gasped as her big toes struck something, probably a rock. They trudged on for what seemed like forever. Finally, they reached their destination. A door opened, and more joyous shouts were exchanged. These people were very happy to see Sarah. All around German songs were sung. Some of the men even reached out and patted Sarah like she had won a prize, or she was the prize.

Sarah tried to remain calm as another man took her arm and led her up three flights of stairs. He kept whispering under his breath how he wished that they hadn't been forced to swear not to touch Sarah in any way that might hurt her or the baby. He kept grabbing her in obscene ways, Sarah slapping his hands away. He found this amusing. Finally, they reached the top of the third flight of stairs. A creaky door opened; Sarah was ushered into a room that smelled of mold. She was stood near a pole, the cold metal stinging at her back. The man wrapped a light chain around Sarah's waist, above her belly. That chain was then attached to another that tied Sarah to the steel pole. The second chain did, however, give Sarah about ten feet of slack.

After the man left, Sarah moved the full length of the chain and felt her way around. There was a couch and a table on one side of the room. The other side seemed cluttered with junk; Sarah couldn't reach the wall. Sarah could reach only one door (though she doubted there was more), but there was a window. It was small, too small to climb through with her belly. Besides, she was blind and three stories up. However, it was not nailed shut. Sarah opened it and felt a cool breeze on her face. She realized that since it was not nailed shut, she must not be within hearing distance of any help. At least she had fresh air, though. Deciding to wait out the events, Sarah knew she would have to be patient and wait for Lucas to find her.

●

Fear gripped his heart; Lucas sat straight up in bed. He had been dreaming of his absent wife. She had been gone for almost a week, no ransom had been asked, no demands made. He was up almost all night, every night, eavesdropping on his father and Jonathan. Owen was trying to decide what to do. They had no idea where to look for Sarah. They knew now that it *was* Krause's mafia who had taken her. The German president had verified that almost all of Krause's men had gone off the grid, some even missing. The ones left behind weren't talking.

Jonathan and Owen had managed to keep the incident out of the press. Luckily, Owen and Jonathan's friendship was well known, so it was not unusual to see him come and go from the White House. Lucas guessed that when anyone came with him, it was assumed that they were meeting with the President about "security" issues. Lucas hoped that his father could keep it on the down low. He hated to think about what would happen if this went public.

Lucas was sure that they had not taken her to Germany. Getting out of the country probably wasn't easy. The van had come from Florida, so the best that Lucas could figure was that they had taken her out of the country through the Florida Keys. He knew that drug traffickers liked to take that way to avoid border patrol. However, no sign of Sarah had been reported by the local law. Where they went from there was a guess. Lucas did know, however, that he was tired of waiting around. His father, knowing Lucas's nature, had told him to stay put, but Lucas couldn't handle it anymore. He had been trained by his father his entire life, not to mention his Army training. Lucas knew that he could find Sarah.

That afternoon, an agent from the FBI came hurrying to the White House. He had a disk in his hands that was contained inside an evidence bag. He told them it was a message for the president. Everyone gathered as Jonathan put the disk in his computer and opened the file. The message started off with a shot of Sarah sitting on an old couch chained to a metal support pole. Lucas thought he would vomit, his knees buckling beneath him; Beth nearly screamed, grasping her husband's hand. The camera stayed on Sarah, while a voice, mechanically distorted, spoke.

In broken English, but with a German accent, the person said, "Leave the press out of this. The girl will not get hurt if our demands are met. Do not come after us. We will make contact in twenty-four hours with our demands."

Beth started to cry. Lucas's body shook to the point he had to sit down. Mona came over and held him. Derek was there as well. Lucas could feel his blood run cold, gasping sobs breaking from his chest. His wife, his beloved wife, was a prisoner; their unborn child, captive. Lucas tried to calm himself. His breath came in a mixture of gasps and sobs.

"She'll be okay," Mona assured, tears in her voice. "I have never met anyone as strong as Sarah. She will pull through. She knows that you will come for her."

"They won't let me," Lucas hissed. "I know I could find her. I love her more than life, and that would guide me. I just need to be given the chance."

"So take the chance," Derek whispered. "I haven't known you that long, Lucas, but I know that you are not the type to do what others say when your heart is saying something else. Go get your wife."

Lucas looked at his friends. They made a point. He knew in his heart that he could find Sarah. He also knew that by the time the service got around to making a deal, Sarah could be dead. Lucas got to his feet and walked out. He stomped over to his truck and contemplated what he was thinking. He couldn't wait any longer. Lucas jumped in, started the engine, and drove back to his and Sarah's house. He considered his options as he packed his bag. Lucas knew that the kidnappers wanted Krause released. The German president would never allow it, even if it meant Sarah's life. So they would have to stall. Soon, patience would be gone, and Sarah would no longer be an issue. Lucas had to get to her before that happened.

●

Sarah had to use the bathroom. Standing slowly, she made her way to the door, bumping the table on her way. She heard the glass of some liquid, most likely water, clatter as it fell to the floor. Knocking loudly, Sarah yelled to whoever could hear her. Footsteps started up the stairs.

"What do you want?" a male asked.

"I have to use the bathroom," Sarah responded. "Please get the woman."

The man shouted in German to the woman. A few moments later she was opening the door. Taking Sarah's hand, the woman led her to the bathroom even though she knew the way. Standing at the door like always, the woman waited for Sarah to finish.

Sarah was glad that she couldn't actually see the woman watching her.

Once back in the room, Sarah settle back onto the couch to sit, as usual. It had been a week, or so she thought, since her abduction. Her captors had not mentioned anything about demands or what they wanted, even though Sarah knew. She began to wonder if they had even made demands yet. Would they call her father? Were they going to release her or kill her once they got what they wanted. How long would it all take? Would her baby be born as a hostage?

Sarah could not bear the thought of never hearing Lucas's voice again, never smell him again, never hold him again. Panic began to seep into Sarah's heart. Willing it down, Sarah tried to think of happy memories. Every memory that came to mind was of Lucas. She remembered the day they had met, that following Christmas, ice skating, their reconciliation, the wedding. All the memories brought her a happy feeling. Lying down, Sarah fingered her wedding rings and then the charm bracelet. Lucas had had it refitted after they had gotten back together adding a diamond charm representing their marriage and another heart once they found out they were expecting. Smiling, Sarah fixed a picture of her husband in her mind and let herself fall asleep.

The woman bringing in Sarah's breakfast startled her awake. Setting down the tray, the woman walked over to where Sarah was lying on the couch.

"We called in our demands," the woman informed. "So far, your father is cooperating nicely. We demanded ten million dollars and the release of our leader. Your father has four days to deliver. If all goes well, you should be home soon. Just pray all goes well. The man running this deal is not a patient man."

"Is that a threat?" Sarah asked.

The woman laughed. "No, I'm just letting you know. I will try to keep you from harm, but the reason I am here is because of my husband, the man running this operation." With that, the woman left.

Sarah was nervous. She knew where her father stood on negotiating with terrorists. She also knew that it might take him longer than four days to gather the money *and* convince the German president to release Krause. Sarah prayed for Lucas to come.

CHAPTER

20

After the demands were made, so was Lucas's plan. Excusing himself, Lucas crept out with a bag to catch a flight. With any luck, he would get to Sarah before the four days was over. Climbing aboard, Lucas was glad he had worn a hat and sunglasses. He still was not used to being recognized as the First Son-in-Law. Being Sarah's husband was wonderful, but he hated the publicity. He only hoped that he wasn't recognized by any of the terrorists.

Lucas stepped off the plane and then rented a car to get to the Florida Keys. Once there, the first thing that he did was dye his hair darker, along with the beard that he had grown due to not worrying about shaving. When he was done, Lucas didn't recognize himself. *It's a good thing Sarah can't see me,* Lucas thought, *or she may not have recognized me. At least I'll smell the same.* Lucas double-checked to make sure he had his cologne.

Taking a deep breath, Lucas set out to find his wife. The first stop for him was the store to buy food and other things for the trip. He wasn't sure where he would have to go or what he would have to do, so Lucas tried to prepare for multiple situations. He bought nonperishable food, blankets, matches, rain gear, a first aid kit, and other things for cross-country travel.

The only real piece of information anyone had was the van's starting point. The insignia Lucas had noticed was one used by three service companies in the Keys: Saturn Plumbing, Orbital Movers, and Solar Home Services. When called, all three had said that all their vans were accounted for. Lucas knew that this didn't necessarily mean that one of them hadn't carried Sarah, even though the FBI had checked locations and uses. He had pleaded with his father to look more into the situation, but he had refused, convinced it was a dead end.

Lucas set off to the loading docks, choosing to start there under the assumption that the Germans would rent a van and then drive it back to get on a boat. He struck gold at the first service company, Orbital Movers, which happened to be at the docks. Apparently they moved more than just land items because they had boats as well. The workers stared as he walked up. One of them stopped briefly to direct Lucas to the manager's office.

Lucas knocked on the door and entered upon invitation. "I'm Officer Lucas James," Lucas greeted, not wanting to use his real name. He flashed his badge. "I need information regarding a van of yours."

"For what?" the manager asked.

"It was involved in a crime."

The manager rolled his eyes and took a breath. "What color and plate?"

"The van was black, the plate was 674 PV, but it was a phony plate."

The manager looked shocked. "I knew it, those bastards. That's one of our rental vans. It was returned about a week ago. The woman who had rented it said she was doing a local job, but when I looked at the mileage, it was way over what she had paid for. By the time I noticed, she was gone. It had a different plate on it when it was returned. It was the one you mentioned."

"Some other officers called here a few days back asking about the van. They were told nothing was out of the ordinary."

"Yeah, well, that's what I get for going on vacation. I just got back today. I rented the van to the woman before leaving. When I got back, this is what I came back to, no one knowing anything."

"Did she have a German accent, this woman?"

The manager thought back. "Yeah, as a matter of fact, she did. She also docked a boat here. The day after she dropped off the van, the boat was gone, or so I was told. She must have left during the night."

"Do you know where she was going?"

"No, I don't. The plate on the boat was for Florida, but that was probably phony too."

Lucas thanked the manager. Just as he was leaving, the manager ran out and stopped him.

"I just remembered," he huffed. "One of my guys thought he heard someone out there one night. He went to look on board and saw no one, but he did see a map of Cuba."

Lucas's heart stopped.

"Did he inform anyone?" Lucas asked a little harsher than he meant. He kept forgetting that Sarah's abduction was not public knowledge.

The manager shook his head. "He didn't really think anything of it, actually."

Lucas thanked the man and went to charter a boat. He had not driven a boat in over two years, but Lucas knew he had to do it. Stopping at a store, he purchased a map and a compass, and quickly mapped out the shortest route, hoping with some luck, it was the same route the terrorists took. He knew he had to play it safe. The very breath in his wife depended on his success. Lucas prayed for God's guidance and hoped his training would help him.

●

Late morning, the day after Lucas left, Paige finally noticed her son's absence. He had left the White House after the message had been watched. He had been understandably upset, so Paige had let him go. She had left him to his misery and fear, but it had been quite some time. It was unlike Lucas to not be involved. Paige was worried about him. So she went to Lucas and Sarah's house, let herself in, and searched the place. Going to their room, Paige noticed a luggage out. Some of Lucas's clothes were missing, the drawers still open. A letter sat on his bedside table.

A sour taste came into her mouth, and Paige desperately hoped the letter didn't say what she feared. With trembling hands, Paige lifted the letter, opened the envelope, and read.

> *Dear Whoever,*
>
> *I have gone to look for my wife.*
> *I get a sick feeling every time I think about her trapped*
>   *like that.*
> *I know in my heart that they will kill her*
> *and my child even if the demands are met;*
> *my father knows this too. I am strong, and if I die,*
> *I promise it will only be after my love is safe.*
>
> *Lucas*

Gasping, Paige ran back out of the house and to her car. Her tears fell unchecked all the way back to the White House. She drove through the gates, slid to a stop, jumped out, and ran up to the house. Hurrying down the halls, she finally found her husband.

"Owen!" she called. "Lucas has gone after Sarah. He's gone!"

"What?" Owen exclaimed in disbelief. "I don't believe he would do that. Where did he go? What is he going to do? What are we going to tell Sarah if we get her back but Lucas does not return?"

"Where do we stand with the demands?" Beth asked Owen.

Owen sighed and shrugged. "Last I knew Jonathan was still talking to the German president. We'll have the money tomorrow afternoon, but without the release papers, we have nothing."

Suddenly, the door to the Oval Office burst open. "He won't do a thing!" Jonathan screamed. Fury mixed with the fear in his heart. "My daughter and grandchild are going to die because he has no spine."

Beth went over and hugged her husband.

"What are we going to do?" he asked.

"Pray," Beth replied. "Lucas has gone after her. He was tired of waiting around. He must have known that things would go bad. Let's just pray he gets to her before the deadline."

•

Lucas arrived on the Cuban shores about twelve hours after he had left home. It was now the early hours of the day, two days before the money was due. Climbing below deck, Lucas knew that he had to get some sleep. However, that was easier said than done. All around him were the sounds of wildlife in the night. He hoped that wherever Sarah was, she was safe. He hated to think that she might be cold or hungry.

What am I going to do if I don't get her back? Lucas thought to himself. *I don't think I could ever live without her. I was without her once, but she wasn't dead. What about the baby?* Pain shot through Lucas like a bullet. Tears fell. *Please, God. Help me find my wife. I don't want to lose her. Guide me in finding her in the safest way for her and our child as possible.*

Trying to relax, Lucas pictured Sarah in his mind. Tears continued to fall as he longed to hold her. He feared for her and their baby. Never had Lucas felt this way before, helpless, yet doing all he could. Memories comforted him, specifically the memory of Sarah in her wedding dress, their wedding night, and then realizing he was going to be a daddy. Lucas closed his eyes.

He had finally slept, but was now wide awake. He had been aroused by a mother herding her children. He could hear her calling to them, giving them orders and their subsequent laughter as they disobeyed. He climbed out of the boat and spoke to the woman in her native tongue, thankful it was one he knew.

"Have you seen this woman?" Lucas asked.

The woman took Sarah's picture from Lucas and studied it. "Yes," she replied. Lucas's heart stopped. "I saw her come off a boat about a week ago. She was with many other people."

"Where did they go? Was a woman with short dark hair with her?"

The woman pondered. "Yes, a woman like that was with her, only one woman. I don't know where they went, but I saw the woman that was with her in the village, that way."

Lucas took off in a sprint in the direction that the woman had pointed. His hopes sprung up as he ran. Lucas thought he could almost feel Sarah's spirit pull him along. The village came into sight. He slowed down so not to seem suspicious. He began walking from shop to shop asking merchants and customers if they had seen Sarah, showing them her picture. He also described the woman who took her, asking about her as well. No one had seen Sarah but many thought they had seen the woman. Lucas knew that he was close; he couldn't believe his luck. Entering another store, he was told that a woman who fit the description was in there yesterday with her husband. He had purchased two automatic weapons. Lucas decided on two pistols and a rifle of his own; and the appropriate silencers, just in case.

The afternoon wore on. Just as Lucas was about to give up, he actually spotted the woman. Diving behind a building, Lucas watched the woman wait outside the gun shop as the man she was with went in. Moments later, the man hurried out, dragging the woman with him. It was unmistakably her, so Lucas followed.

He tailed the man and woman as close as he could, quietly moving from one side of them to the other, trying to avoid being shot at. However, it didn't work. The man, clearly knowing he was there, stopped and fired his automatic weapon. Lucas dropped to the ground. The man cursed in German. Firing had subsided.

Lucas stayed down for a few minutes. Looking up, the couple had disappeared into the trees.

Staying on the heading he was before, jogging quickly, he hoped that the two did not know who he was. If they didn't know for sure that he was actually after Sarah, then she stood a chance. Lucas tripped, nearly falling to the forest floor. But just then, something exploded, sending Lucas careening backward. He slammed into the ground, his head pounding the dirt. Lucas tried to fight the darkness, but it didn't work. He blacked out.

•

Sarah stirred on the couch. It was two days after the demands had been made. The deadline was two days away. No one had spoken to her since the woman; Sarah had no idea what was going on. The night had been restless. No one had brought her dinner last night, and now the baby was in full protest. Besides, she was starting to have contractions again. The clock struck noon. Standing, Sarah moved to the door and yelled for the woman. No one answered; no one came.

What is going on? Sarah thought. *Where are they? I don't like the feeling of no one there.*

Sarah moved to the window and opened it. She could hear a slight rain falling but nothing else. Well, she heard birds and other sounds of nature but nothing of her captors. Sarah knew that they had not left her. Well, she hoped not. No matter how terrified she was about being held for ransom, Sarah knew that she would not survive if her captors were to leave her. She guessed that they hadn't. However, she had no idea where they were.

Four hours passed before anyone was heard from. Sarah knew how much time had passed because of the chime on the clock downstairs; it had chimed four times, meaning four in the afternoon. Suddenly, gunfire sounded in the distance. Sarah ducked instinctively, her heart flying up into her throat. It ceased and was followed by yelling, German cursing. A shrill siren sounded on the ground floor. More cursing. An explosion. The door to Sarah's room opened with a bang. Hurriedly, the woman came in, muttering and cursing under her breath, and took Sarah's chain off. Then, without a word, she ushered Sarah down the stairs and out the door. Terrified, Sarah remained silent as she stumbled along and was led into the trees.

●

Opening his eyes, it took Lucas a moment or two to remember what had happened. The explosion had to have been some sort of warning, something to disable enemies. Lucas stood, wiped the blood from his right eye, and doubled his speed; he had been stupid not to look for trip wires. They now knew he was still in pursuit. He prayed for Sarah's safety. After about a mile of running, a house came into view. Pulling his gun, Lucas crept up to the doorjamb, the door itself stood open. Lucas entered the open front door, ready for anything, his gun held out in front of him. However, the house was empty. Sweeping from room to room, Lucas finally located where Sarah had been held on the third floor. The chains were still attached to the beam. A lump rose up in his throat. All he could picture was his beautiful Sarah in chains, attached to that godforsaken pole in front of him like some dirty beast. Racing back down the stairs, Lucas noticed footprints in the soft earth; he followed.

The tracks stayed clear for about three miles. Deep in the brush, however, Lucas began to lose the trail. The leaves around him all looked the same. He stopped, took a breath, falling back on his training. Lucas closed his eyes and knew that his wife was close. He could feel her. Opening his eyes, Lucas looked around. The jungle trees all looked alike. Vines hung, roots stuck up, and everywhere, Lucas could hear animals moving, birds chirping and fluffing their feathers. It made it impossible to listen for the group he chased. Panic started to rise; Lucas pushed it aside, knowing he had to stay calm. Looking in front of him and slightly left were broken branches. Looking to the ground, Lucas saw a penny. Heading in that direction, Lucas saw more broken leaves and a dime. Coins on the ground of the jungle. How he loved that woman.

•

Sarah gasped, trying to breathe as she was pulled along. She was not only exhausted, but she was still contracting, the constant fast pace was making them worse. Finally, her legs gave out. She slumped to the ground, almost fainting, cradling her belly.

"I have…to rest," she gasped to the woman. The woman informed the men and then told Sarah she had five minutes.

"Why are we moving?" Sarah asked. "Where are we going?"

"My husband said that the gun shop salesman told him some-one was asking about me and you," the woman hissed at Sarah. "Then as we headed back to the house, someone followed. My husband opened fire. The person stopped following until just before we left. One of the alarms sounded, meaning someone had tripped a wire within a mile of the house."

The leader cursed in German and yelled at his wife in their native tongue. "We would not be here right now had you not been seen! How does he know what you look like? Did you not disguise your face at the abduction?" The woman must have shaken her head, for she was slapped in the face.

"Stupid woman," the man hissed. "You may have just lost our deal. I don't know who is following us. I have no idea who we are dealing with or how many. I can't ditch the girl either because it may not be about her."

Sarah couldn't help but smile. *Oh, it's is about me, all right. There is only one, but you should still be afraid,* Sarah thought.

She knew that it was Lucas. However, she feared for his life and for her own. The group began to move again. Sarah, realizing everyone was in front of her, reached into her pocket. Pulling out some coins that were stored in her slacks, she dropped a penny.

She knew that Lucas would come for her. All she hoped was that if the prints grew faint, Lucas would see the coins. A dime dropped next. About an hour later, the quarry stopped to make camp. Sarah heard the leader tell the others that he was sure they had lost their tracker. Sarah knew that just because they didn't see Lucas didn't mean he wasn't there. She was instructed to sit. Bad-smelling food was shoved her way. The contractions were still coming.

•

Lucas finally caught up with the group around dusk. They had stopped to make camp, clearly thinking they had lost him. Lucas quietly circled. He saw Sarah. It took all he had to not cry out to her. She was lying very still; Lucas thought she was asleep, but then she saw her move. The woman had come over to take a dish from her. At least she was being fed. Lucas shifted more to the left. A stick popped under his foot. Sarah sat up. She became very still with her eyes closed. Lucas knew that she was listening to her surroundings; possibly smelling. His cologne. Taking out the bottle, Lucas moved downwind of Sarah and sprayed.

CHAPTER
21

Sarah shifted on the ground trying to relax. The woman came for her dish; Sarah thanked her. Sounds of the night creatures were starting to reach Sarah's ears. The smell of the night surrounded her, damp air leaving a film on her face, the smell of rotting foliage filling her nose.

I wish Lucas were here, Sarah thought to herself. *I miss him so much. I really don't know how long I can handle this. What if he never gets to see his child because he dies trying to rescue me?*

Tears formed in Sarah's eyes. The thoughts that filled her brain were too much for her to handle. Rolling onto her side, Sarah tried to rest. A stick cracked. An animal? Sitting up, Sarah tried with all her might to listen. Was it Lucas? Concentrating, Sarah caught scent of his cologne. Her heart skipped a beat.

The night wore on as Sarah waited, knowing Lucas was there for her. She felt safer just knowing he was in the trees. Sarah couldn't sleep. The anxiety of waiting for Lucas to hold her was physically painful. Tears fell as she laid in the darkness the scent of her love reaching her nose now and then. Fatigue took over; Sarah was soon asleep.

It was the early hours of the dawn when Sarah heard Lucas approaching. She sat straight up and listened.

"What is your problem?" a man asked, heavy with his accent.

"I heard you moving, and it startled me," Sarah covered. "I am sorry." Sarah sat quietly and waited, wondering what Lucas was going to do. She knew that he was terribly outnumbered. A massacre from the trees would work, but Sarah knew that Lucas was not a killer. However, at this point, she was not sure how desperate Lucas was.

●

Lucas tried to control his breathing. His whole body shook with tension. He had felt this way before, deep in the ambushes of war. However, he had soldiers to back him up at that time. Here, only he was around to save his love. He had no idea how he was going to save his wife. She was surrounded by thirteen armed German mafia and the woman. He saw her sit up when she heard him. Freezing, Lucas watched Sarah cover for her startle with the guard. Minutes passed and Lucas saw a woman bring Sarah some water and a nutrition bar. The whole camp was awake now. The woman helped Sarah to her feet and made sure she was okay. The group was making ready to move on. Lucas knew that if he was going to act, it had to be now. He wasn't sure how he was going to succeed given the number surrounding Sarah. So, Lucas decided to just wing it. Hurrying as quickly as he could, Lucas slung himself up into a tree, fit the silencer on his rifle and took aim. Taking a deep breath to steady himself, Lucas squeezed the trigger. The first one fell. He had still been sitting down and slumped right back over. No one noticed.

Lucas took aim again. Another deep breath and down went a second. And then a third. By now the leader knew something was up. Lucas jumped from his position in the tree as the remaining Germans started yelling in an uproar. Sprinting around to the other side of the group, Lucas managed to squeeze off two more rounds into the heads of men holding his wife before things turned nasty.

The last two that Lucas killed had been close to the leader. He seemed to gauge where the shots had come from based on the bodies and soon the air was full of automatic gunfire coming Lucas's way. He hit the jungle floor, attempting to not react to Sarah's screams.

The firing stopped. He heard Sarah scream again.

"Is that your husband out there?" the leader snarled.

"I don't know," Lucas heard Sarah reply, her voice surprisingly steady.

"Well, let's see if we can draw him out." The German laughed and Lucas heard Sarah cry out in pain. It took all of his willpower to stay hidden, to not come out of hiding, guns blazing. He couldn't do that, though. He had to kill off a few more before he stood a chance face-to-face. He dug his fingers into the soft earth to release his frustration over not being able to help his wife as Sarah cried out again.

"It won't work," she suddenly snarled. "If it is Lucas out there, you no good waste of flesh, he won't come out. He knows better. He will stay hidden and kill you all one by one because that was the way he was trained. He knows better than to fight unless he stands a good chance at winning."

Lucas couldn't help but smile, despite the fear in his heart. How he loved that woman. Feisty right down to the very core. And he understood her warning. She knew that there were still too many for him to take on by himself. She was warning him to stay hidden; she was begging him.

Lucas drew his rifle up again. Through the foliage he could just barely get a shot lined up. He squeezed the trigger and blasted another man through the chest. Lucas didn't wait to see him fall, though. As soon as he was sure it was a hit he scampered away because, sure enough, more rounds were released right where he had fired from. Lucas ducked behind a tree and waited out the shots.

Once silence ensued, Lucas glanced around his hiding spot and was actually lined up perfectly to kill two nearly at once. They were standing right next to each other, looking like they had each other's backs. Not so smart. Taking aim, Lucas squeezed the trigger. Just as the second man realized his buddy was down, Lucas got him, too.

More yelling from the ones left, including the woman who was now clinging to the leader in such a way that Lucas suspected she was his wife, or something along those lines.

"Enough!" the leader yelled, loud enough that Lucas assumed it was meant for him, too.

Lucas peered around the tree, not daring to move because of the silence surrounding him. He saw the leader inspect the two newest victims and then he glanced in the general direction of Lucas's hiding spot. He snarled something in German to his remaining men. They started to take action. Lucas remained hidden, until –

"Lucas, run!" Sarah screamed. "Grenades!"

Lucas's heart nearly stopped. He could have sworn he heard the pins fall. Launching to his feet, he barreled deeper into the woods. There was a slight rustle behind him as the grenades sliced leaves on their way to the ground and then the earth erupted behind him as the bombs found their marks. Lucas was launched off of his feet, thrown through the air and slammed back down, the force of the impact bouncing him painfully a few times and rolling him right over a cliff.

●

Sarah sat motionless, silent tears running down her face. She couldn't let herself believe that those grenades had found their mark. Lucas was not dead. He couldn't be. However, her remaining captors were out looking for his body at that very moment. Lucas had managed to kill eight of the men, but what about the remaining five? And the woman? She was currently managing Sarah while the leader paced and the other four looked for Lucas's body.

Suddenly, there was noise of coming footsteps. Sarah listened as the men approached their leader. They spoke in hushed tones now that they knew Sarah understood them, but it wasn't so quiet that Sarah couldn't hear them.

"We looked everywhere, boss," one of the men was saying. "We found where the grenades hit and even where we think he landed. There was a lot of blood. But no body. The only thing that we can figure is that he went over the cliff close to where he landed. It overlooks a ravine and goes down about one half mile to rapids below. No one could have survived that."

"Are you sure he went over?" the leader snarled.

"Pretty sure, boss. There was blood splatter like he bounced, or rolled. Even noticed some on the edge."

"Fine," the leader huffed. "Just get our stuff and the girl and let's get going."

Sarah was numb with disbelief. She couldn't let herself believe that Lucas was dead. He may not have gone over the cliff. Maybe he had just made it look that way. Despair threated to take hold of Sarah as she was dragged through the jungle, but she wouldn't let it. She had been a fighter since the day she was born. She couldn't let that change now. She had to survive for their baby. And she had to believe that Lucas was still alive.

•

Lucas bit back a scream of agony as he caught himself one-handed as he slipped over the edge of a cliff. Glancing down, Lucas wasn't reassured. Sure there was a bottom to the ravine he now hung over but it had to be at least a half mile down and covered in what looked like a raging river.

Groaning in agony, Lucas swung his other arm up, grabbed hold of more of the tree roots that had saved his life and hauled himself up. He nearly blacked out from the pain. As quickly as he could, Lucas pulled out bandages from the first aid kit (miraculously his pack was still on his back) and field dressed his wounds; his entire left side was an enormous abrasion. He was just wrapping up when he heard them coming. Lucas gathered his things, made sure he left no evidence that he had survived and scampered up to hide in the canopy.

●

After four hours, Sarah could go no further. She knew that today was the deadline. She also knew that there was no way her father was able to meet the demands. Once on the next town, the Germans would call to check, and then she would be dead.

Sarah's contractions were still coming, getting closer together. She hated to think that this was early labor. What was she going to do if she delivered her child on the floor of the jungle? Stumbling, Sarah fell to her knees.

"I need to rest," she told the woman.

The men protested. The woman argued with them, informing them that the president would surely want proof that his daughter was alive and well, including the baby, before he gave them what they wanted. This seemed to pacify the men who took advantage of the rest to have a smoke.

Sarah sighed as she settled down onto the forest floor. She couldn't foresee what was going to happen. Tears flowed unchecked and unending down her face. Her heart told her that her husband was still alive, still out there to save her. But her brain was telling her something totally different. Sarah could feel her hope draining from her, the hope of Lucas saving her. Now she was in survival mode. She had to survive to bring life to their child. He or she was suddenly even more precious, even more real inside of her. And still forever on her bladder.

"I need to go to the bathroom," Sarah told the woman, who then informed the men. They told her to take Sarah, but not to go far. The woman grabbed Sarah's arm and lead her away.

"Please take me out of sight of the men," Sarah pleaded.

"I understand," the woman replied. "I wouldn't want them seeing up my skirt either."

They walked for a distance. Getting far enough, the woman told Sarah that she would turn her back. Sarah squatted by a tree and did what she had to do, with a large amount of difficulty. Standing, there was movement near her and Sarah suddenly felt strong arms around her, nearly screaming; she would have had she not immediately recognized his strength, touch, and smell.

"Don't move or speak," Lucas hissed at the woman, moving Sarah behind him.

Sarah heard the woman gasp. No sound came as they stood there.

"Are you okay?" Lucas asked Sarah, tears in his voice.

"Yes," she whimpered, grasping the back of his shirt. She couldn't believe it. She couldn't believe that he was alive. She thanked God that he was, but they were still in very real danger.

"You died," the woman stammered. "They said you went over the cliff."

"I did," Lucas snarled back. "But I climbed back out."

Angry voices suddenly filled the air. They had been seen! Lucas grabbed Sarah, moved her to the side, and pushed her down into the brush. Gunfire rang out through the trees. Lucas left her side. More shots were fired. Sarah stayed down, one arm around her stomach, the other covering her head. Sarah heard the woman scream in pain. The angry German voices were all around her. She had no idea where Lucas was. Was he okay? Would he survive? Sarah was close to hysteria thinking about Lucas in danger.

Someone suddenly grabbed Sarah, but it was not Lucas. She screamed as she was yanked to her feet, a gun barrel pressed to her stomach.

"Come out, lover boy!" the leader called with his thick accent. "Come out or she dies, your baby first."

Sarah heard sticks crack as Lucas (she assumed) came out of the trees. Tears started to run down her face; sobs burst from her lips. Sarah had no idea how many other men there were. Had Lucas managed to kill the remaining four? What about the woman? She could not handle being around if her beloved were to die. Not to mention, she was terrified for her unborn.

"It's just you and me," Lucas growled.

"Yes," the German agreed, "You are quite the hard target to kill. You have killed all of my men, including my wife. In ancient days, it would be only fair that I take yours."

"You kill her, and I kill you. You still don't win." Sarah heard Lucas cock his gun.

The German laughed. "How about we settle this like men? No guns, but still a fight to the death."

Sarah was tossed to the side, falling hard on her right hip. She cried out in pain. She could hear Lucas unload his gun and toss it down. The German went against his word, firing at Lucas.

"Lucas!" Sarah screamed as she heard him dive out of the way, or fall.

The German tried to fire again, but he was empty. Sarah heard him run at Lucas, and Lucas met him head-on, coming with a swift punch to the German. Countering back, the German cussed in his own tongue, and the fight was on. Sarah knew that Lucas would protect her until he *did* die. She prayed that he would win, though she didn't know how big this other guy was. Crawling to her right, Sarah's hand hit the trunk of a tree. She moved her body around to the other side to allow herself some cover, moaning as another contraction came.

All of Lucas's training came back to him, his stealth and strength renewed. The German was tough, but Lucas was younger and faster. A punch came at Lucas's ribs. One cracked. The German's nose broke under Lucas's fist. They fell away from each other. Lucas was bruised, but not beaten. His face was bleeding, his ribs screaming. The German advanced, as did Lucas. He knew he could not lose. Sarah's life depended on him, as did the life of his unborn child. Lucas knew that without Sarah, he would die. She was his life, his love, his very breath. With a yell of fury, Lucas threw himself at the German.

The German and he wrestled to the ground. Lucas took a hit on the face, was picked up, and slammed into a tree. Lashing out with his feet, Lucas caught the German in the chest, and then jumped at him, trying to get his arms around his neck. Just then, the German pulled a knife. Lucas saw it coming and deflected the kill shot, but not enough to keep the blade from slicing into the flesh of his shoulder. Lucas cried out in pain. Knocking the knife from the German's hand, they wrestled some more, the German getting the upper hand as he slammed his fist again and again into Lucas's injured shoulder. Lucas finally shoved him away, stumbling back as well. Lucas spotted his gun and dove at it, shoving the clip back into place. He jumped to his feet to fire just as the German threw his knife, the blade coming straight at Lucas's heart.

●

Skin to skin contact was heard as Sarah hid behind the tree she was next to. Yells of pain could be heard from both men. Tears ran down Sarah's cheeks. She wanted to run but had nowhere to go. Wanted to help but could not see. She wanted Lucas. She could not live without him.

Sarah heard Lucas cry out in pain as his body slammed against a tree; Sarah could hear his skin drag across the bark. More physical struggle followed but then Lucas screamed in pain. They fought some more, and then it sounded as if they shoved away from each other; two sets of feet stumbled in the brush. There was a lot of rustling in the grass. Gunfire suddenly rang through the air.

Silence.

Sarah tried to control her breathing to listen. Her breath was the only one she heard. Crawling to where she had last heard Lucas, Sarah began to panic, sobs escaping her lips.

"Lucas! Lucas! Lucas, answer me!" Fear rose up in Sarah's heart. She couldn't smell him. She couldn't hear him. Sarah stood so Lucas could see her. She felt her way along, unable to find her love, with her hand held out so he could take it. "Lucas, please take my hand. Lucas, answer me! Don't leave me alone. Please, answer me!" A stick cracked. Sarah froze.

"Take my hand, my love." A warm hand grabbed Sarah's.

Screaming in relief, Sarah fell into the safe arms of her husband. Lucas gasped in pain. His right arm gave out under her weight. Lowering them to the ground, Lucas thanked God his wife and baby were safe. Sarah sobbed uncontrollably.

"Breathe, sweetheart," Lucas soothed, trying to keep himself calm as well. "You need to breathe for the baby."

Sarah took a few ragged breaths. "I heard you yell in pain. There was a gun shot. I thought you were dead. What happened?"

Lucas grunted in pain. "He pulled a knife and sliced my shoulder pretty good. I was the one that fired the gun. He tried to throw his knife at me but missed. I had to flip myself out of the way, though, and hit my head. That was why I didn't respond right away. I blacked out a little."

"Are they dead? Are they all dead?"

"Yes, baby, you're safe." Lucas shifted her weight on him, grunting in pain once more.

"Lucas, you're hurt. How badly are you hurt?"

Sarah panicked. All she could imagine was Lucas saving her and then bleeding to death. She got on her knees and ran her fingers over his body. She felt bandages on his left side, through his tattered shirt. His whole right arm was covered in blood.

"It's not that bad. My ribs actually hurt worse." Sarah heard him rip some cloth off his shirt. "Help me tie this, babe."

Sarah helped Lucas tie the shirt on the wound to stop the bleeding. "Are you okay otherwise?"

Lucas looked at his wife. "Never better," he replied, his voice thick with emotion. "I thought I had lost you. I would never be able to live without you." Lucas embraced Sarah again. His mouth found hers.

"I thought you were dead," Sarah choked.

"I'm here now. Don't worry, I'm here."

"I love you, Lucas. Thank you for coming for me. I never stopped praying. I knew you would come. I knew you would come for me." Sarah was sobbing again.

"I will always come for you. Where you go, I will go. If you bleed, I will bleed. If you are sad, I will make you happy. If you hurt, I will ease your pain. If you are lost, I *will* find you." Lucas picked up his wife, gritting against the pain.

"Don't, Lucas, put me down. I can walk, we just may need to rest often. I don't want you to hurt yourself worse."

Lucas set Sarah down, grinning at how considerate she was even in light of the situation. "Take my hand, Sarah. I'm taking you home."

CHAPTER

22

After calming down, Sarah asked Lucas for some water, which he gave her. He then hunted through his things to locate Sarah's watch with the GPS in it. He knew that once he activated it, the signal would be received by every military base and FBI headquarter on this side of the world. That would in turn get a message back to their families where they were. He wouldn't be surprised if the Army showed up to get them, once they were informed what was going on.

After that, Lucas led Sarah through the trees, holding her hand with his good arm. She was trembling terribly, but he assumed it was from the whole ordeal. She was gripping his arm with strength he never knew she had. However, after about an hour, Lucas started to notice how pale she was, how quiet she was. She seemed to be dead-set concentrated on something, and Lucas couldn't figure out what it was. He finally found a spot for them to rest, guiding her to a log to sit on. Sarah shook her head. She stayed standing, her arms wrapped around her belly and her body hunched in on itself slightly.

"I need to lie down," she gasped.

Lucas quickly spread out one of the blankets he had brought and helped her lie down. She grimaced in pain.

"Sarah, what is it? Are you injured?" Lucas asked.

Sarah chuckled humorlessly. "No, I'm not injured, but I am in pain."

"What do you mean? What hurts?"

Sarah groaned as another contraction came. They felt worse now that she was lying down. This was the real deal; Sarah's instincts told her so. Just then, her water broke. Lucas cussed and jumped up.

"Sarah, what is going on?"

"The baby is coming, Lucas. I have been having the contractions for a few days now. Now it is time."

Lucas was horrified. Not only was he going to have to deliver his own child, but Sarah had been walking for the last hour while in labor.

"Why didn't you tell me?" he demanded, moving to his supplies to see if anything would help him. "I wouldn't have made you walk all this way."

"I was hoping it would stop," Sarah gasped, groaning in pain.

Lucas couldn't believe this. Helping villagers in Africa deliver their livestock was one thing. This was his wife and child in his hands. Lucas knew that the basic principles still applied, but that didn't help to calm his fears. As quickly as he could, Lucas gathered the other blankets he had, ripping one of them into baby-sized pieces. He then grabbed the first aid kit and rummaged through that for anything that would help him, like alcohol wipes, string, a knife and a few of those instant chemical heat packs. He was now very glad he had gotten the biggest kit that store had.

Sarah moaned again, kicking out of her pants. "Lucas, the baby's coming," she gasped.

As quickly as he could, Lucas used blankets and his pack to prop Sarah up and then moved into position to help her deliver their child. Sarah was crying, but Lucas knew that it wasn't from the pain. She had to be the strongest person he had ever met. No, this was her "afraid" cry. She was scared, most likely for the health of their child; he could tell by the look on her face.

Sarah pushed with her next contraction, bewildered by what she was feeling. The pain was outstanding, but even stronger than that was the drive to bring life to her child. It was like nothing that Sarah had ever felt before. She pushed again.

"Okay, honey, I can see the baby's head," Lucas said, his voice shaking.

Sarah pushed again and felt Lucas's hands on her as he stabilized the baby as he or she came screaming into the world. The entire jungle filled with the wonderful sound of the baby crying its head off.

"It's a boy," Lucas stated in shock, bringing their son up onto Sarah's chest.

Tears flowed down Sarah's face as she held her child. She felt Lucas dry the little man off, making him cry that much louder. Lucas did a few more things, then took the baby, opened Sarah's blouse, and put the baby right on her bare chest. He then covered them both with another blanket.

"Is he pink?" Sarah asked.

"He's the pinkest baby I have ever seen," Lucas replied. "I clamped and cut the cord. You just have the placenta left, and I am not sure what the protocol is for getting it out. Animals come out with all that still intact."

"Animals?" Sarah laughed.

Lucas snorted. "I helped some villagers deliver goats and pigs while I was in Africa."

Sarah laughed.

Lucas set to work making a stretcher for Sarah to lie on. He wasn't going to make her walk. Besides, her placenta didn't seem to want to come out, and she was still bleeding. It was starting to make him very nervous. By the time Wyatt was thirty minutes old, Sarah was starting to look really pale.

"I have to get you out of here," Lucas said, gently laying her on the stretcher. She had Wyatt still on her chest; he was actually nursing, amazingly enough.

"I'm okay," Sarah replied.

"No, you are not. Your placenta hasn't come out, and I know that's not good. You're losing too much blood. We have to move."

With that, Lucas started to pull Sarah and Wyatt along. He tried to be as gentle as possible, but it was hard. They finally made it to a clearing. Lucas whipped out his cell phone, thankful to tears to see that he had service, barely. He quickly dialed his dad's number.

"Lucas! Where are you?" Owen demanded after one ring. "Do you have Sarah?"

"Yes," Lucas shouted. The reception was really bad. The static was nearly louder than his voice. "We need help. Sarah's bleeding. Send medics to the GPS location on Sarah's watch. Hurry!"

Lucas lost the signal. He prayed that he had heard him. Lucas turned back to Sarah. Her eyes were closed. He rushed to her, feeling her forehead. She smiled softly at him.

"Is Wyatt okay?" she asked, barely above a whisper.

Lucas pulled the blanket down. His son was asleep on Sarah's chest, breathing softly and his body pink and warm.

"He's doing fine," Lucas replied.

"That's good," Sarah replied. "I'm really tired."

"You have to stay awake, Sarah, okay? You have to stay with me."

"I was always with you, I will always be with you," Sarah whispered.

A sob broke from Lucas's lips. He had to keep her with him. Sarah couldn't die now. Not after everything they had been through. Not now that they had their son. He had to keep her alive. He kept her talking for nearly an hour until he heard the most beautiful sound ever. Helicopters.

Lucas jumped up and ran to his pack. He grabbed the flare gun and fired a shot into the air. He then popped two ground flares and launched them into the field surrounding them. Just then the Army choppers flew by, banked, and came back. Lucas cried out in relief. He moved back to Sarah. She was unconscious.

"Sarah!" Lucas choked. "No, please baby, don't go."

Lucas was suddenly aware of the sounds of helicopters landing, the wind from their blades filling the area. He made sure that Wyatt stayed covered.

"Hurry!" he called, waving the medics over.

Lucas picked Wyatt up and moved him out of the way. The medics took one look at Wyatt and then at Sarah who still had blood pooling under her. One of them started poking needles into her arms, pumping her with IV fluids. Another was screaming over the headset to have a surgeon ready at the base for their arrival, blood on hand and the NICU ready. Then the team rolled Sarah onto their stretcher and started to carry her to the chopper.

Lucas lost track of things after that. Time passed disjointedly. He was ushered with Wyatt into another helicopter. They were flown to a hospital in Miami equipped to handle the helicopters landing there. As Lucas was stumbling out, he was greeted by nurses and doctors asking about the baby. They took Wyatt from him, putting him in an incubator-type thing. Then they were asking him about himself. But Lucas couldn't hear them. He suddenly spotted medics rushing by with Sarah on the stretcher, one of them up there with her doing CPR. Blood rushed through Lucas's ears, and he passed out.

Three hours later, Lucas sat outside the nursery. The NICU had deemed Wyatt full-term and as healthy as any other newborn. His temperature was even good. They had transferred him to the step-down nursery almost immediately. Lucas had been cleared medically as well with just a couple of broken ribs and a few stitches to his name. But, Lucas had yet to hear anything about Sarah. Wyatt was currently sleeping in a bassinet, oblivious to the fact that his mother might die.

"Lucas!"

Lucas looked up to see his and Sarah's parents running his way. He dissolved into tears again, explaining to them in broken phrases what had happened. He then took them in to see Wyatt, Beth and his mother picking him up, cuddling him and kissing his face.

"You are a brave man, son," his father said, pulling him into a hug again.

"I'm not brave, Dad," Lucas croaked. "I am terrified. I can't go on if she dies. What am I going to do? I don't know who I am without Sarah."

They waited for another two hours before they heard anything. There were suddenly two doctors in the doorway, one of them in surgical scrubs.

"Mr. Monroe?" the doctor in scrubs asked.

Lucas stood and shook his hand. "Yes."

"I am Dr. Derillo. I am the ob-gyn assigned to your wife's case. This is Dr. Mackey, the internal-medicine physician that was also assigned."

"What happened? Is Sarah still alive."

"Yes," Derillo stated. "She got to us just in time. Another thirty minutes or so and I am afraid that she wouldn't have made it. I had to manually remove her placenta, but I was able to save her uterus, so I believe there will be a good chance you will be able to have more children. She lost a good portion of her blood and is being transfused as we speak. She is on antibiotics as well to ward off infection from everything that has happened."

Lucas sobbed in relief, backing away to fall into a chair. "When can I see her?"

"She's in recovery now," Derillo was saying. "I will have the nurses find you when she is in her room and awake. The entire hospital is on lockdown as well, Mr. President, for security and privacy purposes."

"Thank you," Jonathan replied.

The doctors left.

•

Sarah could feel herself waking up, but she couldn't tell if she was waking up from being asleep or waking up from something else. She felt weird. She was aware, but not totally. She remembered vague things about being kidnapped and giving birth to her son in the jungle. Lucas had helped her. He had said that her placenta wasn't coming out. She had been bleeding. She had been so tired, so cold. Sarah could feel panic starting to build. But then a voice was talking to her and warmth washed through her veins and she was sleeping again.

Sarah woke up again in a different room. She could tell it was different because it was quieter, it smelled different and it was much warmer. A soft voice was talking to her. Sarah tried to listen as the nurse told her what had happened and that her son was doing wonderfully. Sarah asked that he be brought in and asked about Lucas. The nurse said that she would get them both. A little while later, the door opened again, throwing a breeze as it swung open.

"Lucas?" Sarah could smell his cologne.

"Sarah," he sobbed, coming to her side and taking her gently into his arms. "Oh, honey. I thought I was going to lose you, I thought you were going to go where I couldn't follow, where I couldn't come find you."

"Thank you for coming for me," Sarah replied, tears running down her own face. "Thank you for helping me give life to our son. Where is he?"

"Right here," the nurse said, handing Wyatt over to Sarah's waiting arms.

"Oh, my baby," Sarah cried. "I love you so much."

"As do I," Lucas whispered. "As I love you mother and always will."

And then he took Sarah's hand and held it tight, as he always had and always would, while they cradled their newborn son.